The Chalet School series by Elinor M. Brent-Dyer

This is a complete list of Chalet School titles in chronological order. Those titles printed in bold type have been published in paperback in Armada but not all are currently available. Please send a sae to the Marketing Department, Collins Children's Division, for an up-to-date stocklist.

Elinor M. Brent-Dyer

Changes for the Chalet School

ARMADA

First published in Great Britain in 1953
by W. & R. Chambers Ltd, London and Edinburgh
This edition was first published in Armada in 1989
This impression 1990

Armada is an imprint of
the Children's Division, part of
the Harper Collins Publishing Group,
8 Grafton Street, London W1X 3LA

Printed and bound in Great Britain by
William Collins Sons & Co. Ltd, Glasgow

Contents

CHAPTER ONE

"Notice to Quit!"

"Please, ma'am, Commander Christy would like to have a word with you."

Miss Annersley, Head of the Chalet School in England, looked up from the lists she was checking rapidly and gave Gwladys, the head housemaid, a startled look. "What did you say, Gwladys? Commander Christy? Very well; show him in here, please." Then, as the girl stumped off to do her bidding, she shuffled her sheets together and nodded to Miss Dene, her secretary, who was working at a little table in the farther window. "I'm not sorry for the break. We've been mulling over these wretched things until my head's in a whirl and I don't suppose yours is much better. Wait a moment, Rosalie," as that young lady began gathering up her possessions and prepared to depart. "Michael Christy may have something to say that concerns you as well as me."

The sound of firm, manly footfalls prevented Rosalie Dene from making any reply. The next moment the door opened again and Gwladys announced, "Commander Christy."

The Head rose and went to meet her visitor with outstretched hand. "Good morning, Michael. Why the formality? Usually you just wander in unheralded."

Michael Christy, a tall, fair ex-Naval man, grinned, showing a set of magnificent teeth. His blue sailor's eyes twinkled at her greeting.

"True for you, Hilda, but I've come on a very formal business, so I thought I'd better do things in style for once."

Miss Dene once more prepared to go, but he checked her. "No; don't go, Rosalie. I rather think a witness is indicated, though I'm not absolutely certain. Still, you'd better wait."

"A *witness*!" Miss Annersley echoed. "What are you talking about?"

"Well, the thing is I've come to give you folk notice to quit."

"Notice to quit?" Miss Annersley stopped short and began to laugh. "That's really funny, you know."

He stared at her. "*Funny?* Well, I'm very glad you take it that way. I was afraid you'd turn on me and rend me, tooth and nail. But what's so *funny* about it?"

"Haven't you heard from Canada yet? Oh, but of course you haven't."

"Canada? No! Any particular reason why I should? And what the deuce are you laughing at, Hilda? What's the joke in all this?"

Rosalie Dene, who had also chuckled, told him. "Because, if you must know, Madame is writing to give *you* notice that we're leaving at the end of this term."

"Leaving? Then are you going back to Plas Howell? I thought Ernest Howell wanted to sell, lock, stock and barrel?"

"Quite true," the Head agreed. "No; we aren't returning there."

"Then what are you going to do?"

The reply was sufficiently startling. "We're dividing up again. Part – very much the lesser part of the school, we hope – will continue at St Agnes' – Glendower House, you know. The major portion will be going to Switzerland!"

"Good Heavens!" He subsided into the nearest chair and stared at her. "This is certainly news. But why weren't we told before? I mean, you've got young Cherry here. Did you think we wouldn't be interested?"

"The notices have just been sent by post," the Head said. "Yours should arrive by the first post tomorrow. It needn't worry you, you know. Cherry can go to Glendower House with little Gaynor. It's a big place and will easily take quite a large number of girls. Miss Alton hasn't been using anything like all the rooms. Or, if you and Carey prefer, she can come out to the Platz with us. And that mightn't be a bad thing for her, either."

He looked thoughtful. "There's something in that, Hilda. She's making marvellous progress, all things considered. Did you know that she's discarded her crutches at long last? Yes; it's true. And they all say that in time she should be as well as ever again, though there will always be a weakness. What a beastly thing polio is!"

The Head agreed. Then she turned to her secretary. "Rosalie, it's almost eleven. Suppose you go and jog Megan's memory. I could do with a cup of coffee," she added plaintively. "So could you, after the way you've been working all the morning. *You* never refuse, Michael!"

"Not coffee the way Karen makes it," he retorted, laughing.

"Very well, then. And bring some biscuits, too, dear. We had very early breakfast this morning, remember."

Miss Dene nodded and left the room and the Head turned to her visitor.

"It really isn't as sudden as it may seem, Michael – our going, I mean. We've always meant to return to the Alps as soon as we could. The situation in Austria being

11

what it still is, Tirol is out of the question, of course. Even San won't re-open there until the Peace Treaty has been signed, sealed and delivered. There doesn't seem much hope of that as long as Russia remains in her present frame of mind. That being so, and since there is a very great demand for it, we have decided to open at the Gornetz Platz in the Oberland."*

"You mean that place where Dickie and her pals gave their pantomime last Christmas?" he interrupted. "Dick gave us quite a pathetic account of it when she was at home. So that's where Jem Russell and Jack Maynard are taking San, is it? And you're chasing after, I suppose, so that if any of the poor souls have children they want to be near at hand there'll be a good school for them to go to?"

Miss Annersley nodded. Then she explained a little further. "You see, Nell Wilson wrote to Jem that there was a derelict hotel going to be sold that might do. Anyhow, he flew across from Canada and went to inspect and the nett result was that they bought it and already have men at work on the interior, redecorating and doing any repairs that need doing. They hope to be ready for the first patients by the beginning of July."

"And the school goes off, too, in consequence."

"Exactly – or part of it, anyhow. Some people mayn't wish to send their girls to the Continent, even now."

"Then what about Das Haus unter die Kiefern? Will you still keep that on?"

"Oh, yes. It is definitely a finishing school. We couldn't possibly have most of the girls mixed up with the School proper. Welsen, where it is, is a good two hours' walk from the Platz, though it's only about twenty minutes or so by

* *The Chalet School in the Oberland.*

the mountain railway. That part of the school will remain as we began it – a place where the elder girls can have one or two years spent largely in acquiring a few social graces and some idea of culture and their responsibilities. The school itself will be at the Platz."

"I see. But look here, Hilda, what about financial arrangements? How are you managing about them?"

"Jem's seeing to those. In certain circumstances you can arrange for money to be forthcoming, though I believe you have to have a special permit from the Treasury. And, of course, we're not a private concern any longer. It's some years since Madge decided that the whole affair was getting too large for that and turned it into a limited liability company. I have shares in it, myself, and so have most of the staff. I imagine we shall manage through the Swiss National Bank. You'll have to tackle Jem or Jack if you want to have all the details."

"Oh, no. I was only wondering if I could give you a helping hand there. But what are you doing for buildings?"

"Madge has bought three big chalets standing in a little group, and already they are being linked up by means of covered ways and form rooms. I think it will all be rather – pleasant," Miss Annersley added pensively. "I've seen the place, you know. I spent most of these holidays there. And that reminds me: we can take Cherry as she is over twelve; but that's our limit. Gaynor won't be at all welcome, so don't ask. We're taking no one under twelve."

"I don't suppose Carey would agree to her going so far from us. We must certainly think about Cherry, though. I agree with you that it would probably do her a world of good."

"That's what I think. And Michael–" Miss Annersley

13

suddenly came to a full stop and eyed him rather apprehensively.

He looked at her and began to laugh. "I know what's coming next. You want to offer to take the kid at reduced fees. It's like you, Hilda. There's no need for it, though. That, by the way, is largely what I came up to tell you, though I seem to have been side-tracked by your news."

Hilda Annersley sat up in her chair. "Michael Christy! What shock are you going to give me now?"

"Well, I like that! What price the shock you've given *me*?"

"But I thought you'd have had it already in Madge's letter from Canada. *I* wasn't to know that the mail was late," Miss Annersley said defensively.

"Late it is – or Madge missed a post. At any rate, you gave me a shock. Let's have no mistake about that," he told her, his eyes twinkling.

"Oh, very well, then. Suppose you get on with your own story."

"Here comes young Rosalie with the coffee. I'll wait until we're all settled down comfortably with it and then, if you feel faint, Rosalie can hold your hand."

"A lot of use that would be if I really did feel faint!" the Head said scornfully. "Come along with that coffee, Rosalie. We're gong to have a shock and we may need something to pull us together."

Rosalie glanced at the gentleman over her tray. "Hasn't he told you all about it yet? Oh, but I suppose you had to give him our side of it from A to Z first." She set down her tray and began to pour out. "Is it something so frightful that you want me to be on hand?"

"*We* don't think so – or not from one point of view. We were desperately afraid that *you* would, though. However,

14

we might have saved our anxiety, it seems, seeing that you mean to give us the go-by in any case. Thanks, Rosalie; *no* sugar!"

She laughed and handed him his cup, having attended to the lady first. Then she took her own and sat down and looked at him expectantly.

He tasted his coffee. Then he looked at them. "You folk have all been away all the holidays, or you'd have been in all the excitement. As it is, you haven't had a chance to hear our news."

"Tell us something we don't know!" Rosalie retorted. Then, with a sudden thrill, "*Oh!* You *don't* mean you've found your wicked ancestor's lost fortune?"* And she nearly overturned her cup in her excitement.

"Steady on there! If you'd capsized that cup, you'd have had a pretty hot soaking," he said, saving the cup almost by a miracle. "Yes; you've guessed it. It's been such a mild April, that once your little darlings had gone home for the holidays, I got men to work and the treasure has come to light at last."

"Where was it? In a cave on the cliffs as you thought? *Was* the outflow from the pond the way to it?"

He nodded. "Later on, I propose to march you two down to Kittiwake Cove where you'll see a nice little waterfall – or perhaps waterspout would be more accurate – coming from an opening in the cliff."

"How was it we didn't see the opening before?" Rosalie asked practically.

"Because it was overgrown with gorse bushes. We've yanked them away to let the water run away freely. Now for my yarn! Do you remember last Christmas term when Peggy Burnett fell down what was an old well and as a

* *Shocks for the Chalet School.*

15

result the spring that feeds it was freed and the brook returned to its old way?"

"Of course I do!" Miss Annersley said. "Considering the fright we had about her and then about the prefects who discovered the brook in the twilight by falling into it, I'm not likely to forget. I also remember that during that half term, you had Mr Archer down to see it and got the men to dig at the far end of the resultant pond and discovered the old outlet. You told us then that that evil ancestor of yours, Dai Lloyd, must have done the filling-in of the outflow, having first hidden his booty somewhere along the cliff. What I've always wondered, though, was how he got at it when he wanted it."

"There was another entrance somewhere in the shrubbery – at least I think it must have been there. We found about fifty yards of it. The rest had caved in and I didn't see the point of digging it out again. But judging by the direction it took from the cave, that's where it probably came out."

"And you were really right?" Rosalie asked. "You've found the treasure after all this time? This *is* news! Where is it now?"

"Safe in the strong room of my bank. You don't imagine I would keep it over here, do you? Yes; we found it – or what was left of it. I imagine that Dai and his boon companion, the mate, made away with a fair proportion of it. At any rate, we found five empty chests and I don't think any outsiders were responsible for *that*. There were two others untouched. We had to break them open for the locks and bars had rusted home."

"Do you mean you did it yourself? Or did you have to bring a workman in?" Miss Annersley asked dubiously. "I hope not that last. I don't suppose you want your find bruited abroad for the present, at any rate."

"Don't worry! When I said 'we', I really meant that I did it in the privacy of the coal cellar with Carey looking on. The kids were in bed and Dickie was staying at the Bettany's place. She knew nothing about it until she came home two days later."

"Well, what luck?" Rosalie demanded excitedly.

He chucked. "All the luck in the world. I felt like Aladdin in the magic cave. The smaller chest was chock-a-block with jewellery of all kinds. Honestly, you two, you never saw such a collection. Ropes of pearls, mostly gone sick for lack of using; everything you can think of in the way of ornaments – brooches, bracelets, rings, earrings, necklaces – they were all there! Church plate, both gold and silver, some of it heavily jewelled, some just chased; vestments, likewise studded with gems – I rather think Dai must have robbed churches in South America. I wouldn't put it past him! And right at the bottom of the chest a big leather pouch simply crammed with loose stones – diamonds, rubies, emeralds, sapphires, opals – oh, the whole bag of tricks. One great star made of diamonds round a sapphire centre nearly lit up the coal cellar on its own."

"And what about the second chest?" Miss Annersley asked as she held out her hand for his cup.

"Thanks, Hilda. Yes; I could take half a cup more. Oh, that had money. I never saw such a collection of coins in my life! Rose-nobles, ducats, moidores, spade-guineas – the whole shoot, I should think. I've no idea what the value of it all is, but something stupendous, I should think."

"And it's really all yours?" Rosalie drew a long breath.

"Well, I've got to prove ownership. That oughtn't to be difficult, since I can prove descent from Dai himself – collateral descent, anyhow. The kids and I are the only

17

ones left. I know *that*, for before my great-uncle left the place to me, he had inquiries made all over to find out if there was anyone else and they couldn't trace a single soul. I'm not very well up on the law of treasure-trove, but I believe I'm right in saying that I can claim it – or most of it, anyhow."

"What will you do about it?" Miss Annersley asked quietly.

"Well, I propose to sell most of the jewellery. Carey says she doesn't want it – it would give her nightmares to wear it when she thought of how it was come by. Dickie, who is the only other person to know exactly what we found, says much the same thing and, in any case, doesn't care about it. I shall keep a few oddments for Cherry and Gaynor and one or two things for Carey and Dickie. The rest may go. As for the church property, that *can* be restored, thank Heaven! Not to the actual churches, perhaps; but to the Church itself. But after three hundred years or so, I haven't a hope of finding out the rightful owners of the rest. The Spanish Main was the happy hunting-ground of a good many pirates in those days. Dai was only one of quite a crowd."

The Head nodded thoughtfully. "No; I imagine you are right there. Well, Michael, this all means that you are now a wealthy man and can keep up the Big House properly. Now I understand the notice to quit."

"Hold on – hold on! I do propose to keep enough for that and to make sure that the kids will be all right for the future. Now I have a son, I'd like to be able to hand on to him our inheritance. But I've no desire to be a millionaire and I don't want it for Blinkie, either. We haven't had time yet to decide anything definitely and, of course, we must wait and see what the court's decision may be, though I'm not much afraid of that. As for what

18

I shall do with the surplus, it will all go to charities, helping to educate the young, care for the old and sick and helpless. By the way, Hilda, Carey and I want to found a scholarship or two for the school. But we must talk all that over with the Russells and the Maynards as well as yourself before we do anything. And, as I said before, any plans must lie in abeyance until I've proved ownership. Once that's settled, though, that's one of the things we've set out hearts on doing. I don't suppose it'll matter much whether the school's in England or Switzerland so long as the scholarships take the winners to it."

His two hearers were quite agreed about that. If parents did not wish their girls to go to the Continent, there would still be the branch at St Agnes' which was likely to continue for many a long day, as the Head foresaw.

She looked at him with a sudden smile. "You've overwhelmed us," she said, including her secretary in her own feelings.

He stood up. "That's rather how we feel ourselves. By the way, it's no use haring over to see Carey and have a long gossip with her about all this. I've sent her away for a change and a rest. Where? What a question! I ran her and the family down to Penny Rest last week and there she stays until she's got over this excitement. She's not very strong since Blinkie arrived, you know, and all this is, as you say, rather overwhelming. Dickie will go off to Welsen from there and Cherry and Gaynor will be back at school on the proper date. Carey will stay with Blinkie, though, for a week or two until she's more like herself."

"The wisest thing you could do," Miss Annersley assented. "By the way, Michael, you surely aren't going on calling that poor child by that ridiculous name? It's too bad! I thought he was to be 'Francis'?"

"That can wait till he's a little older and larger. Blinkie

will do him very well for the present. Hang it all, Hilda, the kid's just six months old!"

"Then he'll be Blinkie for the rest of his life," Miss Annersley said with decision. "It's all very well saying you can easily change later. You'll find that you can't. Look at yourself. Your real name is Michael, but when we first came here, your wife and Jack Maynard were still calling you 'Tom'. And how you ever got that out of 'Michael' is a minor mystery to me."

"My old ward room name," he said grinning. "It was only when Carey began to realize that quite a lot of people thought I was 'Thomas' and we had some bother over a legal matter that she suddenly decided to use my proper name."

"I see. Well, to go back to first things, thanks for the notice. I suppose you've sent a written one out to Canada? You haven't? Oh, Michael, what an idiot you are! You go home and draft one out in proper form and send it to Madge Russell by the next mail. Otherwise, you may find you're landed with us for the next twelve months or so!"

"Not when I have hers which, you tell me, ought to be here by this time," he retorted. "That'll do us. I'll withdraw my own notice to quit in favour of hers of quitting and leave it at that. Be ready for me at three this afternoon, you two, and I'll be along to show you all the sights – all that you *can* see, that is. The water's flowing again, so I'm afraid you can't visit the cave now. Still, I'll show you the remains of the chests which are still in the coal cellar and take you to view our little water-spout on the cliffs. I think you might ask me back for tea, seeing I'm a grass widower for the moment. Well, I must go now and discuss the amount of manure to be ordered for the garden at Llanywyn –

20

rather a drop from the sublimey to the gorblimey! I'm off!"

And with this, he vaulted out of the open window and vanished, leaving the two women behind him to talk over this startling piece of news.

CHAPTER TWO

Bride

"Here she is – at long last! Come on, Bride! Come and explain yourself! You're most appallingly *late*! What have you been doing?"

"Where've you been, my lamb? We looked out for you at both Bristol and Cardiff, but never a sniff did we get of you!"

"Look here, Bride, what *is* this rumour that's going the rounds?"

Bride Bettany, Head Girl of the Chalet School, niece of Lady Russell and Mrs Maynard and, to quote her chum Elfie Woodward, one of the foundation stones of the school, stopped short in the doorway of the prefects' room and grinned round at her fellow prefects who came crowding round her, all talking at once.

"Hello, everyone!" she said. "Nice to see your dear, ugly old faces again! – *Julie Lucy!* It's never yourself I'm seeing? Are you really fit again?" She dropped the suitcase she was holding and made for a slight dark girl of her own age or a little younger, whose thick black hair curled rampantly all over her head and whose pale face flushed at this greeting.

"Hello, Bride! I can return the compliment you've just paid us. It's nice to see your ugly old face again. The last time I saw you all together, I was feeling like nothing on earth and I didn't care if I never saw one of you again." She finished with a chuckle at this recollection of last term, when she had scared everyone by developing acute peritonitis, which had meant an immediate operation and several weeks of being an invalid for herself.*

Bride did not return the chuckle. Instead, she looked gravely at her friend and considered her. Julie looked amazingly better, but there was an indefinably fragile look about her, even now, after weeks of being at home and carefully nursed. The beautiful blue-black eyes had faint shadows under them and the once brown skin was white and pink and almost painfully transparent.

"You really *are* better?" she insisted. "You still look washed-out to me – except when you're blushing," she added wickedly, as Julie's cheeks went scarlet at her comment. "No, really, my lamb. I mean it. We don't want another shock like the one you gave us last term. What a time that was! We all nearly passed out when you collapsed like that."

Still red, Julie nodded. "I'm practically all right now, though Uncle Peter and old Doc Fuzzey both made me swear not to overdo this term. No tennis for me, or gym or anything like that. That's the worst of having a doctor for your uncle!" she added with a deep sigh. "He keeps *on* at you till you have got to give in. But I really am all right. Never mind me! First tell us how Auntie Mollie is and then see what you can do to elucidate the latest mystery."

"She must have had a dicker to read while she was convalescing," Bride told the rest as she picked up her case again, bore it across the room to a closet where she pushed it onto a shelf and then, having shut the door, turned to face her confrères. "Think she could spell all those long words, folks?"

*Bride Leads the Chalet School.

"You stop blethering and talk sensibly!" remarked a very tall, boyish-looking individual who rejoiced in the name of "Tom", though her baptismal certificate gave her as "Muriel Lucinda". However, she had always flatly refused to answer to either, so even the staff called her "Tom", which had been her nickname from babyhood and might have furnished the Head with another argument against nicknames if she had thought of it at the time.

"How rude!" Bride said with a grin.

"Rude or not, you were asked three questions. Just set your wits to work and answer them, please. First of all, how is your mother?"

"Pounds better." The mischief left Bride's eyes and she spoke seriously. "She really is making marvellous progress. She doesn't get up for brekker yet, but she's down by ten and she's beginning to take up the reins again. Not that Aunt Bridgie lets her do much yet. But she plans the meals and does some light dusting and so on. Doc told Dad privately that if she went on as she was doing, she'd be her old self again by the time the year was up. *And* she's really gone slim again, which is an everlasting joy, for you wouldn't believe how difficult clothes can be when you're out-sized!"

"Good!" It came as a chorus. All the prefects had known that in the previous November it had been touch and go whether Bride and her brothers and sisters would have any mother by this time and they were all genuinely glad to hear such a good report. But now that they had heard this, school affairs pressed heavily on them and Tom Gay once more was spokesman for them all.

"And why are you late? Don't say you copied Peggy's doings and got into the wrong train at Bristol again!"*

* *Peggy of the Chalet School.*

24

Bride laughed at this reminder of something that had happened more than a year ago. "Oh, no; it wasn't my fault at all. As a matter of fact, I don't suppose you could say it was anyone's fault, really. The wretched car conked out when we were halfway to Sheepheys Junction and we had to wait till we could get a tow – which wasn't for a good half-hour. Naturally, we missed the Bristol train and had to wait four solid hours for the next one. Or we should have had to, but Dad decided that the best plan was to hire another car and run us to Cardiff in the hope of joining up with you there. However, it didn't work out like that. We simply couldn't make it, though there were times when I wondered if we'd be landed in the nearest police court for speeding. We didn't reach Cardiff until half an hour after the train had gone, so it wasn't much use going to Swansea. We knew the last school coach would have departed and we didn't want to be hung up there all night. Dad put us on the coastline train and then rang up the Head to explain so that she wouldn't worry. Now you know the yarn."

A small, fair girl with a pointed face and big blue eyes which gave her a kitten-like appearance, smiled at her. "I'm glad it was no worse. When you and young Maeve never turned up at Bristol, I began to be afraid that something awful had happened. I'm glad it was only the car gone wrong."

"If it had been – well – what you thought, I'd have rung you up," Bride said. "What a goop you are, Elfie! You ought to have known that, anyhow."

"I suppose I ought. But if it had – well, there's so much to do at such times that you mightn't have had time or thought for it."

Bride gave her a sympathetic look. Elfie had been motherless from birth, but her dearly-loved stepmother

25

had died in the previous September so she knew what she was talking about better than any of the others. "No; it wasn't anything like that. Just the car gone mad. Now for your third question, Tom. Something about a rumour, wasn't it? You tell me what the said rumour is and I'll tell you if there's any truth in it – always supposing I know anything about it," she added cautiously.

"Well, people are going round saying that there's more than a chance that we may be moving again," Tom explained, sitting down astride the nearest chair back to front, laying her arms on the back and burying her chin in them. "Have *you* heard anything about it?"

Bride looked startled. "No one's said anything of the kind to *me*. Matter of fact, we've been so busy all these hols, making summer frocks for everyone, we haven't had an awful lot of time to talk about school. Did you hear where we're supposed to be moving to? It can't be back to Plas Howell, by the way."

"No? Why ever not?" demanded a girl with sunny brown hair and a smiling face. "What's happened to it?"

"Oh, didn't you know? I should have thought Gwensi would have written to your Beth. She wrote to Daisy Venables and Daisy told us when she was staying with us for Easter. Mr Howell has sold it. It's a convent now – or going to be, anyhow. The Little Sisters of the Poor have bought it and they're turning part of it into a home for old folk who can't manage by themselves. When Peg had read Daisy's last letter which told us that it was all settled, she just said what a jolly good thing it was that we were able to have Big House."

"We'd certainly have had it if we hadn't – unless Madame and the rest had been able to buy," Tom said. "I suppose they could have done that. Only, as we always look forward to going back to Tirol some day, it seems a pity to have to spend money like that."

"Goodness knows when Tirol will be a safe proposition," Bride said gloomily. "Russia seems all set to be as nasty as she can about Austria."

"I wonder what Bethy will think of it," her sister remarked.

"Why don't you ask her?" Bride suggested. "I expect Gwensi will have told her about it by this time. Ask her when you write, Nancy, and see what she says."

Nancy nodded. "I shall certainly do that. All the same," she went on, "it seems to be all over the school that we're due for a move next term."

"But why ever? I thought the Christys didn't want Big House and were only too thankful to have us as tenants," Bride said. "Not that it will affect most of us here. We'll be shifting on to Das House unter die Kiefern in September, I suppose. I'm dying for it! Peggy says they have gorgeous times there and I'd love to see some *real* mountains again."

"You and real mountains!" Nancy scoffed. "Aren't the Welsh Mountains good enough for you? I'll bet you don't remember much about Tirol. You were only an infant when you left there."

"Old enough to have some jolly good pictures of them in my mind," Bride retorted. "The Welsh Mountains are all right; but where the Alps come in, they're mere hillocks!"

"One moment, Bride," said a pretty, fair-haired girl, one Primrose Day. "Your Peggy and Dicky Christy are by way of being pals, aren't they? Did Peg not know anything about it?"

"If she did, Dicky must have told her to keep it dark," Bride said thoughtfully. "Now you mention it, she did have a letter from Dicky the day before they went back to Switzerland, but she only said that Dicky was staying at Penny Rest and would go on from there and suggested that they should meet at Exeter and go on to London together. Oh, and Cherry has cast her crutches at last. Peg read that bit out to us. Cherry was to have a stick, but she's done with the crutches, anyhow!"

"Well, that's good hearing!" observed a tall girl with a clever, thoughtful face. "The poor kid's had a doing, all right. What a filthy thing polio is!"

Before anyone could reply to this, there came a tap at the door and then a sturdy girl of nearly fourteen appeared.

"Is Bride Bettany here?" she asked. "Oh, Bride, the Head wants to see you in the study at once."

"All right, I'm coming," Bride said, standing up and pulling her skirt straight. "Had good hols, Mary-Lou?"

"Super!" Mary-Lou replied. "And the end was the best of all, all things considered," she added with a mysterious air.

Bride lifted her eyebrows at the younger girl's manner, but she merely gave a friendly tug to one of the long fair pigtails hanging down her back, and left the room while Mary-Lou, having performed her errand, scuttered off to join her own clan.

"Hurry back and give us all the gen!" Nancy called after her friend from the doorway. "She may be going to tell you what's going to happen. After all you *are* Head Girl!"

"That doesn't mean that the Head's going to unburden her secret soul to me!" Bride turned to call back. "You'll see me when she's done with me and not before, as you very well know." Then she hurried off along the corridor, past the head of the school stairs and down the great staircase which, by virtue of being a prefect, she was allowed to use. She ran lightly down, crossed the big square entrance hall and tapped at a door to the right of the front door. A deep, beautiful voice bade her enter and she went in to find the Head.

Miss Annersley was sitting by the window, looking out at the garden where spring flowers glowed in the light of the setting sun. She turned her head as the girl came in and smiled at her. "Come along, Bride. I'm sorry I was engaged when you arrived, but I wasn't worrying about you and Maeve after I'd had your father's phone message. What was wrong with the car?"

"They hadn't found that out when we left Sheepheys," Bride explained as she sat down on the window seat. "All I know is that Dad fiddled round with everything he could think of, but he couldn't make her go and *so* we missed the train. I'm awfully sorry, Auntie Hilda."

"Never mind. So long as you've come, that's all that matters." The Head paused and there was silence for a minute or so. Then she said with a smile, "Well, don't you want to know why I've sent for you like this?"

Bride's grey eyes widened. So there *was* something in the wind? She said demurely, "I thought you wanted me to report to you."

"Well, that, of course. I'll see Maeve at bedtime."

"She's grown *again*," Bride said with a chuckle. "Mummy says she's going to leave us all behind. Auntie Hilda," she looked the Head straight in the face, "what is all this about our having to leave Big House?"

"Who told you that?" Miss Annersley asked sharply.

"From what the others have told me, it's all over the place. Is it really true; or is it only a rumour? I know we're not going back to Plas Howell in any case.

Gwensi told Daisy Venables that her brother had sold it and Daisy told Peg who told me."

Miss Annersley nodded. "And did Gwensi and Daisy between them inform anyone else?" she inquired.

"Not so far as I know. Nancy Chester knew nothing about it, anyhow. Nor any of the rest of the crowd. They were fearfully surprised when I told them."

"I see. And do you know what has caused this rumour of yours?"

Bride shook her head. "I haven't the slightest idea. All I know is that when I went to our room, the rest all set on me and asked if I knew anything about it. I didn't, and I told them so; but it does seem to be all over the school."

Miss Annersley laughed and threw out her hands. "Talk of the grape-vine system!" she exclaimed. "It seems to me that you girls have a very good grape-vine system of your own! Yes, Bride, we are leaving Big House at the end of the term; and we are certainly *not* going back to Plas Howell. Where we are going, you will hear at Prayers tonight. I sent for you for quite a different reason."

Again Bride opened her eyes, but she said nothing. She waited with what patience she could to hear the real reason for her summons; but the Head seemed in no hurry to tell her. However, she spoke at last.

"I needn't ask you if you remember Diana Skelton, Bride?"

Bride shot her a quick glance; but she only said, "No, Auntie Hilda."

"No; what Diana did to you last term will, I am afraid, remain in your mind for some time to come, though I hope you will find sooner or later that you can forget as well as forgive. What I have to tell you is about her. And I want to say this, Bride. Sorry as I was for you

30

last term over your wrecked study, I am a thousand times sorrier for Diana."*

"Oh?" Bride murmured. She could think of nothing else to say.

The Head remained silent for a moment or two. Bride could bear it no longer. "Auntie Hilda – what's gone wrong?" she asked fearfully. "I did forgive Diana last term. And on the last night she got hold of me and said she was really sorry and she meant to prove it to all of us by the way she behaved this term."

"I'm glad to hear that, Bride, for Diana will have no chance to prove her words. She is not returning to school."

"But why?" Bride asked blankly.

"Because that is her father's decision. No, child, it has nothing at all to do with what happened last term. So far as I know, Mr Skelton has heard nothing about it. I believe Diana meant what she said to you. I am sure she did. Only she wanted to get clear of all her former ties. In order to do this, the poor, silly girl did something which her father finds unforgivable at present, though I hope that later on he will realize that her actions were partly the result of the spoiling and indulgence she has always had at home."

"But what has she done?" Bride asked. "I – I mean what she does at home hasn't anything to do with us here, has it?"

"It ought not to have. Unfortunately, one other girl, still here, knows all about it and though I have seen her and forbidden her to say anything, I don't know that I can trust her. That's why I am telling you the story so that, if necessary, you can deal with any unkind gossip

* Bride Leads the Chalet School

there may be. Poor Diana is paying heavily enough for her sins as it is."

Bride remained silent. She was trying to think what any girl could do that would make her parents remove her from school at only sixteen. The Head knew this and she spoke abruptly.

"Girls like you, Bride, have a great deal to be thankful for. You have wise parents who have looked after you and certainly not spoilt you. Diana was allowed to go her own way. Unfortunately, it was a way that was very wrong for a little schoolgirl. She has done all sorts of things that girls of your age should know nothing about. Among other things, she has been playing cards for money. She lost a great deal more than she could pay and in order to pay it she took two of her mother's rings and tried to sell them."

Bride gasped. "Whatever possessed her to do such a thing?" she cried. "It was *stealing*! Oh, Auntie Hilda, I knew she was all kinds of an ass, but I didn't think she would do anything so downright *wicked*!"

The Head looked at her thoughtfully. "Bride," she said with a certain sternness in her voice. " 'Let him that is without sin among you cast the first stone.' Have you forgotten that?"

Bride went scarlet at the rebuke. "Auntie Hilda, you *couldn't* expect me to pass over a thing like that!" she protested. "We're none of us angels; but I don't think one of us would do such a thing, no matter what sort of a mess we'd got ourselves into. Why didn't she go to her father and tell him all about it and ask him for the money if it was as bad as all that? He'd probably have been furious with her, but he'd have paid the money and she'd have had to stand the row. I know if I ever got into such a hole Dad would be the first person I'd go to, even though I knew he'd rage at me – or even though I knew that he would be most frightfully disappointed in me – and that would be worse."

"Yes," Miss Annersley said thoughtfully. "I was pretty sure that was how you would look at it. I should have told you nothing about it, but, unluckily, it seems too much to expect Sylvia Peacock to hold her tongue altogether, even though I have got her promise to be quiet about it. Still, knowing Sylvia, I'm bound to say I'm prepared for her to let it slip sooner or later."

She paused and Bride answered at once. "She certainly *will*!" she said emphatically. "If ever there was a leaky cistern, it's Sylvia Peacock! I honestly think she can't help it. The only way you could stop her talking would be to tie up her mouth."

"Well, you may be sure I shan't proceed to *those* extremes," the Head said drily. "But to return to my subject. If it does come out, I want you to be ready to put a stop to gossip. Diana has been both wrong and foolish and I'm afraid she is paying very dearly for it. There is no reason why she should be torn to shreds by you girls into the bargain, and I know how hard people of your age can be. Later, as you grow older, I hope you will learn that there are generally extenuating circumstances if we try to look for them. In this case, much of Diana's folly is the outcome of her upbringing. I want you, Bride, to take time to think how much better you would have been if *you* had been as spoilt and indulged as she has. And I also want you to remember that none of us is faultless and God will judge our sins according to our opportunities and the use we have made of them."

Bride replied in subdued tones. "I'll try. All the same," she added, "there is one thing I shall *never* understand, and that's how she ever expected to get away with such a thing. Surely she knew that her mother would miss the things and make a fuss about them?"

"As I understand matters, she might quite well have got away with it, as you would say, only her father took it into his head to have the jewellery revalued. He wanted to raise the insurance on them. Otherwise, the loss might not have been discovered for months or even a year or two as Mrs Skelton doesn't care for the rings and never wears them."

"Oh, I see." Then, after a moment's pause, "Auntie Hilda, how – how was she found out?"

"The jeweller to whom she sold them recognized them when he looked at them later on. He had actually sold one of them to Mr Skelton. He rang him up and so it all came out."

"And Diana was found out." Bride was silent and the Head watched her curiously. Presently the girl looked at her again. "It's a horrible tale. If I catch Sylvia talking, I'll sit on her good and hearty. But I can't *not* think it was a ghastly thing to do. I don't want to be horrid, but I'm glad she isn't coming back to school."

"Go away, Bride, and think over all I have said to you," Miss Annersley said quietly. "I know it has been a shock to you, but you must learn to meet shocks of this kind now and then, and to be ready to hold out a helping hand and a *friendly* hand if it is asked. And I mean 'friendly'. Now run along. I need not tell you that you are to repeat none of this without my permission?"

"Oh, no; I won't say a word," Bride said. She got to her feet. "Auntie Hilda, I'll try to make allowances for Diana, and I'll certainly put a stop to any gossip about it if I hear any. I can promise you that."

"Very well, dear. I hope the rest will not be too long in coming."

Bride left the room after bobbing her regulation curtsy. On the way back to the prefects' room, she thought to herself that "Auntie Hilda" really did manage to make you feel a complete worm, even when you thought yourself in the right. Well, she certainly couldn't tell the others anything about this. She must just say that it was private business. That would make them pipe down on any kind of questions.

CHAPTER THREE

Future Destination

Bride went up, intending to return to the prefects' room, but when she was halfway there, the ringing of the supper bell diverted her progress to the foot of the flight of stairs leading from the upstairs dormitories.

"Steady!" she called sharply as a bunch of Junior Middles came hurtling down the stairs. "You sound like a mob of baby elephants in a panic! Prudence Dawbarn – get off those banisters!"

A shining light of Upper III who had flung a leg over the banister rail, meekly slid it back and came downstairs on her two feet.

"I didn't know you were there, Bride," she said meekly as she reached the Head Girl.

Bride looked down into the cheeky little face and suddenly grinned. "So I gathered – quiet, there, Mary-Lou – Vi Lucy – Doris Hill! You'll have the house about our ears if you come down like that! – but if you'll think back to previous terms, you'll find that there generally *is* a prefect or two about the stairs and passages when the bell rings for any meal. I know it's first week of term and first day at that, when most rules are in abeyance. All the same, my child, if I were you I'd try to get into the habit of sticking to them as early in the term as possible. You'll probably save yourself any amount of trouble later on if you do. Now you can go!" And she stood to one side and let Prudence – most ill-named of girls – slip past her.

36

In the big dining room, the chatter of two hundred-and-one girls made the meal anything but quiet, once Grace had been said. Rules came into force on the morrow, among them the one that said that Wednesday was a day when nothing but English must be spoken, so the twenty-odd foreigners who were pupils made hay while the sun shone and the British girls were in no way behind them.

Some of the prefects wondered if the Head would make an announcement at the end of the meal, but Miss Annersley knew better. She sat chatting gaily to her staff at the same time keeping an ear open and when the noise rose beyond a certain limit, a touch of the bell beside her reduced it immediately. No one wanted to have complete silence imposed for the remainder of the time.

When finally Grace had been said and such of the girls as were still not unpacked had been gathered in by Matron, the rest went to their common rooms to await the summons to Prayers.

In the big room dedicated to the Middles, a throng stood by the far window, chattering eagerly. A little group of seven had parked themselves in a small recess at the other side of the room. This had a window, as well, for the room was a corner one, looking out on the orchard at the back of Big House, while the side window opened on to the shrubbery. Here, Mary-Lou Trelawney, the acknowledged leader of her clan, had gathered together her special friends. She had something to tell them which she felt they ought to know before any of the others. So she had shaken off various people who came bubbling over with news of their holiday doings, and now the seven who led all the middles except those very superior young persons who were in Lower Vb, were in a compact little cluster.

"Do you really think it's true that we're going to move?" asked Vi Lucy, a frankly lovely thirteen-year-old, as she produced a slab of chocolate from her blazer pocket and proceeded to break it up. "Here you are, everyone; wire in!"

They needed no second invitation. After Prayers, they had to march to the sweet cupboard bearing any sweets they had brought from home, and hand them over to Matron to be doled out, a few every afternoon, for as long as they lasted. It was understood that everything they had brought should be given in, so this was their last chance of indiscriminate feasting.

"It's weird, isn't it?" Ruth Barnes asked with her mouth full of chocolate. "D'you think we're going back to Plas Howell? It'll be rather fun to have the hill to climb again."

"We'll miss the sea, though," Lesley Malcolm said wistfully. "And I do so love it! No chances of boating at Plas Howell!"

Vi Lucy, who had been bursting with some news, swallowed her mouthful and said decidedly, "We aren't going back there, anyhow."

"*What?*" They were all agog at this.

Vi nodded until her bronzy curls tossed wildly. "Yes! I met Betsy just before Abendessen and she whispered that Julie had told her that Bride Bettany said that Daisy Venables had had a letter from Gwensi Howell—"

"Mercy! You sound like THE HOUSE THAT JACK BUILT!" exclaimed Hilary Bennett, a new member last term to their gang.

"Pipe down, Hilary!" Mary-Lou ordered. "Yes – go on, Vi!"

"Well," continued Vi, who was as sweet-tempered a girl as ever belonged to the school, "Gwensi told

Daisy that her brother had sold Plas Howell. So you see we *can't* go back there!" Then she sat back and enjoyed the sensation.

"But – where *are* we going, then?" Lesley demanded, wide-eyed. "And, come to that, why can't we just stay on here?"

"Probably Cherry's people want to come back again," Mary-Lou replied. "I say, you folk, Verity-Anne and I have something to tell you."

"About leaving here, d'you mean?" Hilary asked.

To their amazement, the insouciant Mary-Lou suddenly blushed as she replied, "Er – no; not exactly. In fact, not at all."

"You aren't going to *leave*, both of you, are you?" demanded Doris Hill, suddenly smitten with this awful idea.

Mary-Lou promptly recovered herself at this. "Of course we aren't! At *our* age? Is it likely? Do have a *little* sense, Doris!"

"Oh, I didn't mean leave school altogether," Doris said calmly – she knew her Mary-Lou. "I only thought p'raps your people wanted to send you somewhere else."

"Well, they don't. Ages ago, when I was just a kid, Gran told me that I was staying at the Chalet School until I was eighteen or so," Mary-Lou informed her chum. "They haven't changed about *that*, anyhow!"

"You mean they've changed about other things?" Lesley asked shrewdly. "Well, get cracking and tell us what they are. Or *you* do it, Verity-Anne."

Verity-Anne, a very small person with long flaxen curls hanging to her waist and gentian-blue eyes which gave a rather startling effect to her cameo-like face, went faintly pink, squeezed Mary-Lou's hand and shook her head.

"Oh, I'll tell you," that young person said. "It's just –

we're going to be sisters – step ones, I mean. My mother is marrying her father."

There was a fresh sensation.* Nearly four years before this, Mary-Lou's father, who had been with an expedition up the Amazon, had been killed, together with most of the others, by some wild natives. Verity-Anne's father had been with them as cartographer and he and the doctor were the only ones who had escaped. Verity-Anne had had no home for some months before the news came through, and gentle Mrs Trelawney had taken the child to her heart and home. When Commander Carey came home at last, a badly-wounded man who would never be really strong again, he had had to spend months in hospital and Verity-Anne had remained with the Trelawneys. Later, he had agreed to leave her with them, coming himself to visit her at Carn Beg during the holidays and he and the two Mrs Trelawneys – Mother and Gran – had become close friends, while the two girls were growing up almost as sisters. Now this would set the seal on all that.

Now that she had broken the news, Mary-Lou condescended to enlarge a little.

"You see, Mother and Gran have been alone since Father's death. We've all been tremendous friends and, as you know, Verity-Anne's lived with us straight on. Her father didn't feel like starting a home. Anyway, Gran says that no man is fit to bring up a girl properly." Mary-Lou wound up with an air.

"Daddy *could* do it!" Verity-Anne cried indignantly. "Only it would have meant having a housekeeper and all that sort of thing; and you know yourself, Mary-Lou, that when he first came home, he just wasn't fit to do anything.

---

* *Three go to the Chalet School.*

He could have brought me up quite well himself if he'd wanted to!"

"OK," Mary-Lou returned, quite unmoved. "He could; but he didn't feel like it. Now he's gone and fallen in love with Mother – and I honestly don't blame him!" This with an air of fine impartiality. "Anyhow, they're going to be married the last week in July and Verity-Anne and I are going to be bridesmaids. Carn Beg is heaps big enough for all of us and he won't be going off to America again, 'cos the doctors all say he'll never be fit enough. There's the bell for Prayers at last! Come on, folks; line up! We'll know all about everything very soon now!"

She slid down off the window seat on which she had been curled up and went to assist in marshalling the rest of the gang into line. Silence had fallen on the room with remarkable suddenness. The Chalet School know well enough that certain rules must always be kept, first night or no, and the Prayer-bell meant the end of talking – for the immediate present, at any rate.

Julie Lucy appeared to march them either to Hall, where the Protestants performed their devotions under the Head's guidance, or to the big drawing room where Mdlle awaited the Catholics. Rather to the surprise of the girls in Hall, Prayers began with the beginning-of-term hymns. No new girls ever came until the second day of term so, as a rule, it was left till then and they sang something else. The change in this rule caused a good many raised eyebrows among the elder girls; and Mary-Lou was so surprised that she opened her mouth to remind the Head.

Luckily for her, Vi Lucy was watching and she poked her chum with a hissed whisper of: "Dry up, idiot!"

Mary-Lou shut her mouth with a snap and then joined

in the singing at the full pitch of her excellent lungs, while Verity-Anne's lark-like notes rose from one side of her and Vi's pleasant little pipe from the other. When it was ended, they sat down for the reading. Bride Bettany stood forward and read the parable of the talents, a reading sacred to the first full night of term. But when the Head, having led them in "Our Father" and the Creed followed up with the beginning-of-term prayer, the only wonder was that some of them did not burst from sheer curiosity!

Mary-Lou went so far as to open her eyes and look hurriedly round to see if any new girls were there and she had overlooked them hitherto. How she imagined such a thing could have happened is more than can be explained. However, she gained nothing by it, for all she *could* see were of long standing in the school. There was nothing for it but to bottle up her feelings and try to pay a little attention to the present proceedings.

She was not alone in her excitement. When Bride had gone to the study immediately after Abendessen to ask what passage she should read, she had received a shock on being told to take the parable of the talents. She had been waylaid by Matron on her way back to impart this news to the rest of her peers and only had time to whisper to those nearest her what the passage was before the bell rang and they had to disperse to see that the younger girls went to Prayers decently and in order.

However, no one was any wiser when they rose from their knees than before, and they had to wait until the door at the head of the room opened and the Catholic section of the school filed demurely to seats. Once everyone was sitting down, however, the Head rose from her great chair in the centre of the dais to take her stand by the lectern desk, and a faint sigh of relief went up. They were going to hear the meaning of all these changes at last!

Miss Annersley was a tall and stately person. She was very good-looking in a clear-cut way, with wavy brown hair and a pair of blue eyes that had never yet needed glasses. Her greatest asset, however, was her voice, which was beautiful – deeply pitched and resonant and flexible. The girls always listened intently when she spoke on these occasions, and tonight was no exception to the rule.

Standing on the dais, she smiled at them before she began. Then she said: "Well, first I must bid you all welcome back to school. I hope this will be a very happy term for everyone, especially as it will be our last on the island. I know you've enjoyed being here and having all the fun of bathing and boating, as well as your usual cricket and tennis. Still, we all knew that this was only a temporary home, and now Commander Christy wants his own house again, so we have to seek new quarters. And it really *is* new quarters this time, for Mr Howell has sold Plas Howell as he will never want to live there himself; so we are making a big change.

"I think you all know that we have never given up hope that the day would come when we could go back to our first home in Tirol. We can't do it yet, for various reasons; but we are going to do the next best thing. Next term, we are opening in the Alps once more – in the Bernese Oberland which," she added for the benefit of the younger girls who were looking blankly at her, "is in Switzerland."

There was no mistaking the gasp of delighted surprise that went round at this. Someone began to clap and Miss Annersley gave them their heads for a full minute before she held up her hand as a warning that this noise must now *cease*.

"Well, I see I needn't ask if you like the idea. I'm sure you're all quite as thrilled by it as we all are," she gave a half-turn to include the staff in her statement and they all smiled or grinned back at her. "I must give you one warning, however. I very much hope that *all* of you here who are twelve or over will come with us. Just at present, I'm afraid we can't take anyone younger." Whereat the faces of the two Lower Thirds and several people in Upper Third fell. "Besides this, some of you may have parents who don't like the idea of having their girls out of England under the age of sixteen. I can't tell you anything about that yet. We must wait until there has been time for me to hear from your people. I very much hope that we may be lucky and take everyone here who is of the right age by September with us. Meanwhile, wouldn't you like to know exactly where it is we are going?" She looked at them smilingly and saw the answer in the eager young faces upturned to hers. "We are going to the mountains above Welsen, where the finishing branch of the school has already opened. Our particular part is called the Görnetz Platz, and Peggy and Joan and Dickie and all the other girls who were with us at this time last year know it quite well now."

She stopped again, this time to give the girls a chance to let go and they all clapped vehemently at the news. Bride was grinning at Nancy Chester; and those of them who had sisters or cousins already at Welsen were beaming excitedly.

When she felt that they had relieved their feelings sufficiently, the Head checked them again and proceeded to finish this part of her speech.

"The Sanatorium is opening up there and, as all you elder girls know, the School and the San have always been run in conjunction until the last few years when we have not had quite such close links with it. But now we expect to renew our old custom and, while many of you will not have that shadow on you yet, there will be some who will. We shall not be near San itself. The Platz is three miles or so long and we shall be at one end and San at the other. There will be the whole of Görnetz village between us. All the same, it will mean that if any girl is wanted in a hurry, she can get to San in a few minutes. And now, would anyone like to ask any questions?"

Quite a number of people took up the offer. Mary-Lou set the ball rolling – "She *would*!" as Bride said later on to her friends – and she stood up in her place to ask with much dignity, "Please, Miss Annersley, how do we get there?"

"By train from London. We cross the Channel by the train-ferry and so to Paris. We change at Paris to a train for Berne and from Berne we change again for Interlaken, which will be our nearest town of any size. From there, we take the mountain train up to the Platz." Then seeing the deep disappointment in Mary-Lou's face, the Head asked with some curiosity, "How did you imagine we should go?"

"I only wondered if perhaps we'd fly," Mary-Lou said.

"My *dear* girl! Have you any idea what it costs?" demanded the amused Head.

"Not a sausage!" Mary-Lou returned promptly and thoughtlessly.

No one could help it. The culprit knew as soon as the words had left her lips what she had done and the startling remark together with her expression was too much for everyone – the great room rang with their peals of laughter. The Head bit her lips for a moment. Then she, too, gave way and burst out laughing.

When she had recovered, she looked across at the

abashed Mary-Lou, who was still standing, her face scarlet, and said gently, "Not quite the way to express it, but I see what you mean. No; we aren't flying. It would be far too dear."

Mary-Lou sat down again, still red and hot, and kept herself as inconspicuous as she could until she had cooled off and the others had more or less forgotten her lapse in the eagerness with which they plied the Head with their questions.

Clem Barrass was on her feet asking, "Please, Miss Annersley, isn't there a mountain-path up? Couldn't those of us who liked walk up? We'll all be pretty stiff with all that sitting in trains," she added.

Quite a number of them awaited the Head's reply with some anxiety. Miss Annersley shook her head, however. "Not this time, I'm afraid, Clemency. I hope we shall be able to arrange climbing expeditions for you during the term; but you must be content to use the train when we go up."

Big Tom Gay was on her feet as Clem sat down with a murmured, "Thank you!"

"What will happen to those of us who don't go to Switzerland?" she asked bluntly.

"We are buying Glendower House where St Agnes' now is, and Miss Edwards will stay on at Carnbach to take charge of it, together with one or two others of the present staff and some new members as well. You have all been there, and you know that, at present, we use only about half of it, it is so large. I think that any of you who have to remain in England will find that you still have the Chalet School there, even though it may be much smaller. But that's an adventure, you know. *You* will be the people who will keep up our traditions there. We shall be a much smaller school at the Platz, just at first."

Tom sat down again and Betsy Lucy, who was a shining light of Lower VA, rose to inquire, "Shall we be able to see anything of the people at Welsen?"

"If you mean will they share lessons and so on with you, the answer is 'No', Betsy. If you only mean will you be able to see them on Saturdays and so forth, yes, you certainly will. The Welsen girls often go up to the Platz in their free time. Some of their mistresses will come up to help in our branch of the school and some of ours are going to help with theirs. But you mustn't forget, girls, that the Welsen branch is definitely what we call a *finishing* school. They take subjects that you don't at present; and they have dropped others that you must work at. All the same, I think you'll find that you have plenty of opportunities of meeting relations and old friends, even though you aren't in the same part of the school. Now has anyone anything else to ask?"

A girl of thirteen got to her feet. "Please, what language will we talk?" she asked hopefully.

"The three you use here," the Head told her promptly. "What else did you expect, Emerence? The common tongue in those parts is German, so if any of you have hopes of going shopping, I advise you to polish up your German. Some of our expeditions will take us to the French cantons and then you will need French. And, as I expect we shall be having several foreign girls with us – in fact, I know of quite a number who are coming – we shall keep our English days as well. But for you, the real work is going to be in French and German, so work hard at them, everyone. I can assure you you'll need them!"

Emerence Hope sat down looking very doleful. She hated both French and German and she had been hoping that going to Switzerland meant that conversation in these tongues would not be so necessary, though why she should have thought so, no one could make out. Now, it seemed, she must work twice as hard at them as before. Emerence was a lazy young thing and never did a stroke of work she could help.

"And I thought at least we'd be eased off in *those*!" she groaned to the others later on.

"If you weren't a complete and utter goop," Mary-Lou told her, "you'd have guessed that that was the *last* thing you could expect."

This came later, however. At the present, as no one seemed to have any more questions to ask, Miss Annersley dismissed them; the under-thirteens to bed, the rest to have another hour or more in the common rooms, in which to ventilate their ideas on the latest events in the Chalet School.

CHAPTER FOUR

Term Begins in Earnest

"New girls come today!" exclaimed Mary-Lou the next morning as she sat on the floor, pulling on her stockings. She finished, jumped up and began fastening them, then as no one seemed to have taken the faintest notice of her remark, she repeated it, scurrying into the rest of her clothes at the same time. "New girls come this morning, and this afternoon, *and* this evening. I wonder how many there are and what they'll be like?"

Vi Lucy, just returned from her morning tub, paused to peep through her chum's curtains to say, "There won't be many *this* term – there never are. Mary-Lou Trelawney! You're nearly dressed! And you went for your bath same time as me! How do you do it?"

"She doesn't tub properly," remarked a Welsh girl, one Gwen Davies. "Just splash in – splash out again; that's Mary-Lou's idea of a bath."

Mary-Lou chuckled as she turned her long, light brown hair over her face and proceeded to bang it with her brush. "Oh no, it isn't. I simply don't dither like the rest of you. There isn't time."

"How come you have so much less time than the rest of us?" someone else asked.

Still brushing hard, Mary-Lou replied, "I don't know, but I *have*. Or else it's that I like to get things done and out of the way." She tossed her brush on to the bed, grabbed her comb and parted the gleaming locks before she plaited them, swiftly tying them with enormous brown bows. Then she turned to pick up her blouse, since it was not yet warm enough for gingham frocks.

Vi dropped the curtains and went on to her own cubicle next door, when she said, "Let it go! What d'you think we'll do today, anyone? We don't start lessons until the new girls are all here."

Before anyone could reply to this, the dormitory door opened and Katharine Gordon, the dormitory prefect, came in. Her eyes were gleaming if anyone had been able to see them, and she was grinning to herself. She had just met Bride Bettany, who had passed on to her a message from the Head. Katharine knew that it would be a nasty shock to her lambs, though she herself never minded. She stood still in the middle of the aisle that ran down between the cubicles and said, "All out!"

There was a rustle and several gasps and then the girls appeared between their curtains in various stages of undress. Two cubicles remained still, so Katharine went to investigate. Even as she did so, the door opened again and Verity-Anne Carey shot in, carrying her damp towels.

"Oh, so you're there," Katharine remarked. "Where's Marian Tovey, anyone?"

"She was late," someone explained. "She'll be here in a moment, I expect."

"She had no business to be late," Katharine said tartly. She had no love for the said Marian Tovey, since it was owing to that young lady that she had been reft last term from her own dormitory where three of her intimate friends were, in order to take charge of Leafy dormitory as Marian had proved too much for Gwen Jones, the former dormitory prefect. She was older than Gwen by a full year and, having come from a school where all discipline had been "free", had resented having to obey any orders the younger girl might give. There had been a good deal of trouble over it, one way and another, and finally Matron had moved Katharine to Leafy and sent Gwen to take her place in Wisteria, much to the annoyance of both.

Marian arrived at that moment, so the elder girl said, "You'll be awfully late, Marian. You'll have to hurry. But wait a moment. I've a message from the Head. Listen, everyone. For this term, it's been decided that we need extra French and German conversation. During lessons on Wednesdays – that is, until four o'clock, we are to speak French. Saturday mornings we talk German. That's all. Hurry, all of you, or you'll be late."

Most of them disappeared on the word after casting meaningful looks at Mary-Lou, who was further on than any of them. She nodded and stood still.

"Please Katharine, you don't mean we've got to begin *today*?" she asked. "School doesn't begin properly till tomorrow."

"That's what Bride told me," Katharine informed her.

Not ceasing to button her blouse, Mary-Lou gasped. "But why ever?"

"Don't ask me – ask the Head," the elder girl told her.

Mary-Lou gave another gasp and retreated to her cubicle, where she finished her dressing at her usual railroad speed, stripped her bed and tidied the cubicle. Then she shot across the aisle to see to Verity-Anne.

That young lady was yanking a comb through her long curls in a way calculated to drag half of them out by the roots. She still had to get into skirt and blouse, tie and blazer, and her cubicle work was not touched. As her future relation hurtled in, she turned to give her an appealing look.

"Keep your wool on," Mary-Lou said cheerfully. "I'll see to your cubey."

Strictly speaking, it was against rules; but everyone knew that Verity-Anne had been born deliberate. Not even four years of school had succeeded in making her able to hurry without, as Clem Barrass who lived with the Trelawneys in holiday-time had once remarked, going into a flat spin. As a result, Mary-Lou's custom of helping her out was rather winked at by the authorities. Even Matron, that strict disciplinarian, only said, "It's the only way to have her down on time. I've tried with her for ages and the only result of hounding her on is to make her so nervous that she can't do a thing right. All we can do is to turn a blind eye on Mary-Lou's activities and wait till she's older. She may grow out of it in time."

Now, while her chum finished her dressing, Mary-Lou stripped the bed, "humped" the mattress to let a current of fresh air flow under it, and put away the various things Verity-Anne still had strewn about. When she had finished, she poked her head out between the curtains and announced, "They're lining up at the door. Hurry, Verity-Anne! The bell will go any minute now."

Verity-Anne finished knotting her tie. She snatched up her blazer and wriggled into it and then was prepared to go; but the watchful Mary-Lou checked her. "Where's your Guide badge? And have you a hankey?"

These omissions corrected, the pair finally left the cubicle and dashed to tail on to the line that marched out of the dormitory at the first stroke of the bell. Verity-Anne heaved a thankful sigh. If she had been late she would have had to pay a fine of a penny and her father considered that the official two shillings a week was enough pocket-money for a schoolgirl of fourteen, except for birthdays or special occasions.

52

"And when you've got to put sixpence into each of the Sunday collections, *that* doesn't leave you much to play around with!" Mary-Lou, whose people were of the same way of thinking, had once observed with some bitterness.

Once downstairs, they went to their form rooms where they sat down at their desks. Lessons, as Vi Lucy had said, did not, as a rule, begin the first day of term; so they had no idea what they were expected to do.

Beth Lane, their form prefect, looked round thoughtfully. "No extra desks. *We* don't get any new girls, then."

"It's mostly the kids who do that this term," Mary-Lou pointed out. "Our lot come next term." She stopped to giggle. "I wonder if we'll have any? We may not, you know. The Head said lots of parents mightn't want to let their girls go out of England."

"I hope mine do," Christine Vincent said. "You seem jolly sure about yours, Mary-Lou."

"Well, Mother said I should have a year or two abroad when I finished here," Mary-Lou explained. "I don't suppose she'll make any bones about it coming a little earlier than we expected."

This set them all off, wondering what their parents would do. Some of them were fairly sure that it would be all right and they would go with the school. Others were by no means so certain. Mollie Woods was sure that her father would refuse.

"I'll just have to go on at St Agnes' while the rest of you are prancing up and down the Alps," she said with a sigh that seemed to come from her shoes. "Oh, well, at least we'll have all the sea fun, so that's something."

Doris Hill, who was one of those who felt comfortably sure that she would go, got up and went to examine the timetable.

53

"If this still holds good, we have arithmetic first," she said after a prolonged stare at it.

"Of course it holds good," Beth Lane said. "You ought to know by this time that the timetable works for the whole year. But it doesn't matter. We don't *have* lessons the first day. We honestly don't know what to do until Prayers – except the people who have practice."

The door opened and Miss Slater, the maths mistress who also had the pleasure of being their form mistress, walked in. The whole form rose to its feet, and said, "Good morning, Miss Slater."

"Bon jour, mes filles," Miss Slater replied cheerfully. Then she went on in French, "Have you not heard that French is to be spoken today?"

This was news to a few whose dormitory prefects had not yet been told. The rest went red, shuffled their feet and looked at their desks.

Miss Slater was merciful. "Well, you know now," she said, speaking slowly for the sakes of those whose French was anything but fluent yet. "I came to tell you that Miss Annersley says that you may go out into the garden so long as you keep tidy. You can begin to weed your form bed. Come in the moment the first bell goes; slip on your gardening clogs. Off you go! I'm coming to help in a moment."

It was a lovely April morning, so everyone was pleased to hear this. They hurriedly formed into a line and in less than ten minutes were all standing round the big bed that was their special part of the garden, surveying the results of their month's holiday.

"Well!" This was Mary-Lou, of course. "Did you ever *see* anything like the way those horrible weeds have grown? It was absolutely clear when we went home at Easter and just look at it now! It's dreadful!"

"Miss Slater was right," Beth Lane said ruefully. "We have plenty of work to do. Come along, everyone! We must begin!"

"I certainly should," said Miss Slater's voice as that lady appeared through the bushes. "H'm! Yes; there is plenty of work as Beth says. Spread round the bed, girls, and begin to clear from the edge inwards. Be careful that you don't pull up any flowers by mistake and look where you're going. We have a nice lot of tulips down that side and it would be a pity to trample on them."

They set to work, and by the time the first bell rang there was quite a clearance at the edges of the bed. Miss Slater stood up, dusting her hands together, and marshalled them into line before marching them smartly back to the house, where they fled to their own splashery to wash their hands and tidy their hair. Then came Frühstück, as they called breakfast in recollection of Tirol days, at which they all showed fine appetites. When it ended and they were standing for Grace, the Head reminded them once more that French must be spoken until four o'clock. After that she dismissed them and they went upstairs to make their beds and see that their cubicles came up to Matron's standard of neatness. A walk followed, and when they came back, they were told to go to their form rooms as usual.

Miss Slater was waiting for Upper IVA when they arrived there, so no one could chatter. They went quietly to their seats and when they were all seated, to their amazement she produced the roll-book and called the roll. This was quite new. As a rule, roll-call did not begin until the entire school was assembled. However, there seemed to be so many changes coming, that they just accepted it as another and no one even looked surprised. The bell for Prayers rang as the mistress closed her register and handed it to Beth to take along to the office for Miss Dene to check up. Once more they formed a line and marched off to Prayers. But when that was over and they were all seated in Hall, they learned of yet another change.

"Term begins at once, girls," the Head said. "For one thing, as we are having such a big removal, term must end sooner than usual. For another, we have no new girls this term. Since most of us, I hope, are going to the Oberland, we felt it was better to ask them to wait for the beginning of the school year. That being the case, when I dismiss you, you will go to your form rooms and begin with your ordinary Wednesday lessons. I have one more item of news for you. We shall have no half term, either, though we expect to make our usual expedition on Madame's birthday. But as we are to break up ten days earlier than usual, we must make the most of every moment of our time. Now, that is all. Stand!"

The school rose as one girl and Miss Lawrence, the resident music mistress, struck up a bright march and they went off, beginning with Lower Third and finishing with Upper Sixth. The mistresses followed quickly to their various form rooms. They all knew that the girls, if left a moment to themselves, would be so excited by the latest change that it would not be an easy matter to get good work from any of them. So they had barely time to get out the books they needed for the first half of the morning before they were plunged into the thick of lessons. The staff kept them hard at it and they had to wait until Break before they could air their views on the subject.

Quite a number of people always looked forward to half-past ten; but today, it is safe to say that the entire school longed for it. It came at last, and they went for their milk and biscuits in the dining room. Once those were dispatched, they might go out into the garden as it was a fine morning, and in less than five minutes groups were already forming down the drive and along the paths. Their tongues were instantly loosed and a good many people forgot that French was the order of the day. Several others lost their vocabularies in their excitement and were reduced to wild inventions. This refers to the Middles, of course. Those dignified young ladies, the Seniors, managed better and the prefects were quite fluent.

"Eh bien," Mary-Lou began to a select party from Upper IVA, "this is – I mean – c'est une surpris, n'est ce pas? Rien des nouvelles, et nous allons – is it 'à la Suisse' or 'en Suisse?' I always forget."

No one could help her out. French grammar was beneath their notice just then.

"I wonder – bother! What's the French for wonder, someone?" This was Vi.

"Je ne sais pas," Beth said.

"Eh bien – je wonder si ma mère permetterez moi à allez? Je l'espère! Julie y sera. Peut-être elle agréera que je vais aussi."

"Oh, oui!" Lesley Malcom gushed. "La Suisse sera simplement marvellous!"

"Le français pour 'marvellous' est 'merveilleuse' – je pense," Beth put in.

Bride Bettany was passing and heard all this. She paused. "Don't you people know any more than that?" she asked in excellent French and shocked tones. "You must work very hard this term at languages, that's certain. What do you want to say, Beth and Vi? Tell me and I'll put it into good French for you to repeat."

The pair looked blue. Bother Bride Bettany! Who wanted to spend their Break repeating French sentences and phrases until they were said to suit the Head Girl!

Bride knew what they were thinking and remained

sweetly oblivious to the glances they cast at her. "Hurry up," she said inflexibly.

Very unwillingly, the pair repeated their remarks and she set them right before she gave them a smiling nod and went on to join her own friends. But she had contrived to give them a jolt.

"Pensez-vous que nous aurons parler en français toujours quand nous etes à la Suisse?" Emerence Hope asked in horrified tones.

"No – I mean, non. Er – Mdlle Annersley dit qu'il faut parler en allemand aussi," Doris Hill told her.

"That's worse!" Emerence said despairingly.

It was well for her that only her own gang could hear her, or she would have been made to put the remark into French and repeat it until she got the right accent. This was the rule at the Chalet School and, however much the girls might resent it, there is no denying the fact that they learned an amazing amount by it, not to speak of gaining a very fair accent.

However, Doris's remark had nearly finished them and Catriona Watson only voiced the feelings of all when she said, "Comme faisons-nous?"

"Aussi bien que nous pouvons," Mary-Lou told her. Then, forgetting rules, she added in English, "What a life we're going to have of it this term! I can manage French, but *German*!"

"Prener-garde! Julie vient!" Vi warned her. Julie might be her eldest sister, but Vi knew quite well that that only made her stricter with both Betsy and herself.

Mary-Lou jumped at Vi's warning, but Julie had not been near enough to hear ordinary conversation and, for once, Mary-Lou had moderated her usual bell-like tones.

It was a very difficult day for a good many of them. When you are bursting with excitement, it is hard enough to have to control your tongue anyhow. When you not only have to do that, but also turn your thoughts into a foreign language, there are times when you feel like exploding. At least half of the school felt like that and Clem Barrass expressed it to Betsy Lucy when the end of school brought them freedom.

"I hope I'll never have to go through such a day as this again. *French* – when you're so revved up you find it hard enough to say all you think in English! Cruelty to dumb animals, I call it. Come on, Bets! Let's go and snaffle a quiet corner of the dining room and say what we've had to bottle up all day."

"Let's be thankful," Betsy said as they went off to seek their "quiet corner" at a distant table, "that we didn't have to talk in German! And we might have, you know."

"Today's big thought!" Clem murmured as she subsided into a chair. "Now let's get cracking!"

CHAPTER FIVE

The Prefects Discuss the Situation

While their juniors were greatly intrigued by the present state of affairs, the grandees of the school were no whit behind them, though the prefects, as became such dignified young ladies, controlled themselves in public.

"Prefects' meeting this afternoon," Bride announced to such of them as came within her reach at Break. A fair proportion of the two Sixths took science, and as the laboratory was in the old stables those people were never available until Mittagessen, the authorities, with an eye to wasted time, having decreed that on science mornings they should also have their art and handcrafts lessons, the rooms for those being at one side of the labs. "Elevenses" was partaken of in the domestic science kitchen for the same reason.

Bess Herbert nodded. "I rather thought you would. We shall have any amount to discuss. For instance, I want to go through the libraries. I expect we'll have to leave part of them behind for those who don't go to Switzerland. We shall have to do a lot of sorting out, I may tell you. Jean Donald can tackle Junior Library and I'll see to the rest. I should say most of the Junior books must be left for St Agnes' House. Practically everyone in the two Lower Thirds will be going there, even if it's only for a year; and there'll be a few from Upper as well."

"I hadn't thought about that at all," Bride said slowly. "You're right, of course. Shall we have to tackle the reference library as well, d'you think?"

"I haven't the least idea – not a sausage, as Mary-Lou would say."

The big girls laughed. Then Primrose Day said, "I don't suppose the Ref will be our pidgin. The staff will see to *that*. Just as well too. You'll have plenty on your plate without worrying about that, Bess, even if you *have* got Jean to help with Junior."

Nancy Chester who was with them had been looking thoughtful. "I say," she said, "I've just realized that the same thing will probably apply to the gym and games apparatus as well. We'd better have a good overhaul of the lot as soon as we can manage it."

"I don't suppose we'll have to worry about the gym apparatus," Bride said. "They have their own over there – quite a good gym, if I remember. It used to be a billiards room, so it was a very decent size. But the games stuff – we'll certainly have to divide that. Elfie and the rest of you had better see Burnie about that. She'll give you a hand, I don't doubt."

"Sure she will," put in Julie Lucy, who was with them. "By the way, has it ever struck you people that we're going to be a much smaller school next term? I don't suppose everyone over twelve will be going to Switzerland, and there won't be any Juniors in any case."

They all looked serious over this. They had not considered that side of it until Bess had spoken of the libraries. They were not sure that they liked the prospect very much. They were proud of their school and very proud of the fact that it was a really big one as boarding schools go.

Bride spoke first. "And furthermore," she said, "don't forget that *we* shan't be there, either."

"Oh, my one and only Aunt Sophonisba!" Nancy exclaimed. "Neither we shall! I say, this is going to mean changes with a vengeance!"

"There's one thing," Julie said, as they turned and sauntered down the drive, "and that is all this ought to dispose of Tom's objections, oughtn't it? I mean, if the school at large is going to Switzerland, she might just as well go to the Welsen branch as the one up at the Platz."

"Yes; that's true," Bride agreed. "Good! I'd have hated to miss old Tom after all these years together." —

Bess, who was in many ways the most thoughtful of them all, shook her head. "I wouldn't be so sure about that. Tom's people may decide that she must just go on and finish at St Agnes'. I know they're fearfully poor, for I've heard Dad say so. He always said it was a shame that Mr Gay didn't have a better living after the way he's worked. He's a really good man, you know — a fine preacher and organizer, Dad says. And Dad knows, for they were at Shrewsbury School together when they were boys and they've always remained friends."

The Herberts' father was Dean of one of the smaller cathedrals, so the girls accepted this as being from someone who *knew*. They looked very downcast at her remarks. Tom Gay was a favourite with all of them, so they did not like the thought that their final year at school must be without her.

"Perhaps something may turn up and they can afford it after all," Nancy finally suggested, living up to her reputation as an incorrigible optimist.

"Let's hope so," Bride agreed. "It won't be the same thing without old Tom. There goes the bell! Come on, all of you! Half those kids seem to be deaf when it rings for the end of Break. They need a sheepdog after them every blessed day of the term!"

She went off to duty, followed by the rest, and they were fully occupied in seeing that all laggers were smartly whipped in on time. Then, when the younger girls were safely in their form rooms, the prefects had to hurry to the library, where they had an appointment with the Head on the subject of the romantic poets, and future changes had to be put out of their minds perforce.

There was no time to discuss things before three o'clock that day. However, that hour saw them all assembling in the prefects' room with an hour for the discussion of school business in front of them. Bride sat down at the head of the long table, Primrose and Elfie taking the chairs on either side as befitted the second prefect and the games prefect. The rest merely scrambled for places, leaving Rosalind Yolland, youngest but one of their group, to take the seat at the foot of the table. Everyone was on time for once, as Bride noted with a feeling of relief. This meant that they could get down to business at once. So often they had to wait because one of their number had been delayed by her job!

She waited until everyone was seated and then rapped smartly on the table for silence before she rose and said, "We've no time to lose, so I'm going to ask Primrose to read out the minutes of the last meeting at once."

She sat down and Primrose, who acted as secretary, stood up and read aloud the minutes of the meeting at the end of the previous term. Bride asked if it was their pleasure that she should sign them and did so in short order. Primrose pulled out her biro in readiness to make notes for the report of this one and the company looked very grave and responsible.

"Well," Bride began, "I needn't tell you that we've all had a shock. Last time the school moved, we didn't know anything about it until it had happened.* This time, we have a whole term to prepare. We shall have a lot to do as well. Bess reminded me this morning that, for one thing, the library must be gone over and sorted out and divided. I think we ought to leave most of the Junior stuff here anyhow, seeing that no one under twelve will be coming to the Oberland. And, I suppose, we ought to leave a proportion of the Senior books, too. We don't know that everyone over twelve may be coming. Quite a number of girls may have people who either don't want their girls to leave the country or else can't afford the additional travelling expenses and so on. I don't know anything about that, of course, but I should say it will add quite a bit to the expenses. Anyhow, it's none of our business. All the same, we've got to reckon with the fact that we shall have to allow for it when we begin to sort out. And then Nancy pointed out that the same thing must happen with the games apparatus." She paused, and Elfie, sitting at her left hand, took her turn.

"I quite agree, especially as we don't know whether there will be anyone to play against at hockey or laxe or netball either," she added.

Several faces fell at this.

"Great Caesar's bathmat!" Nancy exclaimed. "I hadn't thought of *that*!"

"Keep calm," Bride said sweetly. "They'll always be the inter-house matches, anyhow."

"Yes, there *is* that," Julie put in a word.

"And what about us?" demanded Lesley Pitt, a tall girl with a clever face. "We'll be there – at Welsen, anyhow. And though Peggy and Dickie and that crowd

* *The Chalet School and the Island.*

64

will have left, there are quite a lot of other girls who will have another year. We'll be able to make up teams from them."

"True for you!" Bride looked distinctly relieved. "Oh, well, then, we can certainly reckon on *some* matches and must take our share of the nets and goalposts and so on with us. I was beginning to think perhaps we had better leave the lot."

"Oh, it won't come to that," Lesley said positively.

"What about the boats?" Elfie queried. "There isn't any sea in Switzerland."

"Maybe not; but what about the lake?" Bride retorted. "There are *two* lakes, as a matter of fact. What do you think the name 'Interlaken' means?"

"Why should it mean anything?" Elfie asked, opening her eyes widely.

"It does, though – 'Between the lakes'. It stands on a kind of isthmus between Lake Thun and Lake Brienz. We'll have to ask the Head, of course; but I expect it'll be all right and we can get a certain amount of boating and swimming, even if it means just one day a week, since we'll have to go down for it. But I do remember that at Tiernsee we always had heaps of boating and swimming, too."

"Oh, cheers!" This came from Nancy and Julie who were cousins. Both lived in the island of Guernsey and both were accustomed to almost unlimited boating and bathing in the summer months, so the prospect of having to give it up again after two years of it and school had, as the former murmured, rather taken the gilt off the gingerbread for them.

"It depends on what the Head thinks about it," Bride warned them.

"Oh, she's safe to agree," Nancy said easily. "I expect,

though, we'll take only two or three of the boats and leave at least two for the others. I say, people, I'm beginning to look forward to all this; aren't you?"

Tom Gay, who had been sitting very silent, looked up. "I'm jolly glad for all you folk," she said, "but even at Welsen you'll be missing me, you know. I'll have to finish at St Agnes'. Please leave us a *few* things!"

Bride looked at her. "I wouldn't be too sure of that, Tom," she said. "You may be awarded one of the schols, you know. No one's said a word about them yet. If you got either, you'd go, my girl, if I had to bang you on the head and drag you after me by the scruff of the neck!"

At this touching picture, all the prefects went off into gales of mirth, even Tom, who had been looking very sober, joining in. She said no more. She had told them all last term that Switzerland would be out of the question for her and why and, from her point of view, there was no more to be said. Nevertheless, all this chatter about the future showed her more plainly than ever just what she would be missing.

"All the same," she thought to herself as she doodled idly on the paper before her, "I must get hold of young Bride and make sure she hasn't been at either of her aunts about me. It's just the sort of thing she *would* do and I'm taking no scholarships that someone else has begged for me and that's flat!"

"What else should we think about?" A very quiet girl, Anne Webster, asked. "I mean, we haven't begun to think about our usual term business yet."

Bride considered. "Well, there's all the stuff here," she said with a wave of her hand that nearly hit Elfie in the face. "The prefect stuff, I mean. Apart from the tables and chairs, every single thing in this room has been

66

given by the prefects at one time or another. The clock, for instance, came from Bette Rincini at the very beginning of things. Aunt Jo presented that bookcase when she was Head Girl. Your sister Beth, Nancy, gave that watercolour sketch of the house the school was in when it was on Guernsey.* We've got to decide whether we take it all or leave part for the prefects' room at St Agnes'."

This was another thing no one had thought of and they all looked round at the various vases, pictures and knick-knacks that adorned the room.

"I suppose," Julie said at last, "that what we've got to consider is whether the – the English branch is going to be more important than the Swiss one or vice versa."

Before anyone could reply to this, there was a tap at the door. Rosalind being nearest, got up and opened it to show Miss Dene standing there with a handful of letters.

"Sorry your post's so late," she said cheerfully. "I had to go over to Carnbach this morning on business and I've only just managed to get it sorted. Here you are, Rosalind. Give it out, will you? Tom, when you're finished here, the Head wants to see you in the study. And does anyone know where Jean Donald is likely to be? She wants to see her when she's finished with Tom."

"I'll look for her, Miss Dene," Bride promised. Then she added eagerly, "I say, I suppose you can't tell us if we're likely to have boating and swimming in Switzerland?"

They waited anxiously for Miss Dene's reply. She considered gravely. "I don't see why not," she said at last. "There are two lovely lakes at the foot of the mountain and we always had any amount when we were at the

* *The Chalet School in Exile.*

Tiernsee. You'd best ask the Head, though. Meanwhile, I daren't stay here gossiping or I'll never get through tonight. Ask me to come some other time." She nodded at them and smiled and then hurried away.

"Not much change to be got there," Audrey Simpson said, laughing. "Never mind those letters, Ros. They can wait. We've only twenty minutes and we haven't done a thing about the usual term's doings."

Rosalind tossed the letters into the middle of the table. "OK. We'll see to them later. Meanwhile, Elfie, what challenges have we had so far?"

They turned to ordinary school business which kept them fully occupied until the four o'clock bell brought their meeting to an end. Then Tom, after smoothing her hair with her hand and making sure that she was tidy, left them to go to the study. Bride, in pursuance of her promise, went off to hunt up Jean Donald, a member of Upper Sixth who had not attained to the honour of a prefectship, though she ran the Junior Library, and ran it well, under Bess.

Primrose reached for the letters and began to sort them out. "One for you, Bess. Madge, a couple for you. Anne – Nancy – Lesley – Julie – here you are. One for Tom and one for Bride from Switzerland – and that's the lot except for my own from Mother."

"None for me?" Rosalind demanded. "Doesn't anyone love me any more? Oh, well, it's early days, yet, I suppose. Mine will be arriving on Monday."

She turned away, laughing, to speak to Audrey.

Bride arrived back, having met Jean Donald on the stairs and given her Miss Dene's message. She grabbed up her letter and tore the envelope open. "From Peggy!" she announced. "Good for Peg! Still, they did go back last week, so it's time she wrote!"

"What does she say?" Madge Dawson asked, looking up from her own epistle. Peggy Bettany had been a much-loved Head Girl the previous year, and most of them had bemoaned the fact that when the finishing branch at Welsen had been opened, she had been one of those who went to it for her last school year.

Before Bride could reply, there came the sound of flying feet along the passage and then Tom literally burst into the room, her eyes shining, her face glowing and her hair all tossed with the speed of her return.

"Hello! Who's left you a fortune?" Nancy demanded as she laid down the brief note from her father.

"No one – at least – well, in one way I suppose it really *is*!" Tom said incoherently. She marched across to Bride and took her by the shoulders. "Bride Bettany, look me in the face and tell me you never murmured the word 'scholarship' to your Aunt Jo!"

"I never even wrote it," Bride assured her. "Not after all you had to say to me last term on the subject! I didn't want to let myself in for battle, murder *or* sudden death! D'you mean she's thought of it on her own bat? Oh, good for Auntie Jo! *Jolly* good!"

Tom nodded. Then she turned to the rest. "I spoke too soon, people. I'm coming to Switzerland after all. The Head's just told me that she's had a letter from Mrs Maynard and she said I was to have first chance of her schol. As you all know, it covers everything – including fares; so I'll be able to come after all. Oh, and Madame has offered *her* schol to Jean Donald, so she's coming, too. Oh, isn't it a set-out."

"You'd better sit down and get off a note to your people at once," Bride said practically. "Here's some paper. Get cracking and I believe you'll catch the evening postbag. It doesn't usually go till the last ferry and that's

69

at six o'clock now that the nights are growing lighter."

"Better see if they've anything to say that you ought to answer," Bess remarked, giving Tom the letter awaiting her. "It'll save time."

She looked excited if anyone had had time to notice. They, however, were all too busy congratulating Tom, who took the letter and opened it, sitting down at the table to read the single sheet the envelope contained. A moment later, she bounced to her feet, sending her chair over, and made for the door.

"Where are you going?" Bride demanded. "Tom – come back, you mad thing!"

"Tell you in a minute!" came back from halfway down the corridor. "Must see the Abbess at once, though!"

"What on earth's taken her?" Bride asked of the rest. "She seems to be off her head with excitement. Matey'll have to deal with her if this goes on!"

Elfie Woodward had had time to see Bess's face. "Bess *Herbert*! I believe you know what it is!" she cried.

The rest gathered round at once to demand an explanation, but Bess put them off. "No; I'm saying nothing. It's Tom's news. But if it's what I think it is, then I don't wonder she's gone all haywire!"

More, she declined to say and they had to wait till Tom came back, still flushed and excited, but rather calmer than she had been. She went across the room to Bess. "Do you know about this? You *do*! Oh, Bess! What a – what a *gentleman* your Dad is!"

Bess nodded and laughed. "Dad hoped it would be all right, but he had to wait for a Chapter meeting before he could be sure. Evidently it is. Oh, Tom, I'm so glad!" She gripped Tom's hand and that young lady wrung the slim fingers until her friend squealed.

"*Tom*!" She rubbed her hand as Tom released it.

70

"What an awful grip you've got! My hand feels as if it had been put through a mangle!"

"But what *is* it?!" demanded Nancy in agonized tones. "Do tell us, someone, before I expire from sheer curiosity!"

Shaken out of her usual calm for once, Tom told them. "Bess's Dad – you know, he's Dean of Minchampton Cathedral? – has offered Dad a really good living in the diocese. Dad's accepted and he wrote to tell me that it was all OK and I was going to Welsen. He's writing to the Head about it, but he had to let me know first. So, you see, I simply had to go and tell her at once so that she can tell Mrs Maynard, for I shan't need the schol after all!" She looked round at them all, her eyes brilliant. "Oh, you folks, isn't life *glorious*?"

CHAPTER SIX

Enter Joey!

"I wish to goodness there hadn't been any need to let the school at large know of the plans for next term!" grumbled Miss Derwent as she looked up from the pile of Upper V essays she was correcting. "The news seems to have gone to their heads – which, Heaven knows, are easily turned at the best of times! – and mere *work* is simply beneath their notice."

Miss Slater, who was ticking – or otherwise (mostly otherwise) the arithmetic of Lower IVb, put down her red pencil and stretched herself luxuriously. "Oh, I couldn't agree more! Their work's gone completely haywire so far. I shall be thankful when this week is ended. Surely, after ten days of excitement over it, they'll calm down and give the things they're pleased to call their brains, to their proper duty! If this sort of thing is to go on for the whole term I, for one, shall have reached the straws-in-the-hair stage long before it ends."

Miss O'Ryan, the history mistress, who had carefully refrained from giving written work to anyone below Lower VI, and had been curled up on the window seat, placidly embroidering a tea-cloth while her confrères sweated and groaned, put down her work with a superior smile. "It was bound to happen. Sure, you couldn't expect anything else from the creatures! Now *I* dished out learning prep, mainly notes and dates, with horrid warnings of what would happen if they weren't known when I asked for them. I decided 'twould be no use to ask them to use their *brains* overmuch for the next fortnight or so, so I've given their memories a spot of work. I saw no reason for loading myself up with piles of written work to no purpose."

Miss Slater gave her an exasperated look. "I suppose Derwent could have managed all right; but just you tell me, Biddy O'Ryan, what sort of prep I could have given the three Fourths in maths *without* making it written. I can't stick to geometry *all* the time, you know."

"What's the matter with revising tables?" Biddy demanded sweetly. "I'm sure the two Lower Fourths could do with tables revision at any time." Miss Slater seemed about to choke with wrath. "Really, Biddy, you haven't much more sense than you had when I tried to drive some idea of maths into your own brain! They've had their tables hammered in until I should think they could say them backwards in their sleep!"

Biddy gave a rich chuckle. "You always did undervalue my abilities!"

"*Did* I? I only know that when you were in the Sixth your ideas of maths used to drive me nearly frantic!" her elder retorted.

"You be thankful you never had Joey Maynard to teach," Biddy replied, quite unperturbed. "I know Miss Leslie who was your predecessor used to come within an ace of murder where *her* work was concerned." She chuckled again and changed the subject. "I say, Slater, have you thought that when we go to Switzerland we shall be missing Jo again?"

"Will you, indeed? *Oho!* That's all *you* know, Biddy O'Ryan!"

The three mistresses, who were the sole occupants of the staff room at the moment, all exclaimed and swung

73

round to face the doorway where a newcomer stood grinning at them – Biddy said later on that the wonder was the top of her head didn't come off! – as she stood with a hand on either stanchion, regarding them with black eyes that danced with mischief.

"Well, I must say you all seem to be utterly dumbstruck!" she said as the trio gaped at her in speechless silence. "*No* one got a word of welcome for a poor prodigal returned home after a year of Canada? Where's the fatted calf? Not to speak of a robe and a ring?"

"J–Joey!" Biddy stuttered. "It's you–r–r–really y–you!"

"Really me myself, large as life and twice as natural. Bridget, my love, I regret to see that you don't seem to grow any larger as the years pass by. If you don't look out my triplets will outstrip you in another year's time. Come here, sugar-pie and give me a kiss like a good little girl and tell me what you mean by it!"

Biddy shoved her work off her lap and came flying across the room. "Isn't it you all over, Jo Bettany – I mean Maynard – to come and give three poor creatures the shock of their lives?" she demanded as she flung herself on her friend. "Oh, but it's glad I am to see you again! The school seems half gone when you're not barging in every once in so often! But where's the family? When did you get back? Are you really in England again for keeps?"

"Wait till I say 'Hello!' to the other two before you begin drowning me in questions," Jo replied after a warm hug. She released Biddy and came to shake hands rather more circumspectly. "Pam Slater! You look as fit as ever and not a day older. Miss Derwent, we did just meet at the end of last Christmas term, you remember? Are you liking the school now you're properly dug in?"

"It's just like you, Jo Maynard, to burst in on us without a word of warning," Miss Slater said pensively. "I've never yet known you do things like an ordinary mortal!" She glanced across at Miss Derwent. "You'll get accustomed to her in time, Derwent. But I must admit she comes as a shock at first. You aren't in a hurry, are you, Jo? Sit down and tell us all the news."

Jo plumped down on the nearest table and smiled infectiously at them. "Where's the rest of the gang? I've seen the Head and Matey and I want to tell my news to the rest of you in bulk, so to speak. As for the girls, I've handed them over to Matey's tender mercies – all five of them."

"*Five?*" Miss Slater gasped incredulously.

"Five! My three and Madge's two. Had you forgotten Sybil and Josette?"

"I really hadn't thought. You gave me such a shock by barging in as you have done. And I wouldn't put it past you to have adopted a couple more girls while you were in Canada," Miss Slater said defensively.

"And me with eight of my own! Oh, no, thank you! Eight'll do me until the twins are well off my hands. Then," Jo paused and her eyes danced wickedly, "I don't mind telling you I've *rather* a fancy for quads, by way of a change."

Her three hearers shrieked violent protest at this, but she paid no heed for her quick ears had caught the sound of footsteps along the passage.

"Here come the rest! *Now* you won't have long to wait! And what's the matter with having quads? It's a perfectly respectable procedure, isn't it?"

Before any of them could reply, the door opened and five or six more of the resident staff poured in, headed by the games mistress, all agog to know what the excitement was. Miss Burnett stopped short as she saw the visitor. Then she uttered a cry and literally hurled herself at her.

"Joey Bettany – I mean Maynard! How simply marvellous! When did you come? How long are you staying? Does the Abbess know you're here? Where are the trips?"

Joey kissed her and said plaintively. "It's the oddest thing. Here have I been married nearly twelve years and yet first Biddy and then you go back to my maiden name. What's gone wrong with your memories?"

"It's the shock of seeing you so suddenly," Miss Burnett said, laughing. "So far as we knew you were either still in Canada or else on the high seas."

"Well, I'm here. And I'll thank you all to remember that I'm Joey Maynard – a proud mamma of eight," she added cheerfully. "Well, let me look at you all! Peggy Burnett, I simply can't believe you're grown up enough to be a gym mistress! Staff baby, aren't you? Mademoiselle!" She pushed Miss Burnett out of the way and went across to Mdlle de Lachennais, who had known her since she was a sinful Middle of fourteen. "Oh, *isn't* this joyful! You don't know how glad I am to be at home again! I've missed you all so much." She bent to give and receive the French double kiss she expected. "You haven't altered a scrap, either. And now let me see if I can remember who everyone is. There've been so many changes on the staff since we went off to Canada."

"Well, I hope it won't be too great a strain to remember me," Miss Everett the gardening mistress said with a grin. "How are you, Jo? You look all right – plumper, too, and with a colour you didn't have when you went away. What a pasty, tallow-faced creature you were then! We were all quite worried about you, I suppose you know?"

Jo laughed. "Oh, I've put on half-a-stone more weight in the year. And you must admit that I'd had something to pull me down just before then."

"I suppose you had," Miss Everett agreed. "All the

worry of Con's sleep-walking exploits, added to that nasty accident of Len's and then having the whole lot down with severe colds up to the moment of sailing almost, quite apart from the fact that your twins were expected before so very long, was enough to make you look like a badly-washed sheet!* And, talking of the twins, where are they? Haven't you brought them with you?"

Jo shook her black head vigorously. "No fear! They are safe in Carnbach in Rosa's charge. You'll see them soon enough. As for forgetting you, Rhyll Everett, I couldn't if I tried. It's a case of once seen, never forgotten!"

"I might have known you'd be insulting if you could," Miss Everett said resignedly. "Well, you'd better go the rounds and then you can tell us all the latest news. You did meet Miss Lawrence at Christmas?"

"I did," Jo agreed, shaking hands with the resident music mistress. "But you must agree that I didn't have more than a peep at you all. –Miss Armitage, I remember you, too. You came to take Bill's place as Science mistress when she went off to be Head at Welsen. And here's an old friend." She beamed at the geography mistress. "Ivy, it's wizard having you back again!"

Miss Stevens laughed. "I find it wizard to *be* back!" Then she added with a twinkle. "I notice you don't talk any less slang than you always did, Jo."

"Yes; I always had a gift that way," Jo agreed, quite unabashed. She turned to the last of the party, Miss Norman, also a very old friend. "Here's the second Ivy! Well, folks, I haven't a fearful lot of time to stay. Ferries won't wait forever, even for me, and I don't exactly want to have to row myself across the Sound, though I expect all the boats are handy and in good order. Sit down, all

* *Carola Storms the Chalet School*.

of you, and lend me your ears. *Waggle* 'em if you can hear better!"

The staff broke into peals of laughter. Miss Norman had once said of Jo that she was like a fresh breeze, blowing all the cobwebs away, and she had certainly contrived to do it on this occasion. They found seats while she perched on her table again and waited for what she had to tell them.

"Now I'll try to answer all the questions that were hurled at me when I first showed up," she said. "Let's see; the first was about the girls. Well, my three and Madge's pair are all with Matey, doing their unpacking, I shouldn't wonder. Ailie is at St Agnes', by the way. You'll see a change in them all, even Sybs. The four younger ones have grown enormously and they've all put on weight, though even now I shouldn't describe any of them as fatties! Mddlle, you'll find that their French is really good, now. They were at a French convent school in Toronto, so they can all gabble like natives by this time. And I don't think any of you will find them behind in their other work. La Sagesse is a jolly good convent and they brought the kids on wonderfully. As for the boys, they've grown, too, and they're all most fearfully independent. All children over there *are* – much more so than the average English child. Stephen is going to be a very big fellow; even Charles has grown quite a lot. As for young Mike, I'll be thankful when he's old enough to go to school with the rest. The only times he isn't in mischief is when he's asleep. As for my twins, at nearly eight months they're a splendid pair, if it *is* their mother who says it. They're teething, but no trouble so far – thank goodness! However, you'll all have any amount of chances of seeing them this term, so I'll say no more. Now what came next?"

"I don't remember," Biddy O'Ryan said, "but *next*

you're going to explain what you meant by your opening remark when you charged in on Slater and Derwent and me. What did you mean by it? 'That's all you know!' What are you going to be up to next, Joey?"

Jo chuckled as she turned brilliant black eyes on her. "I *thought* you'd be dying of curiosity over that! I've a good mind to leave it alone until the next time I come and leave you to stew in your own juice!"

With a bound, Biddy was on her, gripping her by the shoulders and shaking her. Jo was at a disadvantage, perched precariously on a corner of a table, and Biddy might be small and slight but she was very strong.

"No you don't!" she cried, shaking vigorously. "You don't leave this room until you explain yourself in full! So mind that!"

"Pax – pax!" Jo gasped, trying to struggle free. "You'll have us both on the floor, never to speak of making me violently sick, if you go on like that!"

"Promise to tell us?" Biddy desisted for a moment.

"OK then. But let me get my breath first."

Biddy released her and she fought for breath ostentatiously. Then, seeing fresh reprisals in her old friend's eye, she gave in.

"Very well; you shall hear *all*! The San's going to Switzerland this summer. The school's following it – a good part of it, anyway. So are we!"

There was a moment's silence after she had finished. At length Miss Slater asked, "Is this true; or are you pulling our legs?"

"What an improper suggestion! It's true, of course. Either Jack or Jem must be in charge of the beginnings, anyhow. When it's well on its feet, no doubt it can be left to other men. But while it's in its infancy, so to speak, and until it's through its teething troubles, one of its fathers must be on hand – and that's where the metaphor breaks down before any of you can point that out to me." She twinkled at Miss Derwent, who twinkled back as she said, "I *was* just going to point out that it isn't usual for a baby to have more than one father. However, you forestalled me."

"And she practically always does," Biddy informed the room at large. "You've to be up very early in the morning to catch Jo napping. Sure, wasn't she the bane of our lives when we were Middles and she was a prefect?"

"Where you and your beauties were concerned, it was often a case of staying awake all night, Bridget my love!" Jo retorted sweetly.

Before the young history mistress could riposte, Miss Slater intervened. "I've no doubt you were both foes well met when it came to that. In the meantime, this isn't of much interest to any of us except perhaps Mdlle, who, I'm sure, knew all about it. You stick to your story, Jo, and tell us exactly what is going to happen."

"Well," Jo calmed down, "we all talked it over at great length. Jem and Madge really ought to be here for the present. Jem's taking up another idea, you see – no; I'm not telling you anything about *that*! It's *his* affair – and he wants to be here while he's working out the details. There are certain men he wants to consult. As a result, it leaves the Swiss plan to Jack. That means that we shall all go, for I won't be parted from him for the greater part of the year. So we're leaving early in August, and when you folk arrive you'll find us settled down and old residents."

"But won't you miss Plas Gwyn?" Miss Slater asked thoughtlessly.

Jo nodded, compressing her lips. She had grown deep roots at her Golden Valley home where all her boys, with the exception of Baby Felix, had been born and where she had known great joy as well as bitter grief.* To have to say goodbye to Plas Gwyn, even for a limited number of years, was going to be a wrench and she preferred to think of it as little as possible.

"I'm sorry about that, Joey," Biddy O'Ryan said gently. "You'll miss your lovely home at Plas Gwyn."

"Oh, it won't be forever," Jo said, forcing herself to speak lightly. "Jack will certainly have to get the place safely on its feet and that can't be done in one or two years. But we shall come back when we can – probably ten years hence. There's one thing about it," she added. "Margot is very fit and the doctors all think she has completely outgrown her early delicacy, but they all say that it would be as well if she spent her growing years in a drier climate than we enjoy here. The same goes for Charles, though he's never been the anxiety she has. Still, he did have a bad start, poor lamb. And then I've felt a lot better in Canada than I've ever done in England. From that point of view, the Swiss plan is a good one. But, as you say, Biddy, it's a blow having to give up our lovely home, even for a time. We're letting part of it, by the way. Ernest Howell is retiring from the Navy and taking over Howell's church again. Mr Wallace is going to a parish in one of the London suburbs and Ernest likes the idea of taking over the church. The vicarage is impossible for just him and Gwensi – twenty bedrooms, he says, and all the downstairs rooms except the drawing room with stone floors! I believe there's some idea of turning it into flats and building a modern house when he can get a licence. In the meanwhile, they're having the small drawing room, the dining room and the study and the bedrooms over them – oh, and the inner kitchen."

* *Highland Twins at the Chalet School*.

"What will you do with the rest?" Miss Norman inquired with interest.

"Keep them for ourselves. We don't want our family to grow away from their own land and we shall come back for holidays."

"But what about your other home?" Mdlle asked, speaking for the first time since she had greeted Jo. "You have Merry Maids near the New Forest. What, then, do you do with that?"

"Jack's handing it over to the National Trust, lock, stock and barrel – after we've rescued the things we either want or ought to keep. We couldn't afford to keep up *three* places and the girls and I have never been really well there. It lies in a hollow and it's too relaxing. We're taking the old stuff and most of the pictures and so on, and with what's left, I believe they're talking of making it into a kind of guesthouse for foreign notables. Plas Gwyn will be our English home in the future."

"I see. I think you are right." Mdlle had spent a fortnight at Merry Maids on one occasion and she knew that Jo spoke the truth when she said that it suited neither her nor her triplets.

"I know we are," Jo said calmly.

"Well, now we all know that," Peggy Burnett, said, "I'd like to know when you returned from Canada. You must have been back some time if you've got all that arranged. Why haven't you been over to see us sooner? And, while I think of it, why didn't the girls come back at the proper time?"

"We reached Carnbach two days ago. As for our arrangements, those have been going on for the past six months or more as you'd know if you took time to think it over," Jo told her crushingly. "Jack has been back and forward a good deal and we could fix up quite a lot in

Canada. We can all read and write! Any more questions? Speak now, or forever hold your peace!"

"I have one," Miss Lawrence said. "Are you going at once, or can we count on seeing anything of you this term?"

"You people don't listen! I *said* we weren't moving till early August," Jo scolded. "Are you deaf; or were you just not paying any attention?"

"Consider me hiding my diminished head with shame," Miss Lawrence laughed.

Jo suddenly grinned. "OK, I'll answer it. I may go with Jack for a flying visit to the Platz – he has to go almost at once, by the way – but I shan't stay more than a week or ten days. For one thing, I shall be up to the eyes in packing what we're going to take for our home out there."

"Are you living in San?"

Jo shook her black head with its heavy ear-phones of plaits so vehemently that several hairpins fell out and tails of hair appeared. "No fear! Even at the Sinnalpe, which was a lot smaller, Madge and Jem didn't live near San. No one wants children to grow up under the shadow that sort of thing casts. As a matter of fact, Jack's building a chalet practically bang next to the school – 'Make us a willow cabin at your gates,' in fact, as *Viola* tells *Olivia* in Twelfth Night!" Jo chuckled. "The girls will come to the Chalet School, age rule or no, and Stephen and Charles will have to come back to England for prep school in a couple of years' time. I must part with my boys, I know; but I'm keeping my girls. Once we're all safely there, you'll see any amount of me, I promise you. I might even find time to take junior Latin again!"

"Not you – not with your twins on the point of getting on their feet," Miss Slater told her.

"Well, if they're anything like Madge's pair, I *shall* have my hands fairly full," Jo owned. Then she whirled round on Mdlle. "Mdlle, you're awfully silent about all this. Aren't you pleased to know that I'm coming to worry you all day and every day?"

"I was waiting until you had finished talking, chérie," Mdlle said blandly. "Besides, I have asked one question. But now I will tell you that yes, I am rejoiced to know that you will be with us in the Alps. But," she hushed Jo's protest, "if you really wish to catch the last ferry, I advise you to make your farewells, for you have only ten minutes left before it departs."

"Mercy!" Jo bounced off her table. "Of course I've got to make it! The twins will be howling their heads off for me as it is before I can reach home. What's that, Biddy? My hair? O–oh! Bother, drat and drabbit it! Where are my hairpins?"

Biddy scrabbled on the floor and found three. "Here you are. Sure, 'tis time you knew how to fix them so they'll stay in," she said. "Here; take two of mine, or something'll be dropping down before you reach home."

Jo swiftly pinned the heavy plaits into place. "For two pins I'd bob it again! That's done it! Goodbye, everyone! I'll be over again shortly and you all know where we live – or most of you do, and the rest can find out. Please note that you'll all be welcome at any time. I'm off! Ta-ta!" And she whirled out of the room, leaving the staff in peals of laughter over her wild flight.

CHAPTER SEVEN

"Not New Girls At All"

Tea was over and Emerence Hope had run out to the garden. Strictly speaking, this was not where she ought to be, but very few people expected Emerence to keep to rules as a matter of course. She was the product of an early upbringing which had been based largely on letting her do exactly what she wanted. It had broken down on occasion, of course, but those occasions had been few and far between until the day came when she had been bored with life and set fire to the summerhouse at the bottom of the garden for the fun of seeing the blaze.

At that point, the method had ended once and for all. Emerence was an Australian girl and the garden was in Manly, a suburb of Sydney in New South Wales. They had just passed through a bad drought and the result of Miss Emerence's prank had been that not only her own home, but those on either side had been in danger of extinction. Luckily, the fire services had contrived to get the blaze under control in time to avoid the worst; but Mr Hope had been furious about the whole thing. His neighbours had told him just what they thought of his daughter, and the effect their thoughts had on him was to make him send her off, willy-nilly, to the Chalet School in England.

The Head and staff had already known of the affair from Mrs Mackenzie, wife of one of the Hopes' neighbours. Mrs Mackenzie had been Miss Stewart and history mistress at the Chalet School in its early days, and it was her talk that had put the place into Mr Hope's mind.*

Emerence's first term had been eventful, but by the end of it, she had managed to absorb enough of the school's atmosphere to make her slightly more amenable to steady discipline than she had been at first. She still broke rules cheerfully when she felt like it; but then, so did most of the rest of her clan. She had got through the previous term without any major rows and seemed to be in a fair way to becoming a quite normal schoolgirl.

On this occasion, she should have gone straight to her form room to get out her books and pencil-case and generally prepare for "prep", which began at five o'clock. She had been feeling restless and fidgety all the afternoon – a state caused mainly by the fact that they had had sewing and dictation that afternoon and she loathed both – and it had seemed to her that she could never get through the evening without trouble unless she could take a run to shake the fidgets out of her. There was no reason why she should not have asked permission. The authorities were understanding and she would have been sent off at once; but Emerence liked to do things her own way, even though she was slowly learning that it did not always pay to do so, and she had slipped off through the side door while the others went streaming along to their form room.

Having made good her escape, Emerence turned to the left and made her way along the side of the house. She thought she would have a race down the drive to the gate, which led to what the girls called "the holly path" because it was bordered on either side by thick hedges of holly.

* Shocks for the Chalet School.

That would take the fidgets out of her and she would go *straight* back for prep when she returned.

She never got as far as the run – or not just then. As she rounded the corner, a little group of girls came out of the great front door and stood chattering together at the top of the drive.

Emerence stared. They were new girls – at least, she had never seen them before – and the Head had said plainly that there were no new girls this term! She must find out at once what this meant. All thought of her scamper went out of her head and she hurried to find out what it was all about!

Accordingly, the Maynard triplets and their cousin, Josette Russell, standing outside until the Head could come and tell them which forms they were to be in, were startled by the fair, sharp-featured girl round about their own age, who stood with feet planted firmly astride and arms akimbo, demanding, "Who are you? What are you doing, coming out of the front door? Don't you know it isn't allowed? We've got to use the side door – and the back stairs, too," she added with some bitterness.

During her first term, Emerence had had a battle royal with Miss Dene over this very rule and had been defeated with complete ignomiy. She did not love the remembrance in consequence.

The four turned at her voice and Emerence found herself staring at a girl who looked about her own age and three others who, for all their height, were clearly younger. The eldest of the four was very pretty, with silky black curls rioting over her head, eyes of periwinkle blue, and a pink-and-white face that made a charming contrast with her inky locks. As for the other three, they were very much alike in feature; but one had chestnut waves of hair tied back from her face, and dark grey eyes; one was very dark with black hair and deep brown eyes; the last was fair, with golden locks, eyes of forget-me-not blue that had a wicked twinkle in them, and a complexion as lovely as the bigger girl's.

At her remarks, they looked at her and then at each other and the fair girl broke into a bubbling laugh.

"Someone quite new," she said to the others, her eyes dancing.

"Margot – tais-toi!" the eldest girl hushed her. Then she turned to Emerence, who was staring in good earnest. "It's all right; you couldn't be expected to know, of course. As a matter of fact, we're quite *old* girls. I'm Josette Russell and these are my triplet cousins, Len, Con and Margot Maynard. We've all been in Canada and have just come home. Who are you?"

Emerence had heard of the Russell girls, whose mother had started the Chalet School in the days when she was Madge Bettany; and she also knew of the Maynard triplets.

"Oh; I see," she said slowly. "The Dawbarns were saying that you were coming back this term some time."

"Are they still going strong?" Josette asked with a chuckle.

Emerence suddenly echoed the chuckle. "Oh, they're fearfully browned off," she said confidentially. "Last term, we had that weird school from the mainland wished on to us, so we all got shifted round and they even had to make two new forms."

"Well – go on!" Margot said as she paused. "What's that got to do with the Dawbarns? – Oh, I see!" She burst into peals of laughter. "One went up and the other stayed down! Oh, hard lines! Poor old Pris and Prue!"

Emerence nodded, watching her with fascinated eyes.

"Pris went up into Lower IVB and Prue remained in Upper IIIA – they made another Upper III form, you see – and they didn't like it one little bit."

"I guess they didn't," Len Maynard said. "Those two always stuck together like glue."

"We knew about the Chalet School from Tanswick," Josette said in her gentle voice. "Mummy had to agree, of course, before they could come. She didn't exactly like it, but there seemed to be nothing else to do at the time."

"Why didn't she like it?" Emerence asked with some curiosity.

"Because no one wants a lot of new girls the *second* term of a school year," Josette explained. "They lose a whole term's work and it's apt to muddle things up all round. What are those girls like?"

"Some are nice and some are – nasty," Emerence said thoughtfully. "Isn't Bride Bettany your cousin as well? Then one of the big ones was simply *beastly* to her – wrecked her study and everything. Oh, I forgot!" she added with sudden belated recollection. "The Head said we weren't to talk about it any more. Diana – that's her name – said she was sorry."

"I see. Then we won't say anything," Josette said promptly. "Margot – you hear?" She gave her cousin a warning look.

"I won't say anything," Margot promised. Then, "I wonder how much longer Auntie – I mean the Head – is going to be? She sent us out here while they decided what forms they would put us in. Len and Con say they ought to be in Upper Third somewhere. I was in Lower IIB when I left. I've had a year longer in Canada than they have, you see. But now, no one seems to know where we can go as the forms are all so full."

"Where ought you to be?" Emerence asked Josette.

"Upper IV – either A or B; but the Head says they're chockful already. And these three should go into one of the Lower IIIs, I suppose."

"Where are you?" Margot asked suddenly.

"Lower IVA," Emerence said. "There are twenty-five of us and aren't the forms supposed not to have any more?"

Josette nodded. "That's the limit as a rule. I've heard Mummy and Auntie Jo say that if you have more you can't – now what *was* it? Oh, I know, you can't hope to give your pupils indi–indi–anyhow, it means see what each of them is doing and helping the people who are slow or haven't understood."

"Besides," Len put in, "I don't suppose for a second any of *us* will get put into a IV. I was Upper II when we went away last year, and Con was Lower IIA. Margot's told you where *she* was and they don't generally jump you up two or three forms at once. You miss too much – Mamma said so."

"Anyway, the Head did say you three would probably have to be in different forms again," Josette reminded her cousins.

Margot laughed and tossed her golden curls with a wicked air. "Then bags me to be in the lowest form. Work's not my cup of tea at all!"

Emerence glanced at her and suddenly liked her enormously. Work was not *her* cup of tea, either. She forgot the difference there must be in their ages, which was not difficult to do, for she was small for her years and the Maynard girls were all well-grown specimens.

"I'd like Margot to be my chum," she thought. "I haven't got one – not really. She's my sort, I think."

Con, the dark member of the trio, spoke for the first time. "Margot, you haven't forgotten what you promised Mamma?" she said gently.

Margot flushed. "Oh, bother you, Con Maynard! I guess if I've got to go into a lower form and take it easy for this term it isn't *my* fault!" She suddenly spoke with a marked Canadian accent and there was a naughty twinkle in her blue eyes.

Con looked at Len, but the eldest sister shook her head. Before anyone could say anything more, however, there was the sound of quick, springy steps and the Head was with them. She was there before Emerence could remember that she ought not to be in the garden at all, but in her form room, getting out her books for prep. She stood her ground, therefore, and Miss Annersley, on seeing her, left her in no doubt about her conduct.

"Emerence, what are you doing here at this time?" she asked quietly.

Emerence had gone very red. "I – I just wanted – a run," she muttered.

"Then go and take it," the Head said briskly. "You ought not to be here at all, as you know very well, so you must hurry. Off you go!"

Emerence had no choice in the matter – not with the Head standing there looking at her like that. She said, "Yes, Miss Annersley," with the utmost meekness, turned and went racing off down the drive to the gate and back. She made no attempt to rejoin the group in front of the wide door. Instead, she shot off round the house and arrived in her form room with tousled hair and sparkling eyes, the fidgets all gone.

In the meantime, Miss Annersley attended to her other pupils. "Josette, you are to be in Upper IVA," she said. "You'll find all your old friends there ready to welcome you. Go to the office and Miss Dene will give you your books and show you where to go. This house is quite new ground to you and Margot, isn't it? Len and Con will remember it, though."

Josette bobbed a curtsy, saying, "Thank you, Auntie Hilda." Then she ran into the house and was shortly being welcomed by a delighted group of IVA leaders whose chum she had been before the Canadian sojourn.

"Now for you three," the Head said when she had gone. "You may as well know that it's been difficult to fit you in, especially as your time in America seems to have brought you on by leaps and bounds. Len, we have decided to see how you manage in Upper IVB. The average age is a year and a half more than yours, but they already have Heather Clayton and Lydia Sackett who are only twelve at the middle of May, and the work seems to be what you have been doing at La Sagesse, so I think we'll try you there. If you *can't* do it, we'll have to put you down to Lower IVA where Con is going, and as she makes the twenty-sixth, we're overfull already. Still, it is only for this term, so I think you *can* do it."

"Len always was the cleverest of us three," Con suddenly said. "At least," she added conscientiously, "Margot is really that, Papa says; but she doesn't work as hard."

Margot darted a most unsisterly look at her for this, but she said nothing. As she reflected resignedly, it was just Con! Half the time she was mooning about, then she suddenly spoke and said whatever came into her head, quite regardless. "But I wish she'd learn to hold her tongue," the youngest of the triplets thought crossly to herself. "Now Auntie Hilda'll expect me to *work*!"

But Auntie Hilda was speaking, so she gave it up and paid attention to what came next.

"Yes, Con," the Head was saying. "You are to try Lower IVA. If you can't manage the arithmetic, we must send you down to Upper IIIA for that with Miss Johnson, who is new this term. Miss Edwards is over at St Agnes' so we can't have her here, unfortunately."

Con broke into a laugh. "I *am* awful at arithmetic, Auntie Hilda. Mamma says I take after her that way. But I do try."

"Yes; Mother Marie Cécile says so in all your reports," the Head agreed. She turned to the youngest member of the party – youngest by half an hour. "Now for you, Margot. You're going to Upper IIIA and you must give me your word to do your best to work steadily. It's rather disgraceful, you know, that you should have to be two forms below Len who is the same age. All the same, until you learn that odd spurts won't really get you anywhere, I'm afraid it will have to be. When we start again in Switzerland, we'll see if we can put you in the same form as Con. If not – and hers will be the lowest there – it's going to mean that you'll have to come back to England and go to St Agnes' branch instead. It all depends on yourself."

Margot's eyes filled with horror at the thought. "But, Auntie Hilda," she said, "we've been apart for a year and – and – Auntie Madge was a dear to me and I loved part of it, but it was – just *awful* being without Len and Con! You don't know how glad I was when Mamma brought them all to Toronto!"

Miss Annersley smiled rather grimly, but she said no more. She and Jo had talked it over and she knew what Jo's plans were for her girls. All the same, she had insisted that this spur to Miss Margot must be applied.

"It isn't that she lacks ability, Jo," she had said. "In some ways, she is even cleverer than Len, who is a really clever child. But she's mentally lazy. While she was so frail, I didn't like to push her; but now Jack tells me that it won't hurt her physically and is the best thing for her character. I shall tell her my plan and we'll hope that it makes her work. If not, however much you object, I'm afraid it's going to mean sending her back to St Agnes' for a term at least. You think it over and you'll see that, for her own sake, we can do no other."

Margot took fright at the Head's silence. "Please, Auntie Hilda," she urged, "I just *can't* be left behind when the rest go to Switzerland."

"Well, you know how to avoid it," Miss Annersley said, hardening her heart against the three; for Len and Con were also looking at her anxiously. "Work steadily all this term and deserve to be put up to Upper IIIA and you'll come like the others. Keep slacking off, and you'll be left behind. Now, I've nothing more to say about it at present. It's time you were in your form rooms. Run along to the office and get your books and then you can go to your form rooms and begin work."

She turned to go and speak to Griffiths the gardener and the three were left, looking at each other.

"We'd better go," Len said. "Margot, it won't be hard – honestly it won't. It only means doing your work as well as you can all the time and being careful not to make silly mistakes. Con and I will help you when we can."

Margot looked at her sisters with a woebegone face. "But it *is* hard!" she burst out. "You two *like* work, but I don't and you don't *know* how hard it is for me to have to remember that I've got to work all the time! I wasn't born that way and you were and I think it's wholly unfair of Auntie Hilda to talk like that and say she won't ha–have me in S–Switzerland if I *can't* do it."

"Don't cry," Len said. "Anyhow, Margot, if you think, you'll know it's not true to say that you *can't* do the work.

You can if you try – and it's only for this term, anyway. Things may be different by next."

Margot gulped madly for a moment and drove the tears back. Then she said, "Anyhow, I d–don't believe Mamma w–will agree. She s–said when she c–came to Canada that she w–wouldn't p–part with any of us again! I'll ask h–her!"

Her sisters made no reply. For once, Con had the tact to hold her tongue and Len rarely burst out with her inmost thoughts. But both of them knew that if the Head stuck to her word, their mother would agree with her in the end, no matter how much she might protest at first. Margot knew it herself if she took the time to think. At present, she was filled with glee at her own plan. She pulled out her handkerchief, wiped her drenched eyes and turned to the house.

"Yes," Len said. "We'd best go and ask Aunt Rosalie for the books and things. The prep bell went ages ago!"

They went to the office where they were given their piles of books and sent off in short order, Rosalie Dene saying, "You'd better hurry or you won't be able to finish. Josette was here ten minutes and more ago."

She saw Margot's eyes, but thought it wiser to say nothing. She had been present at the interview with Jo and she fully agreed with the Head's dictum. Though she rarely did any teaching, there was not much Rosalie did not know about most of the girls.

Len and Con took Margot along to Upper IIIA and left her at the door, Len going next door to Upper IVB, while Con ran along to the room which Emerence had entered half an hour before. She looked up eagerly as the door opened, but it was only Con who came in, and quiet Con had no special appeal for a young firebrand.

Emerence turned back to her arithmetic with a feeling of disappointment.

Miss Norman was taking preparation. She looked up at the newcomer and smiled. "Welcome back, Con! Now where – Oh, yes; we can find room for you beside Emerence if she moves her desk a little nearer to Angela. Take that spare desk in the corner, Con, and set it up. Christine, you run along to the store room and bring a chair, please. The rest of you, go on with your work. You can talk to Con later."

Emerence moved her desk; Con brought the spare one and set it up; Christine Dawson, a bright-looking young person of twelve, dropped her pen and went flying to bring a chair from the store room. Ten minutes later, Con, having been shown the work she had to do, was hard at it. Miss Norman looked round her flock, saw that her lambs were, outwardly at least, working, and returned to the correcting of Upper IIA's compositions with a fleeting wish that schoolgirls would consult a dictionary occasionally and not guess at words they didn't know.

Con started on her arithmetic and was thankful to see that the exercise was on a rule she had done the previous term at the convent. She was a neat worker and, once she was certain of anything, could be relied on to do good work. As a result, she got all her five sums right and Miss Slater thought next day that it would be quite possible to keep her where she was.

French was the next subject she tackled, and after a whole year in a French convent, what Lower IVA had to do was baby work for her. Geography proved much worse. The girls were beginning on India this term. Con had no difficulty in drawing the sketch-map demanded; but when it came to inserting the courses and names of the five most important rivers, she was reduced to the Indus, the Ganges and the Brahmaputra. She had to leave it at that, though she worried and frowned over her atlas for some time.

Emerence, giving her a side-glance as she wrestled with her own map, felt a little more interested in her. Geography was a hated lesson with the Australian girl. If Con Maynard also found it difficult, there must be something more in her than Emerence had thought. Con, glancing up, caught her eyes and gave a puzzled smile. Then she shut her mapping-book and atlas and picked up the anthology from which they took their repetition.

They had to revise the first two verses of Barry Cornwall's THE SEA and learn the third. Con had never seen the poem before, but learning by heart was easy for her. She settled down and, by the time the bell rang for the end of preparation, had got the first two verses into her memory, and knew the last sketchily.

"P'raps I can finish it off before school tomorrow," she thought as she carried her books to the locker given her and stowed them away. "It's a lovely poem. I like the *rushing* way the words go, like waves tearing in and breaking on the rocks."

Then, having finished, and Miss Norman having left the room, she turned to be mobbed by all those of the others who knew her.

"When did you come?" Ruth Barnes demanded.

"Well, we reached England two days ago," Con said, "but we went to Plas Gwyn first as Mamma wanted some things from there. We only got to Carnbach this afternoon. Mamma brought us over after tea."

"Did you like Canada, Con?" Christine asked. "And haven't you *grown*! I believe you're the tallest in the form."

Con laughed. "We've all grown. But so have you.

I nearly gasped when I saw Ruth and the twins." She beamed on Ruth and the Carter twins. "You two especially. You were just *shrimps* this time last year."

The leggy pair looked at each other and grinned. "You should hear Mummy talk about our dresses and coats!" Angela said with a chuckle.

"She can't be any worse than Mamma," Con said decidedly.

"Now then, you kids, I suppose you know that you ought to have been out of here five minutes ago," said a fresh voice; and the girls turned to see Julie Lucy in the doorway. "Hurry up and clear out," she continued. "The bell will be ringing for Abendessen in a moment."

They turned to do her bidding reluctantly. None of them wanted to get across a prefect – *any* prefect. They would, on the whole, have preferred to have trouble with a mistress. Con, having performed her duties, went to smile at Julie.

"Hel–*lo!*" the young woman exclaimed. "Con Maynard! When did you come back? Is Sybil here, too?"

Con noded. "Yes; I expect you'll see her at teatime. Mamma brought us over after early tea." She suddenly began to chuckle. "Such a funny thing, Julie! We were outside and that new girl, Emerence Hope, saw us and thought *we* were new! She told us we must use the side door *and* the backstairs."

Julie laughed. "And then you told her that you were quite *old* girls, I suppose? That would be a drop for Emerence. Are you ready, Con? Then you'd better hop off and tidy for Abendessen." She turned to the others. "Hurry up, you folk! You'll be awfully late!"

There were squeaks as they did their best to obey her. Con stayed where she was, brown eyes gleaming with fun. Julie looked down at her and suddenly realized that she hadn't very far to look. "Merciful Heavens! How you've *grown*!" she exclaimed. "Are the rest as bad?"

Con nodded. Then she said, "Wasn't it fun about Emerence, Julie? She really thought we were new girls!"

Julie nodded; but all she said was, "I told you to go. *Scram!*" Con turned and fled on the word.

CHAPTER EIGHT

A KNOTTY PROBLEM

By the time the Maynards and the Russells had been back at school a week, it was plain to everyone that Margot Maynard and Emerence Hope had struck up a violent friendship, despite the three years' difference in their ages.

No one was very pleased about it. The staff considered that either alone was bad enough; what the pair of them together might evolve in the way of wickedness was hair-raising to think of! The prefects were of much the same opinion and demanded to be told why Margot couldn't be satisfied with her sisters; or else choose someone with a *character* for her special friend.

Jo Maynard herself, on hearing the news from Biddy O'Ryan, who had come over to have tea and inspect the twins, became very worried.

"It isn't that I mind their having bosom pals apart from each other," she said, serious for once. "On the contrary, I'm all for it. It was all very well their sticking together like a bunch of barnacles while they were *little* girls. I wasn't really sorry about that as it gave me the chance to impress home training and home ways of thought more firmly on them. Now that they're growing up, though, it's high time they branched out and had their own separate friends. I was delighted when I saw it beginning to happen at La Sagesse. But I'd a lot rather my bad Margot hadn't chosen to pal up with another desperate young criminal like Emerence. She's quite bad enough without anyone to egg her on! And," she added, "from all I've heard, I should say that the same goes for Emerence herself."

"Too right it does," Biddy said ruefully.

"Well, there you are, then! Here – take Felicity a moment while I fill her bottle, will you?" She dumped the snowflake fair baby into Biddy's arms, outstretched to take her, and turned to fill the feeding-bottle.

Biddy sat cuddling Felicity and murmuring love-nonsense to her. When Jo brought the bottle, she held out her hand for it. "Let me give it to her, the baby angel that she is! Sure, Jo, 'tis a mystery to me how you've managed at all, at all!"

"Managed what?" Jo demanded. "All right, Mamma's little man! He shall have his bottle, too, in just a minute." This last to Felix who was murmuring.

"Why, to have two silvery-fair babies like these two! I know Margot and Michael are both fair, but they're *golden*. These two are like little stars." She laughed, and added as she moved the bottle and held up the baby on her arm for a moment's breather, "But 'tis sweet they are, the pets!"

Jo laughed. "Sometimes I think them the sweetest babies I've ever had. But on looking back I find that I've said much the same thing about all the others – except the girls, of course. As they were the first, I couldn't make the comparisons with them." She sat down, after lifting Felix from his cot and began to feed him. "And that brings us back to Margot and her latest craze. I don't see what I can do about it, Biddy. I *don't* want them to miss all the fun I've had with Frieda and Marie and Simone – nor all the joy, either. A friendship like ours is one of the greatest joys life can bring. Even though we're all right apart now, it still lasts and I rejoice in their happiness as

101

I know they rejoice in mine. I can tell you, I was thrilled to the last toenail when André wrote to tell me that they had a son at last! I know both he and Simone had begun to fear that Tessa was to be an only child and that hadn't been their idea at all."

Biddy nodded. "Oh, yes; you four believe in families, I know. Marie has four now and I wouldn't put it past her to go and try to beat you, even now. And Frieda has her three. 'Twas always a grief to Simone that she seemed to have stopped short with Tessa. Now she has her little Pierre, she'll be as proud as a cat with two tails!"

"Oh, prouder!" Jo said. Suddenly she gave her wickedest chuckle. "Did I ever tell you what I did when I heard of Pierre's arrival?"

"You did not. What was it – something awful, seeing it's you!"

Jo chuckled again. "I went round the shops and bought the very largest hat I could find and sent it to her! It swamped *me*, so what it was like on *her* small head, I just wouldn't know! And the letter I had back from her! I've got it somewhere. I'll fish it out and you can read it."

Biddy joined in her chuckles before she said, sobering down, "We're side-tracking. Let's get back to our present problem – for a problem it is, I can tell you."

"I know it. I've told you I don't see what to do about it. They *must* make friends off their own bat. They've stuck to each other long enough. Up to this year, they've always shared everything. Why, when we got to Toronto, one of the first things I heard was Con telling Margot about Tom's dolls' house that she won at the Sale just before we left, and assuring her that it belonged equally to all three of them. It's always been 'ours' where any of their possessions were concerned until the beginning of last

102

term at La Sagesse when they began to chum a little with other girls. Then we came home and the Canadian friends were left behind. But though both Con and Len spent part of their time on the boat writing to Cordélie and Marie-Adelaide, I noticed that Margot wasn't bothering about Amélie and it rather worried me. I don't think the other two have chummed with anyone here so far; but when I was over yesterday, Emerence was all that Margot could talk about. She's got it hot and strong – at the moment, anyhow."

"That sort of thing was bound to come," Biddy said. "You know, Jo, I can see a huge difference in them since last year. That last term at the Chalet School they – I mean Len and Con, of course, seeing Margot was in Canada – were still *little* girls, with little-girl ideas and little-girl ways. Since they've come back, though, I can see that they're real schoolgirls now. You've lost your first babies, my dear."

Jo nodded. "I couldn't agree more! I saw it happening before my eyes. Canadian children are very much more independent and mature than ours at the same age. Madge had warned me of it and I'd made up my mind to it before ever we sailed. That's one reason why I'm glad for them to make their own friends. But oh, how I wish Margot hadn't fallen for Emerence!"

They had to leave it at that. As Jo had said, there was nothing she could do about it, since the pair were at the same school. All the same, everyone hoped for the best and prepared for the worst.

Meanwhile, the two friends were together every chance they had – and in the summer term there were far more chances of that sort of thing than at any other time. The girls were out-of-doors as much as possible and, when they were not playing cricket or tennis, there were plenty of opportunities for friends to be together, even if they were not in the same form.

It had *one* good result – and one bad one. Margot wanted to be with Emerence in form as well as out of it. As she was clever and Emerence had only average ability, she quickly realized that, with steady work on her part, it was an even chance that she could achieve it. Accordingly, she set herself to do it and the consequence was, that as the weeks passed, it was soon plain to everyone that she was well on the way to promotion next term.

The monkey had imparted her ideas to her chum, however, and Emerence promptly slacked off so that there should be no question of a remove for her when the time came. From being somewhere around fifteenth or sixteenth in the fortnightly lists, she dropped to being twenty-fourth or -fifth in a form of twenty-six girls, while Margot herself went sailing gaily up to the top of Upper IIIA, displacing Jane Abbott and Stella Porter, who had usually shared that place between them but now had to be content with second or third. As neither had been at the school before Margot went to Canada two years before, neither liked it and they both worked to the limit of their powers in a wild attempt to beat her.

"Margot Maynard's doing very well," Miss Norman said one afternoon at the end of May when she had a "free" and was taking it in the rose-garden which, by common consent, was the staff's favourite stamping-ground in summer. "They've certainly taught her to *work* at La Sagesse. She always was clever, but now the young demon seems to have learnt to slog as well."

"Demon," said Miss Slater bitterly, "is the operative word – unless you like to put it even more strong-ly!"

"What do you mean?" Miss Norman asked, sitting up

104

as far as she could sit up in a deck chair. "What's biting you, Slater?"

"So you haven't jumped to it yet?"

"Jumped to *what*? What is there to jump to?" Miss Norman demanded, wide-eyed, while Miss Annersley, who was also free for once and had joined her staff in the garden, said nothing, but listened with all her ears.

"Tell me this," Miss Slater said. "What sort of work is *Emerence* doing?"

Miss Norman looked thoughtful. "Simply vile!" she owned.

Biddy O'Ryan, who had been lounging in a deck chair, preparing a lesson on the growth of Parliament in the Middle Ages for Upper VA, shut her book with a bang and joined in. "Her work for me is about the worst I've ever had to correct. All the same," she began to laugh, "she *does* contrive to be funny on occasion. Yesterday, I gave her form a 'spot' test. Among other things I asked for a few lines on Henry VIII – they're revising the Tudors this term – and what do you think I got from Miss Emerence?"

"What?" half-a-dozen voices chorused this with eager anticipation.

Biddy stooped down and fished in the case at her feet. "I've got it here. I'll read it to you." She sorted through some sheets of examination paper and finally picked out one. "Here we are!" Then, with a perfectly grave face, she read the following effusion: 'Henry VIII had a bad character. He was very cruel' – incidentally, she spells it c-r-e-w-e-l- 'and he executed a lot of people because he wanted to be Head of the Church and they said only the Pope was that. St Thomas More was one and another was his own grandmother' – and where she got *that* from, goodness only knows!" Biddy paused in her reading to inform them. "It wasn't from me. – 'He is called Henry VIII because he had eight wives. The last one was called Katharine Parr, but he called her Fatima because she was so fat and he said she was a Flanders mare. He died before she did.' There! How's that?" And Biddy dropped the sheet and looked benignly round on her auditors, who one and all seemed to be in the throes of incipient convulsions. "I haven't had time to talk to her yet, but there's going to be *one* very sad girl in this establishment by bedtime tonight."

"She's mixed him up with Bluebeard!" Miss Norman gasped faintly in between her peals of laughter. "She must have gone mad!"

Miss Slater sat up. "Mad my foot!" she said simply. "She's as sane as anyone else and knows quite well what she's doing – though I don't doubt that it was Margot Maynard who put her up to it. That kid's got too many brains for her own good!"

"Put her up to *what*?" Miss Derwent demanded as she dried her eyes. "What bee's buzzing in your bonnet now, Slater?"

"No bee at all! What those two are trying to do is to ensure that Margot gets her remove next term and Emerence *doesn't*. That's their little game!"

"I rather thought that was what they were at," the Head said pensively, speaking for the first time. "Well, I'm sorry, but they're going to find that it's a game that more than two can play."

"What are you going to do about it?" Miss Slater asked bluntly.

"When I've had the half term reports, I shall send for Emerence and warn her that unless her work improves all round, I shall not consent to her going to Switzerland with the rest but shall leave her at St Agnes' for the whole of

106

the next year." She wound up with a gentle smile.

Biddy whistled. "*That* will take the wind out of their sails! I wonder what the result will be so far as young Margot's concerned?"

"There will be *no* results there," the Head said sweetly. "It won't affect her work in the slightest. Margot already knows that if she doesn't do well this term, *she* will be left behind."

"Jo won't agree to that," Miss Norman said instantly. "One of the first things she said to us when she came back was that she would never again consent to parting with one of her girls until they were grown-up."

"Jo will listen to me. However she may feel about it, as Rosalie said to me on one occasion, she does take her motherhood very seriously, mad though she may be in other ways. She cares too much for her children not to sacrifice her own feelings if it's for their own good. Margot is far and away the most difficult one of her family – unless either of the twins turns out to be another demon. It depends very much on how Margot is handled at this stage whether she grows up as we all want in the future. Jo knows that and, whatever she may have said, she will agree to leave her bad daughter behind in England if it should prove necessary."

"Poor Margot!" tender-hearted Miss Norman murmured.

"*I* think it's 'Poor Jo!'" Miss Slater retorted. "However, Margot would certainly hate to be the only one of the family left behind and all the rest going off to the Alps, so she'll probably see to it that it doesn't happen if she can help it. But I wouldn't have a child like that for all the tea in China!"

"You don't like Margot, do you?" the Head asked, looking meditatively at her.

Miss Slater reddened. "I'm not at all fond of her. Len is a clever child and, what's more, she's a steady worker. Con isn't good at maths, but she does try. But Margot – she can do almost anything she likes if she chooses to work. The trouble is she works for her own ends only and she lets me see it every time."

"At not quite eleven! In fact, at barely ten-and-a-half!" Miss Norman said scornfully. "Margot may be a clever child, but she's not as subtle as that. Oh, Slater, what a biased creature you are!"

Miss Slater said no more and the bell rang, taking her off to supervise Preparation for all Junior Middles in Hall. She knew quite well that the Head deprecated her way of disliking girls who showed their distaste for her subject, but she was very much one-track minded and it was part of her make-up. When she had first begun to teach, she had honestly tried to overcome it. Of late years, she had given up the effort.

The rest of the staff were also on duty elsewhere. Biddy, Miss Norman and Miss Derwent went off to help with junior tennis and Miss Everett had a gardening class with Upper VI. The Head was left alone in the rose-garden, since she was still free until Rosalie Dene should call her for an interview with a prospective parent. She lay back comfortably in her chair and thought over all she had learned this afternoon. She was not over-troubled about Emerence. She knew that she could deal well and faithfully with that young lady and no one would intervene. When the girl had been sent to school she had been placed unreservedly in the hands of the school authorities, the only proviso being that they should do their best to reform her. It was on those terms alone that she had agreed to accept her, for Emerence came with a reputation that fully justified Jo's description of her as a "young criminal". The first term had been eventful: but the second one had not been so hectic and, until Margot had arrived to upset her again, Emerence had given every sign of settling down into being neither better nor worse than most schoolgirls.

"I can deal with both Margot and Emerence," the Head thought as she gazed dreamily across the garden at the glimpse of blue sea to be caught between the trunks of the trees. "All the same I hope – I very much hope that Margot will continue to behave herself. I don't want to have to make trouble for Jo. Her married life has been very happy on the whole, but there have been one or two bad patches and I should hate to create another. I know she isn't too pleased at having to leave England again so soon."

A light footstep sounded beside her and she turned to smile up at Rosalie Dene, who had come to fetch her to her interview.

A sudden inspiration came to her as she stood up. "Rosalie, would you like to do something for Jo?" she asked.

Rosalie's blue eyes opened widely. "Of course I would!"

"Well, then, could you have a talk with Margot Maynard?"

"Yes; but what about?" Rosalie asked. "I know she's working well. I've been amazed at the way she's gone up in form since she came when I entered the fortnightly lists."

"Her work is good," Miss Annersley said grimly. "The trouble is she's trying because it suits her own ends. Unfortunately, Emerence–"

Rosalie interrupted her with a peal of laughter. "Oh, I know about that, too. *And* I know what they're playing at – the imps!"

"Ah! Then I needn't say any more. Emerence is going to be severely warned that unless she pulls up in her work, she hasn't a chance of coming to Switzerland with us. At the same time, if Emerence chooses to work – and I'm pretty sure she will – it won't do if Margot slacks off because there's little or no chance of her being in the same form as Emerence next year. If Emerence goes to Switzerland, she will move up, you know, and however hard Margot may work, I don't think she'll be ready for Upper IVᴮ."

"Len's there already," Rosalie said doubtfully.

"Len has always worked steadily and her foundations are good. Margot has had spurts – few and far between, into the bargain. Her foundations are shaky and I won't promote any girl to a Fourth unless she knows her early work thoroughly. I'm afraid that Margot is inclined to be superficial and that won't do. Now, if she doesn't work steadily, I have warned her she must stay behind at St Agnes' for another year. That would come very hard on Jo, who has had to do without her for a year already, and I don't want to have to enforce it. Will you have a chat with Margot and see if you can get it into her head that sudden flashes of brilliance don't really get you anywhere in the long run. She may take it more readily from you than from me. After all, to her you are mainly 'Aunt Rosalie'. I may be 'Aunt Hilda' out of school; but in it, I'm 'the Abbess'–"

"How *did* you know?" Rosalie gasped, turning scarlet.

Miss Annersley laughed, a clear, ringing laugh. "Oh, my dear girl, I've known that for ages – since long before we left Tirol! Let me finish, or my visitor will be turning restive. As 'the Abbess', I'm bound to talk gravely about work and Margot will see it in that light. You rarely come across them officially, so she might be more inclined to listen to you."

Rosalie, now returning to her normal pink-and-white, nodded. "I see. Yes; I'll do that, certainly. May I take them all for a walk after tea? They would only be playing about the garden and I have the excuse that I've never had a chance to ask them about their Canadian adventures. I think I could manage it that way. And if her sisters are there to absorb my pearls of wisdom as well as herself, Margot isn't so likely to get her back up as if I take her off alone."

The Head nodded. "A very wise idea! Very well, my dear. Take them by all means; but don't make them too late for prep, please. Now I must go."

She turned and ran lightly as a girl from the rose-garden, leaving her secretary to follow more slowly, turning over in her mind what it might be advisable to say and what she had better avoid like the plague.

CHAPTER NINE

The Tennis Pairs

Miss Dene duly kept her promise to the Head. After tea that day, she called Len Maynard to her, bade her find the other two and all three come with her for a short walk as she wanted to hear about their Canadian adventures.

Len ran off gleefully and presently appeared with her sisters and the whole party set off along the one main road which ran across the island from St Briavel's village due south to the Merry Maidens, a reef of sunken rocks which had been a death-trap to shipping all through the centuries. The girls, however, loved to hang over the stout fence on the cliffs above them and watch the seas restlessly circling the wicked rock-teeth that were never more than a couple of feet above water at the lowest tide.

When the triplets had hung over the fence to their hearts' content, the secretary quietly changed the conversation which, so far, had been about Canada.

"Canada – and now Switzerland," she said. "You girls will be far-travelled before you reach your teens. At least," she added, "I suppose you all *will* be going to Switzerland with the school?"

"Oh, yes," Len said. "Mamma must go because of Papa and, of course, we'll go, too."

"But not necessarily with the school," Miss Dene said calmly.

The three stared at her. "But of course we shall!" Len said. "Where else could we go, Aunt Rosalie?"

"Well," Rosalie said, "you know that you are a good deal younger than the lowest age and if it weren't for the fact that none of the other parents seem to want to send their girls abroad before they were twelve, it would have been very awkward to have you three. As it is, it isn't going to matter, so long as your work's up to standard. That's up to you three, of course."

"Oh, I guess it would be all right, anyway," Margot said. "Mom would see to that OK. She says it's bad enough having to part with the boys when they're prep school age, but she's keeping us girls with her."

Len gave her sister a very straight look. "You *are* a rotter, Margot. Mamma told us we weren't to call her 'Mom'."

Margot shrugged her shoulders. "Well, 'Mamma' is so old-fashioned," she retorted. "It's daft, using a word like that."

"She said we could say 'Mother' if we liked," Con reminded her sister. "But she did say she wouldn't have 'Mom' at any price."

"Then that settles it," Rosalie interfered firmly. "And as for trying to insist that the school has you if you're not ready for it, you ought to know your mother wouldn't do it. So it would mean either a Swiss school or St Agnes'."

Margot glanced up at her from beneath long lashes, but said nothing. Len took it up, however. "I don't think Mamma would awfully like us to go to a Swiss school, Aunt Rosalie."

"I don't suppose she would," Rosalie agreed. "However, if you all work as you are doing, I don't see any reason why you shouldn't be able to go. I know you're very young for your forms – at least, Len and Con are; but you seem to be able to do the work. As for you, Margot, go on as you're doing and you'll be up with Con next term and the question need not come up."

Margot sighed. "I do so loathe having to keep *on* slogging," she said. "I like to put on a spurt for a while and then sit back for another while."

Len gave her an anxious look. "But you *will* go on digging in, won't you?" she asked. "Mamma would hate having to leave any of us behind. You don't want to make her unhappy, do you?"

Margot thrust out her lower lip. "*Who's* going to make her unhappy?" she demanded in shocked tones. "I never said I *wasn't* going to work."

"No; but you do like to do things in bits and pieces," Con said. "Oh, Margot, you've done awfully well since we came back. Do go on with it. You can, you know. Papa says you're the cleverest of all of us."

Margot smirked complacently. Then her eyes clouded. "It'll be an awful bore, though. I guess I'll have to take it out on something else, that's all."

"Time we were going back," Rosalie said. "I mustn't make you late for prep."

Len and Con held their tongues about school for the rest of the walk. After more than ten years of living with her, they knew their Margot and her terribly quick temper. She was very much better than she had been; but she was still apt to blow up, as their father said, if you said too much to her. As for Margot, she had made up her mind to tackle her mother on the point the first chance she got. She did so, but obtained no satisfaction.

"Yes," Jo said. "I did say I wouldn't be parted from you girls again as long as you were school age. All the same, I was wrong to say it. If it's to be for your good, I shall agree to leaving any or all of you behind. I can't just think of what *I* want, Margot. I've got to think of what's best for *you* and put my own feelings into my pocket. I had to do it two years ago when I let you go off to Canada with Auntie Madge. I simply hated it at the time, but now when I look at you and see my Bouncing Bet instead of the little misery I sent off I'm more thankful than I can say." She smiled at Margot infectiously. "Anyhow, sugar-pie, so far as I can understand, it depends on yourself what happens. Go on working as you've done all this term and you'll go up with a bang next and no need for anyone to worry about St Agnes'."

Thereafter, Margot worked; and when Emerence, looking very woebegone after a serious interview with the Head, came to tell her that their lovely plan was at an end, so far as she was concerned, she said briskly, "OK, then. You must slog and so must I or they'll be leaving *me* behind. It only means that we shan't be together in lessons, and after all you can't really have much fun then. We'll make up for it out of 'em though, or my name's not Mary Margaret Maynard. I guess it would be a lot worse if one of us was left behind in England and, mind you, that's what they'll do if we don't watch out."

That was the end and no one had to complain of the work of either thereafter – or not more than was quite usual.

This was as well, for summer had come in the third week of May with a rush of blazing sunshine, after bright but chilly days for the first three or four weeks of term. As a result, the girls found their spare time well filled with tennis, cricket, swimming and boating. The Guides began to talk about their weekend camps and no one had much time to waste on anything but normal school activities. Gingham frocks were the order of the day and stockings and shoes were discarded in favour of sandals, and everyone was warned that hats must be worn when they were in the sun.

The prefects were hard at it, deciding on their teams. The cricket First Eleven was little difficulty as seven of last year's colours were still at school and the last four places nearly filled themselves automatically from the Second Eleven. The tennis pairs, however, were another matter.

The Games Committee held a special meeting on the Saturday of that week to discuss the question. Their first tennis match would come off on the following Wednesday afternoon and they wanted to give a good account of themselves.

As this was their last term on the island, Elfie, the Games Prefect, had set her heart on their winning all their matches. This meant that every available moment saw girls at the nets or on the courts, and Miss Burnett complained bitterly to her peers that she couldn't call her soul her own, for she was always being called away to pronounce on the play of someone!

"Miss Burnett is doing remedials," Elfie said when the committee had all assembled. "She told me to carry on and she would come when she could. As this is a special meeting, we won't bother with the last lot of minutes, but get down to work at once. The chief job is settling the tennis pairs."

"Pity we had to lose Peggy, Daphne, Nita and Natalie," Madge Dawson sighed.

"Well, we have so we must fill in their places," Elfie said. "Luckily, we will have Blossom and Katharine. Katharine's almost as good as a pair in herself; and Blossom's come on enormously since last year. Have you noticed her drive, anyone?"

"And she's considerably steadier than she was," Bride added. "As for Kath Gordon, she's due for Wimbledon before she's twenty or I miss my guess."

"Yes; she's an absolute gift," Elfie assented. "All the same, that gives us only one pair – and you, Madge. We've three more to find and then three second strings. We can't waste time, so trot out your proposals, folks!"

"We've got yourself as well," Madge retorted. "I suppose you haven't forgotten that you were first reserve last year?"

"I haven't," Elfie said briefly. "I can't work up to match standard, though."

"Why not?" two or three voices demanded at once.

"My idiot ankle's giving me trouble again," she told them, still curtly.

"Oh, hard luck!" Nancy Chester exclaimed.

"Elfie, do you mean that tendon you hurt when you had that fall all those years ago at Plas Howell, and Daisy had to carry you miles through the snow, is playing you up *again*?" Bride demanded.

Elfie shook her head. "No; it's a bone that was slightly displaced. I'm going into hospital in the summer to have it put right. I slipped on the stairs at home these hols and that did it. But it means that I can't do anything very strenuous this term. So you'll have to count me out of any teams."

The girls voiced their sympathy. Elfie was a keen player and for her to have to miss a term's games would be a great trial for her.

"Well, we can be thankful it's your ankle and not your brains that's affected, I suppose," Bride said. "Well, Elf's out of it, then. And so's Julie. Why on earth did you want to go and have a septic appendix last term, old thing?"

"Wanted? Talk sense!" Julie retorted. "I never wanted it. And I'm as sick as any of the rest of you about not being allowed to play. Doc's a fussy-gussy; and Uncle Peter's another! They both put the wind up Mummy, though, and she made me promise faithfully I would do as they said."

"Well, it's no use talking. We'll just have to put up with it, then."

"It's an awful pity Di Skelton left as she's done," observed Ruth Lamont, who represented Lower Vb. "It was the one thing she really loved at school and she was a demon player on her day. We could have done with her very nicely. I simply don't understand why she left like that. Last term she was talking about having a year at the Welsen branch. She said it would be just her cup of tea – all the *finishing* ideas, you know – and then she just lights out and leaves us cold like this and no one seems to have any idea *why*."

Bride flushed faintly at this, but the others were too busy calling Ruth to order to notice. Elfie banged on the table with one of the junior cricket bats lying on a nearby locker, and when she had silence reminded them that there was no time for mere gossip.

"You can discuss Diana another time. At the moment, I want to decide on the pairs and three second strings. So far, we've Katharine and Blossom, with Madge for good measure. I'm out and so is Julie. Hurry up and make some proposals. We can't stay here all day."

Nancy stood up. "I propose Bride," she said. "She's come on enormously since last year, especially in service. She's really better at tennis than cricket and if it comes to a question of which, I think she ought to go hot and strong for tennis. We've two or three other good bowlers, and fielders can be trained; but we are short of outstanding

118

players – apart from Kath and Blossom and Madge."

With one accord the 'Committee turned to stare at Bride, who got to her feet looking red with embarrassment. "If that's what you all think," she said, "I'll willingly stand down from the Eleven. I love cricket; but I like tennis as well, and if you do want me to be in the pairs I'll do my best."

She sat down amidst an outburst of clapping and Elfie pounded her on the back. "Good for you, Bride! The Eleven will miss you; but we really do need you for the tennis, so I'll put you down with Madge pro tem."

"Well, that gives us our second pair," Audrey Simpson said. "I'd like to propose Ruth for one of the third. We've seen her play and we know she's good and keeps her head and she doesn't poach!"

"I'll second that," Julie put in; and it was carried promptly.

Ruth, new the term before, but already very keen on her school, turned as red as Bride had done, and looked pleased. She was not outstanding like Katharine and Blossom; but she was above the average. The girls all liked her and she had her meed of clapping when she accepted.

"Five of the six!" Nancy exclaimed. "We're getting on! Now who can suggest who for the last of the pairs?"

It was difficult. Several names were proposed; but Annis Lovell was really a cricketer; Clem Barrass was a swimmer and other summer sports came a long way behind with her; Rosalie Browne played a very pretty game, but she lacked the stamina needed for matches; the same could be said about the Ozanne twins, who were cousins to the Chesters and the Lucys, and quite good, but apt to tire easily.

"Besides," Julie said, "Uncle Paul has been raising the

119

roof about their work. He seems to have just wakened up to the fact that they're three years older than young Betsy and in the same form, with her skating about the top and them quite happy to be somewhere in the middle of it."

Nancy twinkled across the table at her cousin. "So far as that goes, they're older than we are. Vanna and Nella take like easily and it's mad of Uncle Paul to raise the roof over their reports at this late date. He should have done it years ago when we were all Middles. Anyhow, Vanna is really inclined to be delicate since that bad go of measles she had when she was fourteen. I often think Nella could have done a good deal better, but she sticks by Vanna. They're seventeen in October. It's too late to change them now. But anyhow," she added, "they've no more real stamina than Rosalie, so I think we can wash them out."

Elfie turned to Ruth. "What about your lot, Ruth? We haven't had much time to know their play. Can you suggest anyone?"

Ruth shook her head. "Janet Overton can play brilliantly on her day; but it *is* on her day and that's not good enough for matches. Janice Richards was promising last year; but she's only fifteen and there, again, I think she lacks stamina. The rest come more or less in the ruck."

"What about Carola Johnstone?" Bride suggested. "She's a hefty specimen and she plays quite a good game. I should think if we give her a trial she'd play up and find just the little bit extra she needs. We all know she's mad keen on the school!" she added with a wicked grin.

The rest chuckled. Carola had quite literally gate-crashed the school four terms ago, running away from the cousin who was her guardian as her parents were in Central Africa, and a trip to Jamaica as well, so that she might be a pupil of the Chalet School.* After a good deal of bother for all concerned, she had been accepted and anything she could do for the school would be done with all her might.

"It's an idea," Elfie agreed. "Carola played well last year and she's even better this, so far as I've been able to judge. I wonder? What do the rest of you think? Shall we try her? As Bride says, she'd do her best and she has an excellent service and isn't too bad in a rally."

"*And* she can keep her head," Nancy said. Then she added, "So long as she doesn't forget!"

They all laughed at this. It was Carola's favourite excuse on most occasions. However, she seemed to be growing more level-headed, so it was finally decided that she should be tried and they drew a long breath as they realized that the pairs were settled, at any rate.

When it came to the second strings, they found they had six names to choose from, all being much of a muchness.

"Not a pin to choose between them," Elfie said rather despairingly. "How on earth are we to decide?"

"Write their names on slips, put them in a hat and blindfold someone – our one and only Mary-Lou, if you like – and let her draw three," Nancy proposed.

"Don't be an idiot!" the games prefect said scornfully. "You can't decide anything like second strings for the tennis pairs in that hit-and-miss fashion."

"Fix up matches for them against the pairs and choose the three who play best," was Bride's much more reasonable idea.

"That's more like it!" Elfie pulled a pad towards her and began tearing a sheet off it into slips. "Who shall play with who?"

* *Carola Storms the Chalet School.*

Primrose Day, who was out of it since she was a swimmer like Clem and captained the swimming, looked up. "Bride and Madge – Kath and Blossom – Ruth and Carola. I should write those on slips. Who are your choice for second strings?"

Elfie handed her the list and she scanned it closely.

The door of the gymnasium, where they were holding their meeting, opened at that moment and Miss Burnett, accompanied by Miss O'Ryan, came in. The girls heard them, looked up and then rose to their feet.

"Well, how are you getting on?" the games mistress queried. "Got anything settled?" She took the list Elfie handed to her and looked at it. "Oh, good! Tennis pairs all settled. What are you doing now?"

"Second strings – but there are so many that seem to be about level that we can't decide," Elfie explained as the mistresses took their seats and the girls followed their example. "We've six at least. Bride thought we might try them against the pairs and choose those that do best."

"With one eye kept firmly on those who don't come up to scratch," Miss Burnett said. "Sometimes people rather fall down on an important occasion until they're accustomed to an audience. I don't think you could do better, Elfie. If you like to try that out, Miss O'Ryan and I will umpire and I'll get someone else for the third match. Then you people can divide your forces among the courts and take notes. How will that do?"

"Oh, thanks awfully, Miss Burnett," Elfie said fervently. "That would be a huge help. It's so easy to miss points of play when you're keeping score."

"Very well, then; we'll do that. Now let me see who you've chosen."

They handed her the list and the two mistresses studied it thoughtfully.

"Jean Ackroyd," Miss O'Ryan murmured. "Yes; she plays a good game, though there's not much sting to her service. Betsy Lucy – Meg Whyte – Kathleen Norman – Freda Lund – Oh, Elfie, *would* you? I mean, Freda is coming on at wicket-keep and she's good for ten or a dozen runs as a rule. I'd leave her for the cricket if I were you. Don't you think so, Miss Burnett?"

"I do. And put Susan Dagleish in her place, Elfie. She's good now and she's going to be very good presently. She places her balls well, and she's not afraid of playing at net. Haven't you seen her?"

Elfie shook her head. "She hasn't been playing when I've been coaching. I'll change Freda for her, though. Freda plays tennis quite well, but I've noticed that she's got the makings of a wicket-keep and we can do with one. Then I've put Sally Winslow down. She's very steady and occasionally she sends over an untakeable service. The only snag with her is that she's still rather young, and mayn't be able to stand up to match practice."

Miss Burnett laughed. "Sally's on the small side, but she's as wiry as they come. Try her, by all means. Now let me see the court's chart. Ye–es; I think we'll get leave-off for everyone's prep tonight and have the tests immediately after tea. Will that suit you?"

No one was disposed to quarrel with this except Ruth, who had General Schools Certificate in July and felt nervous of her chances of passing. However, Miss O'Ryan, who knew about it, put in quickly, "I think we'd better ask for just those we need, Miss Burnett. Ruth, perhaps Miss Burnett will excuse you as you have that exam coming along. We'll find someone to take your place."

Miss Burnett agreed, so Ruth looked relieved. She had heard from her father that if she did well in Schools, he would send her to Switzerland. If she did not, she must go on to St Agnes'. She was anxious to remain with her own particular set who were all going, so she was working to the top of her bent.

Miss Burnett stayed to make one or two slight arrangements about the evening and then the meeting was closed and the Games Committee departed to other chores, feeling that a good piece of work had been done that afternoon.

The tests were easily arranged and, in the event, Betsy Lucy, Meg Whyte and Susan Dagleish were finally appointed as second strings. The rest were ordered to practise as much as possible in case there should ever be any need to call on them. It did not seem likely, but none of the Games Committee had forgotten what had happened in the previous summer, when none of the proper second strings were available at the beginning of a match and Nita Eltringham, one of the pairs, had fallen and dislocated her collar-bone. Katharine Gordon, who had already played her match set, had had to go on the court again, and altogether it had been a trying time for those responsible.

The pairs and their second strings settled down to work hard and the result was that the school managed to win the match on Wednesday. It was a hard struggle, for the big convent school had one outstanding player and several who played exceedingly well for schoolgirls; but, as the Head of their games said to Bride when they were going to tea after the match, Katharine Gordon and Blossom Willoughby were both something out of the common and had simply walked away with their set.

"And the rest of you are jolly good," concluded Josephine O'Donovan generously.

On the Saturday, the First Eleven defeated Dumbarton

House, a much smaller boarding school from the mainland, by twenty-seven runs and five wickets. So the school had made a good beginning. They knew they would have a tough fight of it with Campden House the following Saturday, however. It was a much larger school and always did well in its matches.

"Still," said Audrey Simpson that evening, when the visitors gone, they were taking their ease in the garden and waiting for the tennis folk to return from their match against Carnbach High School, "I hear they have lost that demon bowler of theirs – what's the girl's name?"

"Jessica Mallory," Elfie answered. "She's gone to Bedford to train for P.T. And the Sacred Heart have lost Genevieve Leycester. She didn't bowl leg-breaks like Jessica, but her balls came down on you like – like thunderbolts. Tom was the only one of our lot who could do anything with them."

Tom, sprawled full length in a deck-chair let down to its furthest limits, grinned amiably. "So long as you stood up to her, there really wasn't anything in her bowling," she said placidly. "I grant you it was fast, but there wasn't anything *tricky* in it. I've played a lot with boys, remember, and I've had to stand up to just as fast bowling before."

"A good thing you felt like that!" Elfie said with emphasis. "The rest of us were scared stiff of her; but I seem to remember that you took seventeen runs off her in two overs. I'll bet Joan was glad of you that match!"

Tom contented herself with another grin before she sat up to wave a welcome to the tennis pairs who hove in sight just then, escorted by Miss Derwent, who went on into Big House and left them to join their compeers and announce that they had won again – though by the skin of their teeth.

125

"The High School has hard courts," Bride complained, "and when you're accustomed to playing on grass, it gives you a terrifically fast game."

"What are the scores?" Elfie asked.

"Six-four – seven-six – six-three. I'm dead!" And Bride flopped back in her chair.

"I wonder what the kids are doing?" Nancy Chester said thoughtfully before anyone could reply to this. "They seem awfully *quiet*! Anyone know where they are?"

" 'Go and find out what Master Alfred's doing and tell him to stop it,' " Lesley Pit murmured. "Do sit quiet while you can, Nance! Someone will be in charge of the little dears, never fear!"

"The Fifths are mostly in the orchard, arranging for their 'do' next Saturday evening," Rosalie Brown said. "And Miss Slater and Miss Stephens took all the Thirds off to Kittiwake Cove after tea."

"And anyway, the Junior Middles will be on their best behaviour," Bride remarked. "They're having a trip over to Brandon Mawr next Saturday and they know that if they want to go, they've got to have clean sheets to show. I overheard Priscilla Dawbarn warning young Prue about that on Wednesday just before our match began. They lost their turn last summer, thanks to smashing that kitchen window during their green apple battle, so they've never seen the place yet. I should imagine it will be a case of 'peace, perfect peace', so far as that crowd are concerned until the trip is over – and thank goodness, too!"

The prefects fully agreed with this but, as the warning bell for Abendessen rang just then, they had no time to discuss it further. They picked up their chairs and cushions and strolled back to the house, and the question of the Junior Middles' treat was forgotten in the interest of their own concerns.

CHAPTER TEN

Junior Middles' Treat

No one among the Junior Middles wanted to miss the treat of a trip to the two bird sanctuaries so close at hand. Everyone knew that bad behaviour and careless work might very well put a stop to *her* share, so, for a whole week, the school at large enjoyed comparative peace and even work improved. As a result, when the Saturday came and the motor launch, which was always used to take them across to either Brandon Mawr or Vendell, tied up at the old quay down in Kittiwake Cove, most of them were present, including Emerence and the irrepressible Dawbarns. Five unfortunates had been left behind in San with various ailments; and Peggy Harper, who was another imp of the first water, was expecting a visit from her mother and had to stay behind, much to her disgust; for, as she remarked to her own gang, "If only Mummy hadn't fixed on today and come next Saturday instead, I'd have had *two* treats!"

The staff, however, breathed more freely on learning that they would not have to worry about the fourth worst girl in the school.

"*That's* something to be devoutly thankful for!" remarked Miss Norman, throwing grammar to the winds in her relief. "Look here, Jeanne, if I take on the Dawbarns and Biddy sees to young Emerence, can you deal with the rest? I don't think you'll have much trouble with them so long as their ring-leaders are skewered down with a watchful eye or two."

Mdlle broke into her pretty laugh. "But, Ivy, chérie!" she protested. "Why should you and Biddee have all that trouble? Me, I can take my share."

Biddy O'Ryan, who was the other mistress on escort duty, gave little Mdlle a look of affection. They were old friends, and in her own salad days Biddy had been one of the Frenchwoman's brightest pupils. "Sure, didn't ye have all the trouble going when *our* lot were at school?" she said. "No one could be saying we were a set of little angels – not with any truth – and now it's time you sat back and let *us* take all the trouble."

"Hélas!" Mdlle cried dramatically. "Am I then so old a woman that you must treat me as an invalid? Consider, Biddee, that all my teaching life has been spent in the Chalet School and I was very young – younger even than you – when I first joined it."

"I wasn't thinking of that," Biddy said. "Only that, when you can, you ought to take life a little easily now. Jo told me that you were our first French mistress and the only one until Mdlle Berné joined us when St Scholastika's became part of the school. The thing that matters now is that I, at any rate, should try to pay back some of what I owe ye. I'll see to Emerence."

"Please, will you have me, too?" asked a fresh voice from behind them as they stood near the foot of the path that led down to the cove from the cliff-top. "The Head seems to think that with *this* crowd an extra policeman is needed."

"I don't blame her at all, at all," Biddy grinned. "We're glad to have you, Rosalie – Emerence Hope!" She broke off her talk with Miss Dene. "What are you doing? If you fall into the water, you'll go straight back to school to Matron with a request that she puts you to bed for the rest of the day!"

Emerence, who had actually been preparing for a leap to the deck of the little vessel, turned very red and tried to hide herself behind Ruth Barnes, who was bigger in every way than she. The rest, warned that the staff had no intention of forgetting them, stood quietly until the gangway had been run out. Then Mdlle took charge and marched them aboard, instructing them to sit down and remain seated until the sea trip was ended.

The mistresses followed them aboard and disposed of themselves among the more tiresome of their pupils. The motor launch was safe enough, for the men made the run almost daily and knew all about the currents; but with a set of young demons like this, the staff preferred to play for safety.

"And even so, I'll bet you we have at least *one* scare before we get home again," Miss O'Ryan murmured to Miss Dene as that lady settled herself down with a Crater twin on either side.

They cast off and presently they had rounded the cliffs and were running due west through the Sound which separated St Briavel's from the mainland. They chugged past St Briavel's village, keeping parallel to the shingly beach, and when they had reached the northern end, settled down on a western course.

"Why didn't we just go round by the Merry Maidens?" Emerence asked Mdlle who was sitting beside her. "Wouldn't it have been shorter?"

"That is true, ma petite," Mdlle said. "But it would not have been very safe and, as you see, we turn south here to pass between the Wreckers and the Callachs – see; those great rocks where nothing grows – and if we had taken the other route, we must have gone far away round them because of the wicked current and so it must have been a longer passage. Now we go right round Brandon

Mawr and you will have a good view of the cliffs where the seabirds nest. Regardez, mes enfants," she went on, raising her voice so that all could hear. "Regardez les oiseaux de mer."

The girls turned with one accord to survey with awe-filled eyes the mighty granite cliffs that towered out of the sea almost vertically. The air was filled with the noise of water and the mewing of seagulls which swooped down on the little craft in search of food. No one had anything for them, for Mdlle forbade the opening of the picnic hampers, though the birds circled the boat, shrieking and scolding all round the island to the tiny harbour which lay at the northern corner, sheltered from the western gales by a long, narrow promontory and from the northern ones by the mainland.

Then they saw a green streak in the waters which were blue as the Mediterranean on this sunny day, and knew that it was the Wreckers' Race which they must cross before they could enter the harbour at Brandon Mawr.

For a short distance the launch held steady on her course. Then she suddenly swung round and, with throttle fully open, cut right across the Race at right angles. For a few minutes they pitched violently; but it was a few minutes only. Then, before anyone had time to think about being seasick, they were across and slipping through quiet water to the small stone quay where Kester Bellever, the bird-watcher, was waving welcome to them.

The girls knew him well, for he was a great friend of the school and came twice a term, as a rule, to give them talks on the birds he loved. He was a somewhat short, thin man, with thick curly hair, turning grey and usually in need of cutting, and a short beard. He had been in the Navy during the war, and his sea-blue eyes had the far-seeing look of the sailor. His attire was wildly unconventional, consisting of a pair of elderly grey slacks, a striped shirt, collarless and open at the throat, and a pair of rope-soled shoes which he always declared were the safest footgear for his job.

He shouted a cheerful greeting to them as the launch drew into the quay and then tossed the great hawser, wound round a stone set securely under the fall of the cliff, to the men who quickly coiled a turn or two round the bollard. Ten minutes later, and all the passengers were ashore. Mr Bellever had a few words with the men on the launch before she cast off and chugged away for the journey to the mainland. Then he turned to his visitors and after a few lively exchanges with those he knew well, suggested that the first thing to be done was park the hampers and other impedimenta at his house.

"I thought we'd do that first," he said to Mdlle with his shy smile. "I've got some jugs of goat's milk waiting, for being on the sea makes you thirsty. When we've had that, we'll take them round and show them the sights. After that, I think we'll have dinner because I want to take them over to Vendell earlyish. Most of them have been here before; but except for Cherry," he smiled down at Cherry Christy who was clutching his hand rapturously, "none of them have seen the other place. I told the Parrys to have the launch back here at two. I want the girls to see the marshes where the wild geese come and breed in season."

Mdlle looked relieved at this programme. She had been to the smaller island two or three times and though the cliffs were moderately steep at one part, most of the shore was shingle with patches of sand, where the girls could not easily run into danger. They would have plenty of fun, gathering shells and hunting for bits of rare crystal, cornelian and amber which were to be found among the

131

shingle if you were lucky. Besides that, Vendell produced some wild flowers that were rather rare elsewhere. She felt that even the Dawbarns and Emerence could hardly get into trouble over there, and said so to Rosalie as they toiled up the zigzag sandy path that led to the top of the cliffs in the wake of their pupils.

"I wouldn't be so sure," Rosalie said thoughtfully. "There are some girls who could get into mischief if you tied them up in the middle of a field, and those three are among them. However, we can only keep an eye on them and hope for the best! Sit down on that rock a moment, Mdlle. This *is* a pull up! What a glorious view there is from here!"

They all reached the summit at last and Kester Bellever, with Cherry still clinging to him, led the way to his little stone house with its roof of deep thatch literally tied on by thick ropes that criss-crossed it everywhere. It stood in a dip in the ground, giving it protection from the great north and westerly storms that swept across the sea in winter. All round it was a garden, gay with such hardy flowers as nasturtiums, marigolds, love-in-a-mist, garden daisies and thrift in front. At one side was a healthy-looking kitchen garden, producing potatoes, greens and salads of all kinds, and turnips, carrots and onions. At the back was a big, heavily-wired run where some hens and a lordly cock lived. There were two or three batches of golden chicks running about and the girls crowded round with cries of delight.

"Why don't you let them run loose all over, Mr Bellever?" Clare Kennedy, a shining light of Upper IVв, asked inquisitively.

"Because of all the wicked pirates we have here. The black-backed gulls, for instance, love a nice plump chicken

132

for dinner."

"Oh, the horrid things!" Prudence cried. "How can they – such darling babies, too!"

Kester Bellever laughed. "To the black-backed gull – and others of the same gentry – a chicken is just a good dinner. Besides," he added, twinkling at her, "you eat chicken yourself, don't you?"

"Ye–es," Prudent admitted, "but not babies like this."

"Exactly. Well, the gull has a big tummy to fill and while he prefers a nice, tender chicken, he doesn't turn up his beak at a fine plump fowl either. So I keep my poultry well-protected as you see. This outer door is shut firmly behind me before ever I open that inner one. I'm taking no chances. I've been had before. Now come and park your baskets and try my goat's milk and then we'll take a trot round and see what we can find."

They crowded into the little house where Cherry Christy, who was Mr Bellever's adopted niece, enjoyed herself playing hostess. She had spent many a day over here or at Vendell with him when she was convalescing from the bad attack of poliomyelitis which had turned her from a merry, jolly little roundabout into a thin, miserable creature who hated all strangers. It was nearly two years now since Cherry had first met Mary-Lou Trelawney and her gang. They had made friends with the little crippled sister of Dicky Christy, and as a result of their treatment, Cherry had first agreed to come to school and then settled down happily and learned to forget that she wasn't like the others. Mary-Lou and Co. now reckoned among the Senior Middles, for most of them were fourteen. Cherry's birthday did not come until mid-October, so she had been included in this expedition while the rest had not.

There was little enough time for the house, and ten

minutes later they were all streaming across the rough, hillocky turf towards another hollow, where shielded from the worst weather was a very large wired-in run which, Kester Bellever explained, was where he put his fowls when they needed a change. There was also a big old nanny-goat who could be guaranteeed to look after herself and who had supplied the milk they had just drunk.

"I keep the kids down at Vendell," her owner explained before he led his visitors to the south side of the little island where the ground sloped down to cliffs that were a mere thirty-five or forty feet above the sea. Here he halted them and told them to listen, hushing Cherry when she would have burst out excitedly with some information.

The girls stood silent, listening for they knew not what. Suddenly, Prudence gave a squeak. "Oh, Mr Bellever! One of your cocks must have got away! Listen! I can hear it crowing under the ground somewhere!"

Cherry broke into a peal of laughter while Kester Bellever said, "Those are the shearwaters, Prudence. You know that they nest in burrows in the ground, don't you? I told you so last term. This is their colony and all this part is simply riddled with their tunnels. At the other end of the island you'll find the puffin burrows. The rabbits use them in winter, but in spring they have to clear out for the birds."

"What are puffins like?" Emerence asked.

"Parrots – of a sort. Their other name *is* sea-parrot. They have great rainbow-hued parroty beaks and orange legs and feet. They live on fish, of course, and one of the foulest-smelling places I know is a puffin burrow."

"Oh?" Emerence said. Then she asked, "What other kinds of birds do you keep here, please?"

"Ravens – kittiwakes – gulls of all kinds – swallows –

swifts – martins. We have all those. By the by, our martins are sand-martins and make their nests in the sand. I'll show you later on if we have time. Two at a time only, mind! You must wait for your turns. Come along!"

He swept them off to the west coast where they lay down, two at a time on their tummies, with himself between each pair and Miss Dene at one side and Miss Norman at the other while Mdlle and Miss O'Ryan held the rest in check. It was an awe-inspiring experience, looking down that sheer, tremendous drop to the sea, with the narrow ledges littered with the untidy nests most seabirds build and flocks of birds darting and screaming about and above them.

"Are they being insulting?" Priscilla asked her host when she was on her feet once more. "Don't they *shriek*? Do they think we'll hurt their babies?"

"Quite likely," he said. "Well, you and Norah are the last, so suppose we see about dinner now. Time's going on and the launch will be here before we know where we are. Mdlle, what do you say?"

Mdlle quite agreed. She knew that the girls were safe enough, but she was not sorry when they left the great, menacing cliffs and their noisy inhabitants for the rough pasturage outside the stone wall that enclosed the garden, and camped down for their meal. It was not that she minded heights in the least. She had been a member of the French Alpine Club for many years and was an experienced mountaineer. But she was always nervous of what might happen to the girls on these expeditions and preferred to have them where they were safe.

Lunch was a lengthy meal. In the first place, they were all blessed with good appetites, even Cherry, nowadays, and did full justice to the sandwiches, hard-boiled eggs,

135

fruit pies, cakes and bananas which Karen had packed for their midday meal. These they washed down with delicious home-made lemonade and afterwards, while the grown-ups enjoyed the coffee brewed by their host, the girls were allowed to run down to the beach and see if they could find any special pebbles or crystal chips. They were still employed on this when the launch appeared, and their elders, who had been keeping a look-out for her, came down the path and hustled them aboard her for the run to Vendell.

That was fun, too, and new to everyone but Cherry. They landed safely, and while they scattered about the shingle beach, hunting for more stones and shells, Mr Bellever held a short, low-toned conversation with the Parry brothers before he rejoined them and the *Silver Lady* chugged gaily off.

"Make the most of your time," he warned his guests with a glance at his watch. "They're coming back for us at half-past five and it's nearly three now."

Mdlle gave a quick exclamation. "So soon? Mais – j'ai crû qu'on retournera pour nous à sept heures."

He nodded. "I know. But Evan Parry doesn't like the look of the weather signs and I knew you'd rather be safe than sorry." He had turned and was leading the way to the marsh where the wild geese found sanctuary. "Can't they picnic at Kittiwake Cove when we get there? That's near enough to home for you to get there in a few minutes or so, if weather really comes."

Mdlle nodded. "But yes; they can do that. And, truly, you are right when you say that I should choose to have them all safely at St Briavel's before any storm could arise."

"It's not storm so much as fog that he fears," Kester Bellever replied. "However, he doesn't think it'll come

136

down before evening. Still, we don't want to be caught here in a fog. Neither do we want those children to have the frightening experience of crossing in a thick blanket, though I don't really mind it much for myself. – Yes; run and pick what flowers you like so long as you don't yank them up by the roots. Oh, and keep off the marsh."

The dozen or so thronging round him set off. They knew, for Cherry had told them, that not only were sundew and bogbean to be found, but in the marshes they could gather kingcups, as she called marsh marigolds. Two or three others were not near enough to catch what he said; among them, Priscilla, who had set her heart on gathering a good bunch of marsh marigolds for the form room.

She caught a gleam of golden yellow, shrieked to her twin to come on and help gather, and sped hotfoot for her quarry. Being Priscilla, she never troubled to look where she was going, and she bounded off the dry margin of the marsh on to a tuft near the edge and then tried to leap to another near which was a handsome clump of the flowers. That was where her foot slipped, she overbalanced in her efforts to get back and, with a wild yell, fell headlong into the marsh.

The others, seeing what had happened, also yelled at the full pitch of excellent lungs, and Kester Bellever had to bawl for silence as the disturbed geese rose with a thunder of wings and went off honking their disgust at this interruption of their quietude. Meanwhile, the bird-watcher had reached the terrified Priscilla. He knew his marshes and he thanked his stars that the accident had happened just here where the mud was viscous and unpleasant, and not at the other side where it was deep enough to be dangerous. He speedily dragged her back to dry land, where she burst into tears while everyone promptly retired, the smell of the mud being thoroughly unpleasant.

The first thing Kester Bellever said when Priscilla was safe was, "Stop that noise, all of you! Do you want to frighten the birds away? Stop it I say!"

So imperious was his voice, that even Priscilla stopped in the middle of a yell and fell to whimpering. She was mud from throat to toes and there was even mud in her hair. Luckily, Miss Annersley had ordained that they must all wear slacks for their trip and the slacks were of blue jean which would stand any amount of boiling and brushing. The trouble was that Priscilla could hardly disport herself in her vest while the mud was being removed from her outer garments, and that was about all she had on underneath.

"It's all right, Mdlle," Cherry said, coming forward. "I left a frock here the last time I was over and Priscilla can wear it. It'll be a bit *short* for her," she added dubiously, regarding Priscilla's leggy length.

"Never mind, so long as she's decently covered," Miss Dene put in. "May we take her to your hut, Mr Bellever, and see what we can do with her? And stop that silly noise, Priscilla. You've only yourself to blame."

Priscilla stopped her whimpering, though she thought Miss Dene was one of the nastiest people she had ever met for being so unsympathetic. That lady whisked her off, together with Cherry, while Mdlle, after issuing a stern warning against the marshes, let the girls go on with their flower-picking and pebble and shell gathering.

In the event, when they all came together an hour later for tea, Miss Dene arrived on the shore, accompanied by a vision which reduced them all to shrieks of laughter. Cherry was built on a miniature scale and the Dawbarns were sturdy young folk. The blue gingham frock Cherry had offered was a good four inches above her knees, though Miss Dene had unpicked the hem to make it rather more decent in length. It was so tight that it could not be made to fasten across her chest and the secretary had been forced to employ her handkerchief to make a kind of front. The sleeves, as Priscilla said, were cutting into her arms and she had to move as little as possible in case she burst it. Miss Dene had taken her down to the shore and given her a thorough bath, including her hair which had had to be rinsed in the tiny spring that seeped out of the rock near the hut and it was still damp – which meant that it curled in tight rings over her head, so that Priscilla was *not* looking forward to bedtime when it must be combed out. Altogether, a more awful young fright had never yet graced a Chalet School picnic. Priscilla was thankful to slink behind Ruth Barnes and hide herself as far as possible.

Tea over, the girls wanted to go off again, but there was no time for it. The launch came into sight and when she had tied up to the tiny landing, the elder Parry observed that the fog was a-comin' sure enough and they'd better look slippy and get aboard. Mdlle and her colleagues took no chances after that. They marched the girls on to the launch, and almost before they knew it, she was standing out and Vendell was being left to starboard. Towards the open sea, the horizon had a misty look and the younger Parry opened his throttle and sent the little *Silver Lady* cutting through the slowly-heaving water at top speed. He made no attempt to round the cliffs at Kittiwake Cove either, but ran them to the ferry landing at St Briavel's village and they had to walk the mile and more back to Big House through a clammy white cloud that soaked them thoroughly, though no one had much chance of feeling cold, for Kester Bellever led the way and he raced them along the road at such a pace that more than half of them were well-winded by the time they entered the holly avenue. They reached Big House wet, glowing, and able to assure their host when he said good-night and turned to seek shelter for the night at the Christys' house that, to quote Maeve Bettany, they had had a wizard time and one of the things they would most miss when they went to Switzerland would be him and his birds.

CHAPTER ELEVEN

Joey Brings News

By the time what should have been the half term holiday had come, the girls mostly knew whether their future for the next year lay in Switzerland or at St Agnes' on the mainland.

The majority of the Seniors would go either to the branch at Welsen or the new one at the Görnetz Platz, though Margaret Benn and Gwynneth Jones of Lower VI would pass on to St Agnes'. Half-a-dozen or so from Upper V would be there as well; and quite a number from the two Lower V forms. In Upper IVA, the only other form which might have been expected to send the greater number of its members to Switzerland, there was, as Bride Bettany said, weeping, wailing and gnashing of teeth, for quite a number of parents refused to allow their girls to go abroad before they had reached the age of fifteen, and among those so affected was Doris Hill, a prominent member of what was known in the school as "Mary-Lou's gang". Doris had been certain beforehand that she would go and the decision of a firm parent to keep her in England until she had, as he said, had a chance to develop some idea of responsibility, brought bitter grief to her crew.

Another small coterie was broken up when Dr Jones set down a large and solid foot on Gwen's ideas and informed her that she was staying in England until she was seventeen. As Christine Vincent and Catriona Watson were both going, this meant the breaking up of a promising friendship which had lasted since the three had joined the school as Juniors of eight. As Gwen said, writing was not the same thing as seeing your chums every day!

Jo Maynard, having come over with her babies to pay a visit to the school at large and unburden herself of several pieces of news, overheard Gwen's wails and stopped short in her journey across the great front lawn to disabuse the three of this idea. Her arms were filled with the twins, and as she paused beside the garden bench they looked up and then jumped to their feet with eager requests to be allowed to hold the babies for a moment.

Jo was happy-go-lucky and the twins as placid a couple as ever entered the world. She let Gwen take Felicity and Catriona lifted Felix off her left arm and cuddled him while Christine waited for her turn.

"What was that I heard you moaning about just now, Gwen?" the complaisant mother demanded as she sat down among them. "Hurry up and tell me, for I can't stay here more than five minutes or so."

"Well, I think I've reason for moaning," Gwen said. "Dad won't let me go to Switzerland for another two-and-a-half years. Catt and Chris *are* going and it means we'll be parted. I know we can write, but it isn't the same and – and we've been chums all these years."

"Give Felicity to Christine," Jo said. "It's her turn. As for your friendship breaking up because you're parted, do you mean to tell me it's as poor and weak-kneed a thing as all *that*?"

The three went pink before her scorn. "It *does* make a difference, Mrs Maynard," Christine said. "Now, we see each other nearly all the time. But then we'll be miles apart and there isn't a lot of time for letter-writing at school."

"All the same, my dear, if your friendship is really what it ought to be, you'll find it'll stand the strain. You all know that *my* three friends and I are chums still, even though it's four years since I saw Marie and quite two since I saw either of the other two. We haven't so much time for writing, either, and anyhow, Simone always was one of the world's worst correspondents. The other two aren't so bad. Don't worry, Gwen. You'll find that you can make time for a few lines most weeks and so can the others, who anyhow will want to send you picture postcards of the place. Now give me Felix, Catriona, and hand over Felicity, Christine, for I must go. Cheer up all of you! You've half this term left, anyway, and you never know what may happen in the future!" And with this, Jo tucked a baby under each arm and left the trio oddly comforted by her offhand remarks, though, as Gwen said, it would take a dozen traction-engines and an earthquake to make her father change his mind and she didn't see herself reaching Switzerland before her seventeenth birthday, anyhow.

Jo's path lay along the wall which shut off the sunk rose-garden from the rest of the grounds. It was a hot day and the babies were heavy, so she made no attempt to hurry herself. As she strolled along, thankful for the shade afforded by a clump of tall horse chestnuts, her quick ear caught Miss Slater's voice. Evidently that lady was holding forth about something. With a grin, Jo laid her babies carefully down on the soft grass where they rolled and chuckled, parted the branches of a yellow banksia rose that grew here, and peered down to behold a group of the mistresses, all lounging in deck-chairs or hammocks, and all talking vigorously, considering what the weather was like.

"You mean to say you *aren't* coming to Switzerland!" Miss Derwent was exclaiming incredulously. "But why on earth not?"

"I simply can't face having to live where I've got to talk either French or German most of the time," Miss Slater said defensively.

"You funk!" That was Rosalie Dene from the standing hammock in which she was swinging luxuriously. "Fancy missing the mountains and lakes for a silly reason like that! Oh, Slater, you *are* an idiot!"

Miss Slater's quick temper rose at once. "Thanks for the bouquet! I suppose it hasn't dawned on you that I *may* have other reasons besides hating foreign languages? Where I'm going, I shall be head of the maths department and can run it to suit myself and that'll be a change after all these years of being just an assistant mistress!"

"This is where I pitch in pronto!" Jo murmured to herself as she let the rose-branches slip and picked up the twins. "What is that ass Slater doing?"

She set off at a faster pace and thus missed what came next. Biddy O'Ryan, who was sitting at a rustic table, supposed to be correcting Lower VI essays, glanced up as the maths mistress finished her speech, mischief in her eyes.

"Oh, *no*!" she said in awed tones. She tossed down her pencil and jumped up. "I say, you people, do you think we *ought* to be lounging about like this in the presence of anyone so important?"

"Lounge?" Peggy Burnett was quick to take the hint. "Of course not! We ought to be *kneeling*!"

The three younger mistresses promptly plumped down on their knees before the embarrassed Miss Slater, heads bent meekly, hands folded before them.

"Please, Teacher, be kind to us!" Miss Derwent wailed.

"Remember we're only humble assistants and you're going to be Head of a department!"

"You'll condescend to let us know how you're getting on sometimes, won't you?" Peggy Burnett added.

Miss Dene had been keeping her eye on Miss Slater. Now she intervened. "Get up, you goops! Enough's enough–"

She got no further, for at that moment Jo appeared at the head of the brick steps leading down to the garden and gasped, "Merciful Heavens! What *are* you all playing at? Here," she went on, coming down, "anyone want a baby? Don't all speak at once and don't scrap over them! Jeanne, would you like your god-daughter? OK; here you are." She laid Felicity into Mdlle's outstretched arms, handed Felix to Rosalie Dene and then dropped into a chair and mopped her face. "Whew! How hot it is! I'll say this, when England sets out to have a summer, she *has* a summer! Well, how's everyone?"

Biddy had jumped to her feet. "What are *you* doing here? Go away! You've got chickenpox at home – or is it measles? Something infectious, anyhow! You're a danger to the public! You oughtn't to be here!"

Jo chuckled. "My lamb, if it really *had* been that, you wouldn't have seen the tip of my nose for ages as you very well know. I rang up Rosalie this morning, though, and told her that Jack had come home last night and wanted to know if I had no more sense than to mistake nettlerash for chickenpox or measles. Didn't you tell them, Rosalie?"

"Jeanne," Rosalie said. "There hasn't been time to tell the babies."

"OK," Peggy Burnett said, unperturbed. "I'm the real staff baby and Biddy and Ruth come next. Well, 'tis glad I am 'tis no worse."

"Have they got it badly?" Miss Derwent asked, turning from worshipping little Felicity.

"Steve's covered. Charles and Michael have only got it in patches. Jack mixed them a cooling lotion and also gave them a very nasty but effective dose of something. They'll be all right again soon, only they've got to keep off sweets and have less strawberries while the rash lasts. But I had a fright, all right. I didn't want the twins to start anything when they have their hands full with their teething. Well, now that you know that, suppose you tell me what the performance I saw just now was all about. Had you been ticking that lot off for the good of their souls, Pam?"

Miss Slater went scarlet. "No; though I certainly should have done so if you hadn't arrived when you did. The silly young asses were putting on an act because I'd just told them that I'm not coming to Switzerland when the rest of you go. I've got a job as Head of the maths department at Selling Grammar School, not far from where I live. It's a big school – between six and seven hundred pupils – and I'll be head of the entire maths staff which numbers six besides myself."

Jo raised her eyebrows. "Not coming with us? D'you really like the idea of a berth like that better than Switzerland and all the fun of a new beginning?"

Miss Slater nodded. "Think it over a moment, Jo. I'm thirty-five now. If ever I want to get a post as Head somewhere, I've got to make a change. And though I enjoy a holiday abroad, I'm not so mad on the Continent as to want to spend most of my time there. I've been here ten years and I feel I'm getting into a rut. If I don't make a break now, I never shall."

Jo gave her a curious look before she said, "I see. If you feel like that, I agree you're wise to make a break now when the school is making a big break, anyhow. But I'm sorry, Pam. I'd have liked us all to go together."

"I've got to think of the future," Miss Slater defended herself. "It's all very well for people like the Head and Matey and Jeanne here. As you've said more than once, they are foundation stones and would probably hate to go anywhere else. But the school had been in existence years before I ever joined it. I've been happy here and I'll always be interested in what happens; but I want to be on my own. I hope to put in two or three years at Selling and then I'll have a shot at a headship. I've quite a few theories I'd like to try out."

"In maths teaching d'you mean? Or school in general?" Jo queried.

"Mostly maths, of course; but there are one or two other things I'd like to try, too, and I don't fancy they'd be acceptable here. So I'm leaving." Her tone added, "And that's that and I don't want any more talk!"

Jo nodded and said no more on the subject. Instead, she said lazily, "I've really come to bring you people a piece of news – several pieces, in fact."

The mistresses were all attention at once. Jo frequently brought news and it might mean anything from a decision to alter all the textbooks in the school at one fell swoop to the engagement, marriage or career of an old girl or mistress. There was never any saying.

"What's the first?" Rosalie Dene asked.

"Well, first of all, Gillian Linton – Young, I mean – has had a son."

"Not really?" Biddy cried. "Oh, Jo, how lovely! When did he arrive?"

"Early this morning. Jack rang me up about eight to say that he'd come a couple of hours before and all was well. I think myself," she added calmly, "that Gill might have managed a girl for the first. However, they seem to prefer boys in that family. Joyce's baby last autumn was another boy, you may remember. That gives her two sons to one daughter. Gill told me last week when I saw her that she wanted a son, so she's got what she wants."

"What's his name to be?" Peggy Burnett asked.

"Robert after Gill and Joyce's father, and Clement after his own daddy. Peter's first name is Clement. That's where Clem Barrass gets her Clemency, you know, seeing as he's her godfather. He'll be called Robert."

"That," said Miss Derwent severely, "is a most entangled sentence."

"Oh, well, you all know what I mean. Jack came home about noon and said Gill was in the seventh heaven and he was a *huge* baby – weighed ten pounds, if you please!"

"I'm so glad for Gillian," Mdlle said. "She has had a sad life, la pauvre!"*

"Yes; but now, as the Italians would say, she's eating white bread," Jo returned quickly. "And Peter takes great care of her and she hasn't to worry over Joyce any more."

"And that must be a *big* relief!" Miss Slater said with emphasis. "When I first knew them, Joyce seemed to be the be-all and end-all of Gillian's life. And I don't want to be unkind, but a more accomplished little piece of selfishness than Joyce Linton used to be I never yet encountered!"

"Joyce has altered and improved," Jo said gravely. "Her little girl is very delicate and they've had a lot of trouble with her. In spite of what I said just now about the Lintons preferring boys, Joyce really does adore her little Jocelyn and all the anxiety over her has finished off

_____
* *The Chalet School and the Lintons.*

148

that hard shell of selfishness Joyce had ever since I knew her, too."

Biddy glanced at Jo and changed the subject. "That's one piece of news and a very nice one, too. What's the next?"

The gravity left Jo's face. "It's another baby. I'll give you all three guesses whose it is. My god-daughter, by the way," she added airily.

"Your god-daughter? Then it must be Frieda or Marie or Simone. *Don't* say Simone has had *another* baby?"

"When Pierre isn't a year old yet? Have a little sense, Bridget mine!"

"Marie, then?"

Jo grinned and looked knowing. "Not just yet awhile. Ilonka is only eighteen months old. But by the time she celebrates her second birthday, I wouldn't mind betting there's another baby there, too. No; it's Frieda – after five years. Gretchen was five last March and she had another daughter on Friday of last week. Bruno wrote to me and I got the letter this morning. They've asked me to choose her second name, seeing that she's to be Josephine after me as Gretchen was named for her grannie and Madge."

"What have you chosen?" Peggy asked eagerly.

"Sent them a choice of three – Anna – Simonette – Carlotta. I'm *rather* hoping they'll pitch on Carlotta. Bruno's second name is Carl."

"Carlotta Josephine," Miss Derwent said, trying it out. "Or is to be Josephine Carlotta?"

"I can't tell you. Bruno didn't go into any details of that kind. But he said the whole family was thrilled to the limit and Frieda says she means to get level with me sooner or later. Let her try – that's all!" And Jo grinned fiendishly. "I shall go for those quads next time and *that'll* make her think again!"

149

"Don't be so foolish, my Jo," Mdlle said, laughing. "You have had triplets so you have beaten everyone else. Tell us, instead, what other news you bring."

"Well, you'll see!" Then Jo condescended to continue. "Well, if I don't get in first, someone else certainly will, and I do like to be first with all the titbits. It's about the Graves."*

"The Graves?" Biddy looked vague. "That rings a bell, somehow."

Jo glared at her. "I should just about hope it did! Really, Bridget!"

Peggy Burnett chipped in. "Hilary Burn! What's she doing now?"

"It isn't what she's doing. It's what they're going to do."

"Another baby, I suppose? Aren't the second generation crowding along?"

"Well, there will be one – in October. That wasn't what I meant, though."

"Let's see," Miss Slater spoke thoughtfully. "Dr Graves gave up his practice and they went out to South Africa, didn't they, to stay with a brother of his. Hilary never was much of a correspondent, and in any case, her real chum here was Renie Bell who left the same term – *and* for the same reason. You'll have to tell us, my dear. I suppose Dr Graves has settled on a new practice. Where is it – Carnbach, by any chance?"

Jo shook her head. "Oh, dear no! Far otherwise! Jack and Jem have invited Dr Graves to join the staff at the Görnetz San and he has accepted."

"But this is news indeed!" Mdlle was sitting up, her black eyes sparkling with delight. She had always been

* *Carola Storms the Chalet School*

150

very fond of the said Hilary Burn, who had been at the Chalet School as one of its best Head Girls and later joined it as P.T. mistress. Hilary had left the previous summer to be married to Dr Graves and they had seen practically nothing of her since then. If she were to be at the Görnetz Platz, the old friendship would be renewed.

Jo glanced at her. "Yes, Mdlle, you always did think Hilary the cat's whiskers, didn't you? Well, we're getting her back again, and if you're so glad, so am I. I always liked her from the time she was the Peri in that show of theirs at our Fairytale Sale of Work – remember?"

"When you did your best to murder Bill,"* Biddy struck in with a chuckle.

Jo made a gesture reminiscent of tearing her hair. "Will that affair *never* be forgotten? If I've told you once I've told you fifty times that it was Corney Flower's fault, bouncing off the step-ladder as she did. Anyhow, Bill was none the worse for it – and thank goodness for that!"

Miss Derwent sat up, interest in her eyes. "What's all this about?"

"I'll tell you later on," Biddy assured her. " 'Twas a near thing – but funny," she added.

"I suppose it's no use trying to forbid you," Jo said resignedly. "OK; tell it if you must. Well, the Graves are going out almost at once. When Jem bought the hotel for the San, he also bought a couple of chalets to house the assistant staff. The Peters are going next week as Frank Peters is one of them, and the Graves will be following a week later. Oh, by the way, Helen Graves – Phil Graves' sister, you know – is also going as Matron."

* *The Chalet School and the Lintons.*

"Quite a family affair," Miss Slater said. "I'm almost sorry now that I took this other job. However, it's too late to do anything about it, and after all I can always come out for a holiday and see you all."

"Mind you do," Jo replied.

"Then is that all the news?" Rosalie Dene asked, breaking a long silence.

"Yes, I think so. Isn't it enough for you? Anyway, I ought to be going to look up my offspring. I haven't seen them yet and it must be nearly four o'clock by this time. Give me my babies, please."

Jo stood up and held out her arms; but Mdlle shook her head. "I will carry my god-daughter to the house for you, since I am free. The others have duty when the bell rings."

Jo laughed. "I can see you spending every spare moment you have at our place once we get settled in. I won't have Felicity spoiled, Jeanne."

Mdlle laughed. "I shall not spoil her. But you must permit that I take much interest in my own godchild. There is the bell, and Rosalie is on duty so you can take Felix, my Jo, and let us go up to Big House. Hilda will wish to hear all this news you have given us."

Jo took Felix from Rosalie, who yielded him up and then went off to see to Lower IVB collecting their tea so that they could have a picnic beside the brook. Biddy went with her and the others slipped off to attend to their duties. The two left alone stood looking at each other with smiles.

"I think," Mdlle said as she turned to lead the way up the steps, "that once we are all safely settled in Switzerland, we shall be very glad of the many changes the removal brings us."

Jo, following her, nodded. "Especially as Frieda and

Marie hope to come to stay near by for the winter months – which I did *not* tell the others. I thought Biddy and Peggy, at least, had had enough excitement for one day. I've written to Simone, too, to beg her to bring Tessa and Pierre and come as well. Who knows, Jeanne, we four may yet be all together again, even if it's just for a few weeks, as we used to be in the old days of the Chalet School!"

CHAPTER TWELVE

Expedition

Ever since the school had opened, it had been the custom to mark the birthday of its founder by an expedition. Sometimes the whole school went together. More often, of late years, the various divisions had separated as there were so many of them. This year the Juniors were to go to Pembroke Castle, while the Middles visited the Cheddar Gorge. The Seniors' expedition was to the great Bournville factory near Birmingham.

It meant a long day, for they had to be at Carnbach by half-past six in the morning, where the motor-coaches would meet them, so Matron ordained bed at half-past eight for everyone the previous night. The staff who would escort them called them individually, since there was no need to rouse the younger girls who would have breakfast, or Frühstück, at the usual hour.

The Seniors rose and washed and dressed as quietly as possible when Biddy O'Ryan, Rosalie Dene, Miss Derwent and Miss Armitage slipped from bed to bed at half-past five in the morning. Ten to six saw them all downstairs in the dining room where they had Prayers before sitting down to a good meal. There were to be no halts on the way for even coffee, and they would carry packed lunches to eat as they went. It was a very long drive and they must be at the factory by two sharp.

"Don't you wish *you* were coming, Matey?" Bride asked of that lady as she passed up her cup for more coffee.

Matron shook her head. "I'm thankful to get you all out of the way to give me and the maids a chance to see to sorting out some of the household linen. How I'm ever to get through all I have to do before the twenty-eighth is more than I can tell. Here, take your coffee, Bride, and stop asking silly questions."

"No change from Matey," Nancy murmured to her chum with a grin.

"Didn't expect it," Bride replied with a return grin.

Then they had to stop talking and attend to business. Miss Annersley, who was coming with them, had arranged for one of the ferries to be at the landing-stage at twenty past six, and they knew they must not keep her waiting. Beds had been left for once, Matron engaging to ask the maids to see to them as there would be no time for the girls to do so and she flatly refused to have any beds made that had not been properly aired.

By ten past six they were marching quietly over the lawn and the sleeping younger members of the school never knew when their elders left. Bride and Nancy led the way, with Miss Derwent near and the Head acted as whipper-in together with Miss O'Ryan.

"Isn't it a gorgeous morning!" Bride sighed as they left the entrance gates and walked quickly down the highroad. "Cooler than it's been for ages, isn't it? There's quite a decent breeze from the west."

"It'll rain by night," Nancy the weatherwise remarked as she turned to look towards the west. "Look how clear-cut the hills are across the Sound. That's a sure and certain sign of rain to come."

"Not before time either," remarked her cousin, Julie Lucy, who was immediately behind them with her own great chum, Madge Dawson. "If the drought doesn't break soon there won't be a thing left in the garden. Even the brook is lower and the pond's shrunk quite a foot."

"Don't worry," Nancy told her. "When it comes, it'll be a downpour. Did you see the moon last night? Tipping right down instead of up as she has been."

"The courts are cracking," Bride said. "As for the pitch, I'm thankful that the Cwyst High match had to be scratched. What that fast bowler's balls of theirs would have been like on it I shudder to think!"

Elfie Woodward, walking behind Julie and Madge with Tom as her partner, struck into the conversation. "There's a lot in what you say, Bride, but all the same, I'd have loved to be able to play that match. They beat us by three wickets and five runs last season and this was the only match we could fix up with them. Then they had to go and start a scarlet epidemic and had to scratch.

"Oh, well, they might have beaten us again, so we've escaped that, at least," Bride said philosophically as they reached the landing. "They've still got that girl – what's her name – Gwladys Pugh, wasn't it?"

"It was," Elfie said as they filed on board. "And, of course, they have Margiad Evans and Myfanwy Griffiths and they're really outstanding as batsmen. Just the same, I'd have loved to have tried to beat them."

"Well, you can't have everything," Tom said as the Head came aboard and the ropes were cast off. "We've ten days' extra hols so let's be thankful for that. Off we go! It's quite cool in the water, isn't it?"

"You won't find it so cool at Bournville," said Miss Dene, who was standing near. "You'll be thankful for your cotton frocks then, I can tell you."

"Oh, I'm not complaining," Tom told her as she looked down at the mistress from her length of six feet. "It's a change for the better, really, after all the heat we've been having. Coo! Isn't she making it this morning? We're nearly there already."

In fact, the ferry, instead of circling round the other islands, had taken a straight course across the water and they were landed well before half-past six. The motor-coaches were waiting down on the quay and Miss Annersley, anxious to get off as it was a very long run, quickly apportioned them.

"Prefects, you take the small one. All the rest of Upper VI go with them and Valerie Arnott – Madge Herbert – Annis Lovell – Ruth Wilson – Rosalie Way and Gwynneth Jones. Take the hampers with you and all the raincoats. Now for the rest of you!" And she set to work with vigour.

"Which of the staff is coming with us?" Bride asked when everything was in and they were all seated. "Have we left a decent seat for whoever it is?"

She was answered by Miss Derwent, who poked her head in at the doorway to say, "You people ought not to need a mistress, so we're sharing with the others. You can go ahead, Williams." This last to the driver who, nothing loath, let in his clutch and rolled slowly and ponderously off the quay and up the long High Street of Carnbach, making for the open country where he quickened until they were bowling along at the speed limit and making good time, since the roads were still very empty at this hour.

For the first twenty or thirty miles, they went within sight of the sea. The sunshine roof was pushed back as far as it would go and the girls revelled in the cool breezes. Presently, however, they turned north-east to run through the mountains towards Brecon. Here, they had to labour up one of the steepest hills they had so far encountered, run through the town where signs of bustle had begun and down through Hay and across Herefordshire. The drivers had worked out the route very carefully and they found themselves constantly quitting the main roads which were growing very busy as the morning went on, and taking all sorts of short cuts. However, they reaped the benefit when noon saw them past Worcester and trundling along the Birmingham road. Here, they stopped admiring the scenery – as Tom said, there was precious little to admire just here – and ate their lunches. Gradually, the country vanished and they were running through small towns where the gardens were looking very sorry for themselves after more than three weeks without rain. Finally, as a clock somewhere near solemnly chimed two deep strokes, they drew up outside the factory and all tumbled out, thankful to stretch their legs a little.

The other two buses were not far behind; then, forming into line behind the Head, they entered the factory. Inside they were greeted by a pleasant-faced young man who ushered them into the factory's own theatre, where, as they were to learn, the employees had lectures and concerts, as well as plays and operas given by their own Dramatic and Operatic Societies which were flourishing.

Quite a number of parties were already seated there. The girls were shown the block of seats intended for them, and a few minutes later a gentleman appeared before the heavy curtains on the stage and explained that they must split up into groups of six each. The official cicerones would take charge of the parties and show them round everywhere. When the tour was over, they would return to the theatre, where they would see a film of the cacao plantations belonging to the Company, and get some idea of the planting, cultivation, harvesting and packing of the beans, after which they would be taken to the staff canteen for tea.

It looked like a full programme, for someone had told Elfie that they would have to walk five or six miles during the course of the visit. However, they had no chance to talk, for the same young man who had welcomed them came and touched Bride on the shoulder and asked her to lead the way after the first guide who was waiting for them.

Bride, Elfie, Nancy, Tom, Lesley and Primrose made up one group and were led off by the small and very pretty person who was waiting for them. She was very erect and sure of herself in her smart guides' uniform of chocolate brown overall with cream collar and cuffs. When they were all outside in a wide hall from which equally wide corridors branched off, she gave the girls an interested look.

"All from school, aren't you?" she said. "What fun for you! Well, come this way, please. Now in this case you see samples of the chocolates and other things we used to sell here before the war. At one time you could have bought any of our goods at these counters, but it had to be stopped then and we haven't begun it again, so far."

"I suppose it would have meant an awful lot of bother with sweet coupons," Bride said thoughtfully.

The girl nodded. "You've said it! Now come this way, please." And she led them into a great room or shed, filled with sacks piled high. "These are sacks of cacao beans as they come from the plantations." She took a handful from a great container and held them out for the girls to see. "This is one of the storage rooms," she went on, tossing them back. "When the beans are needed the sacks are loaded on the motor-trolleys and wheeled away to a lift where they are taken upstairs to a roasting room. There they are roasted, being kept moving all the time so that they roast evenly. This way please."

She led them up a flight of steep, iron-edged stairs, and into the room where the beans were being slowly and thoroughly roasted in a huge machine.

"Why must they be roasted?" Nancy asked.

"Well, partly to make them fit for grinding and partly to begin to extract the oil from them. They are full of fat, you know."

"What happens next?" Tom queried when they had all solemnly stared at the roaster.

"Grinding. This way, please. They are put through this mill first and are ground into chips – like these." She took a handful from a box and they all examined the small chips, still so unlike cocoa as they knew it. "Then they go through another mill where they are further broken down and finally through one where they are pulverised and become powder – like this." She lifted a lid and showed them a very dark powder.

"Cocoa, in fact," Lesley laughed.

The girl shook her head. "Oh, no; not yet! There's a lot to be done before they become the cocoa you buy and have for breakfast or supper. You wouldn't like it at all if it was left like that."

"It looks awfully like ordinary cocoa," Elfie said, surveying the powder. "It's darker than usual, but that's all. Why wouldn't we like it?"

The girl laughed. "It hasn't been sweetened yet, for one thing. It's terribly bitter as it is. And for another thing, you've got to get rid of the grease. I told you the cacao beans were full of fat. Haven't you ever heard of cocoa-butter? Theatricals use it to take off their grease-paint. And it's used in making chocolate, too. If it was left in, your cocoa would be so oily it wouldn't be fit to drink. This is just the raw article. What you get has been properly refined and sweetened. You'll see presently."

She turned and led them off and Primrose Day, walking beside her, glanced down at her with a friendly smile. "I say, couldn't we know your name? It seems so rude to keep on saying 'you' all the time. We'll have heaps of questions to ask, I expect. Tell us what to call you and we'll tell you our names."

The girl smiled back. "I'm Miss Nichols," she said.

The girls promptly gave her their names, and thereafter, though she frequently lapsed into her official manner, she often forgot and was as friendly as they could wish.

"Come along," she said. "We've lots to see yet. And please do ask me any questions you like. I'll answer them if I can." She paused and opened a half-glazed door, ushering them into a room that was very warm and full of the rich smell of chocolate. "Now here we have the place where the powder is turned into chocolate. Look!"

The girls pressed forward eagerly to gaze at the stream of rich brown chocolate pouring from an immense container to pass over rollers so that it looked like a miniature brown waterfall, thence passing on down large pipes.

"It looks like an open sluice at a reservoir," Bride observed. "Is this what you make chocolates and chocolate biscuits with?"

"Yes – after it's sweetened," Miss Nichols explained. "This is unsweetened chocolate and very bitter." She suddenly laughed. "We shouldn't sell much if we used it like this!"

The girls laughed with her and sweet-tooth Nancy said, "I remember someone gave us some bitter chocolate once. Urrh! How I hated it! And what a horrid shock it was when I bit into it!"

"What did you do with it, then?" Tom asked with interest.

"Oh, Dad had it. He rather likes bitters, you know. He bought us some *proper* chocolate instead."

"I think," Miss Nichols said firmly, "that we ought to move on now. There are other parties waiting to come in."

Bride glanced round and saw a party of ladies standing outside. She gave Elfie, who was inclined to linger, a little push and they all followed their cicerone to a huge kind of shed where the noise, as Tom said later, was simply terrific. This was to be expected, since it was the place where the cocoa and drinking-chocolate tins were made.

Miss Nichols led them to a great machine at one side and they stood and watched a man feeding narrow strips of tin-plating into it. A conveyor-belt carried the strips up to a cylinder where they were swiftly twirled round into shape and passed on to another part which clapped a base on and sealed them. Then they were carried on down the other side to pile into baskets of stout wire netting. When a basket was full, a man standing by swung it off and on to a motor-driven trolley while another basket slid into place at once to be as swiftly heaped up.

"But these are *round* tins," Lesley Pitt said, when they had gazed their fill and were being led off to see the filling of the finished tins. "Are the squarey ones made in the same way?"

"More or less," Miss Nichols replied. "The principle is the same, though. If you've seen one, you've seen the lot. Be careful of the floors," she added as Bride slipped on the greasy floor and was only saved from going headlong by Tom's strong arm. "You see they're iron-plated here, to take the weight of the trucks and trolleys and they get oily and it's easy to slip if you don't look out. Now here's the filling department. The tins are set upright on the belts and travel along until they are under the filler which drops

162

the exact amount into each tin before it passes further on, where its lid is put on. Then it goes to be labelled and sealed and then it's ready for the market."

The girls hung over the great machine, marvelling at the precision with which it worked. They could have stayed twice as long, watching the river of slowly-moving tins, each being held long enough under the filling machine to be given its proper quota of cocoa before passing on down the belt to be sealed and labelled. Miss Nichols knew exactly how long they should spend in each department, however, and she moved them on relentlessly to the next room, where they saw the sealing and labelling, after which the filled tins were dispatched onwards to tumble into cases which, as they filled, were removed and loaded on to the inevitable trolley. When that was piled so high that the girls wondered how the top cases should remain safe, it trundled off, the driver giving notice of his coming by shouting when necessary.

"How on earth do they manage to pack them up like that without half of them collapsing when the thing moves?" Tom asked.

Miss Nichols laughed. "But, of course, the packers know exactly how many cases each trolley should carry, and besides they know how to pack them safely. Now shall we go and see the printing works?"

"Do you mean you do your own printing as well?" Primrose asked incredulously.

"Oh, of course! We do *all* our work," their small guide said proudly. "We even have our own railway system which takes the loaded trucks to the goods yards in the city where they are dispatched all over the country – except what goes for export. I'll show you that later on. Turn round this corner. Now here we have our printing works. We'll go along this gallery and you can look down and see what's being done."

She led them along a gallery from which they could look down on the people busy below and see how they were printing great rolls of purple paper for the boxes of Milk Tray chocolates, as well as long strips for the others. Miss Nichols explained that the firm employed their own designers for chocolate-box lids and also for the advertisements. She took them to some show cases where they saw examples of what had been done, and admired the really artistic reproductions. Then she marched them off to see how chocolates were "filled", as well as the making of the fillings themselves.

This came first and they were shown great pans of pink or orange filling, and further along others of toffee. The fillings were made in huge containers from which they poured into the pans when they were ready, and these, when full, went on to the cooling department whence they emerged as paste.

"Pink – oh, raspberry or strawberry, I suppose?" Nancy queried. "Look at it, you folk! But however do you get it into the chocolates?"

"We don't," Miss Nichols said. "It's allowed to set to a paste and then moulded into the various shapes and put on trays which pass under containers full of liquid chocolate. The chocolates are *coated* fillings, you see. But actually, these are for chocolate biscuits. Come and see how they are done."

The biscuit room was a fresh thrill. Men filled trays with the shapes of biscuit paste. As the trays were filled, they were set on the conveyor-belts which bore them very slowly to the ovens. These were enormous cylinders through which the trays passed from heat to heat until they emerged at the other end, baked.

"Are they heated by electricity?" Tom asked.

Their guide nodded. "Oh, of course. Come outside and see what the ovens look like there."

The girls gazed up at the huge, shining cylinders which rose far above even lengthy Tom's head. Then Miss Nicholas took them to the room where the biscuits were finished and they saw men spreading orange or raspberry paste on one small oblong, clapping another on top and placing the finished article on a tray. It was then borne away to be coated with chocolate, after which it went to the cooling chamber to set.

They thought they must have seen practically everything now, but she bore them off to the box department where they saw piles of flat pasteboard which were folded into shape, put into a machine and covered with one or other of the well-known paper coverings and then made ready to be rolled away on hand-trucks to the filling and packing department.

"Goodness!" Nancy exclaimed. "How do they do it so quickly?"

"Plenty of practice!" Bride retorted. "Have you forgotten the White Knight?"

"That's from 'Alice', isn't it?" Miss Nichols said. "I love that book."

"Who doesn't?" Then Bride asked a question she had been longing to ask from the first. "Do you do any of this or are you just a guide?"

"Oh dear, no!" Miss Nichols replied. "I work in the decoration department. I was busy there all the morning. You see, they choose out so many of us from each department and train us to show parties round. We work in shifts, of course – so many of us one day and a different lot the next. We have heaps of visitors. Several big groups every afternoon, so we need a good many guides."

"Do you enjoy it?" Primrose asked.

Miss Nichols looked at them sharply. She saw nothing but friendly interest in the girls' faces, so she replied as simply as the question had been asked. "Yes; I like it very much. It makes a break and you know how it is. Any work gets monotonous if you're doing it *all* the time and a break is fun and freshens you up. But I love my job," she added. "I wouldn't like to do anything else. Now I'm going to take you to my own department and you'll see what I do."

She took them to a great room where girls and women in white overalls with white caps on their heads sat at tables, and each with a little wooden spatula in her hand. Trays of chocolates, smooth as they had come from the coating machine, stood before them and, as they slowly passed, the workers marked them with a twirl, a twist, bars or lines, or elipses. It was fascinating work to watch. A quick turn of the hand and a curlicue would appear; or two strokes and a couple of small ridges were running down the top of the chocolate. The girls noticed that each worker made only one kind of mark and the speed at which they worked was amazing.

"That's what you do, Miss Nichols?" Tom Gay asked. "What a job!"

Tiny Miss Nichols – she was even shorter than Elfie – had to look very far up to smile at tall Tom as she said, "That's right. I was doing it all the morning and I love it."

"Are you allowed to eat any?" Nancy asked longingly.

"Sugar-baby!" Bride teased her chum; but Miss Nichols only said, "When you get the smell of chocolate all day, you soon lose your longing for a lot. I've even heard of people who say they can't bear chocs. I'm not like that, but I certainly don't want many. Now we'll go and see

166

them weighed and packed. This way, please." She led them out of the department and then, with a smile, asked, "Are you getting tired? It's a lot of walking and, of course, so many of the floors have the iron runways and they're hard on one's feet."

"Never mind; it's jolly well worth it to have seen all this," Lesley said, as they turned into the weighing and packing department.

This was another room where women only seemed to work. Some sat before weighing machines, weighing the chocolates for the different-sized boxes. As soon as one lot was correct – and, for the most part, the workers knew to the last chocolate how many should go to each – it was swept off the scale to another who quickly dropped each chocolate into its paper cup and tucked it into the box, which was then passed on to receive its sealed cellophane wrapper. The workers moved with almost incredible rapidity and the girls literally gasped at the speed with which the boxes were finished and piled up ready to be borne off by the inevitable trolley.

"Now that's all the work," Miss Nichols said as she called them off to make room for another party. "Now I've something nice for you."

She took them into a wide corridor where tables stood, bearing dishes loaded with all kinds of chocolates and chocolate biscuits. She held them out to the girls, inviting them to take two from each dish and presently they had quite a selection. Now they knew why they had been told the night before to take a paper bag each in their handbags.

"What a lovely idea!" Elfie cried as she twisted the corners of her bag.

Miss Nichols explained. "Years ago, before the war, the firm always gave visitors a box of chocolates to take away

167

with them. We couldn't do that while sweet rationing was on, and we haven't gone back to it yet. In the meantime, they like you to have a few samples."

"Well, it's a jolly good scheme," Nancy grinned. "Is this the last?"

"No; I'm taking you to see our swimming bath. Then we'll go back to the theatre for you to see the film. When that's over, I'll meet you again and you'll have tea in the canteen. Come along; we go outside to get to the swimming bath."

After the heat of the factory, it was a relief to breathe the open air. Miss Nichols led them across a kind of broad alleyway, talking all the time of the way the great firm of Cadburys' looked after their work-people. She explained that they had their own doctor, dentist and nurses always in attendance. The firm had provided playing fields of all kinds where everyone could play.

"And we've heard of Bournville village," Bride said. "Do you all live there?"

Miss Nichols shook her head. "A lot do, of course; but quite a lot of us come from further out. *I* live in Halesowen," she added, "and travel every day."

Then they had reached the magnificent swimming bath where Miss Nichols pointed out the chute down which the used suits and towels went to the laundry to be washed and dried, ready for when they should be wanted again. When the girls had finished exclaiming and voicing their admiration, she took them back to the theatre where they found two or three parties from their own group already waiting. Miss Nichols reminded them to look out for her when the film ended and left them for the time being. But when the film was over, she bobbed up beside Bride and haled them off to the canteen where a magnificent tea of bread and butter, jam, scones and cakes awaited them.

168

That really was the end of it. When tea was over, they were shown to the cloakroom where they washed, tidied their hair and generally freshened up. Then they said goodbye to their little guide and piled into the motor-coaches which were waiting on the parking-ground.

"We're the first off," Bride exulted as they rolled away. "Just as well, considering how far we have to go! I say, folks, hasn't it been a gorgeous expedition for our last in England?"

And with one accord the entire coach-load responded, "Rather!"

CHAPTER THIRTEEN

Enter – Lady Russell!

" 'Blessings brighten as they take their flight!' " Mary-Lou said it in such lugubrious tones that there was every excuse for the open-mouthed amazement with which her gang stared at her before exclaiming with one voice, "What's *that* in aid of?"

"Well, it's just struck me," she explained. "We're leaving the island for good in an awfully short time now. Do you folk realize that we have only four weeks of this term left? Then we go away – and that's the end of us on the island."

Cherry Christy, who had tailed on to their crowd this term, glared at her. "And I s'pose I haven't ever said all you crowd must come and stay with me in the hols, have I?" she demanded with a killing attempt at sarcasm. "Or p'raps you didn't hear me? Or is it that you don't want to come?"

Mary-Lou regarded her calmly. "You'll hurt yourself if you go on like that. Of course we heard you and of course we mean to come – that is if your mother agrees. I wasn't talking about that at all. What I meant was that we shan't come back here again as a *school*. No need to go up the wall about that!" She grinned at the crushed Cherry and then added mournfully, "All the same, though it'll be fun to stay here in the hols, it won't be the same and I hate changes!"

"Who's that grousing?" Clem Barrass suddenly arrived

among them. "Oh, you, Mary-Lou. I might have known! This is just the way you went on when you first heard that you were leaving Polquenel – remember?"*

"I was a mere child then," Mary-Lou returned with all the dignity of fourteen. "Just the same, I *don't* like changes, not really – and you know it!"

"OK then. Ask Auntie Doris to let you stay in England and go on at St Agnes'," Clem said unkindly, for she knew very well that Mary-Lou would have shrieked with horror if this had been suggested. "In the meantime, you and Vi and – let's see – Doris Hill and – oh, bother! I'll have to find someone else. You three pop off to Fiction Library, anyhow. You'll see why when you get there. I must scram!" And she turned and left them gaping after her.

"What's the idea of that?" Vi Lucy wanted to know.

"No idea. We'd better go, anyhow. Clem never said if it was mistresses or prees that wanted us," Mary-Lou replied, pulling her tie straight. "Am I decent, someone? Is my hair tidy on top?"

"You'll pass with a shove," Cherry told her by way of paying back the squashing she had just had. "So'll Vi and Doris."

"Come on, then!" And the leader of the clan turned and went off towards the house where she and her chums met Clem with Beth Lane, just going in.

"What's all this in aid of, Clem?" she demanded.

"You folk are to go and help decide which books of Junior Fic. are to be left for St Agnes' and which you'll take," Clem said. "Hurry up! Jean and Bess are waiting and it'll be a longish job, anyhow."

They scuttled at that. Jean might be merely a member

* *Three go to the Chalet School.*

of Upper VI, but Bess was a prefect and, as such, not to be kept waiting. They found the two big girls in the room devoted to the Fiction Library. One half was given up to Senior Fiction and the other to Junior. In that part, besides Bess and Jean, there were also a selection of Junior Middles and Juniors and they were obviously the last.

"Here you are!" Bess said. "Then I'll go and get on with the other chores, Jean. You don't need me, do you?"

"No; I can manage all right," Jean said. "Sit down on the floor you four and pay attention to me."

They squatted down, and when they were ready she set to work at once.

"These books are to be divided. We have two or more copies of quite a number of them, as you know – Kipling and Arthur Ransome and people like that. But there are a lot more that we've only one copy of and a good many of them are out of print and can't be renewed. So it's only fair to give both lots a chance of choosing. I'll read out the list and you'll take it in turns to choose. Doris Hill and Beth Lane, you're staying, aren't you? Then move over to the other side. *Now* are you all right? St Agnes', you're having the first choice. *Bevis; the story of a boy.* Do you want it or not?"

Opinion was divided, but at last it was decided to keep it. Then the future members of the Swiss branch were given their chance to claim *The Girls of St Bride's* for which they all promptly shrieked as it was a favourite with them.

As Jean had said, there were quite a number on which to vote – mostly school stories and the lighter adventure stories; though there were most of the Andrew Lang fairy books as well and there was bitter competition for these last.

172

It had been a grey day, for Nancy had prophesied truly when she had said there would be a break in the fine weather. Even as Mary-Lou and Co had entered Big House, the rain had begun to fall and the girls were not sorry to be turned on to beginning preparations for the removal so imminent. While Jean coped with the Junior Library, Elfie and the rest of the Games Committee joined Miss Burnett in the gymnasium and they routed out all the games apparatus and went through it. Some of the gymnastic apparatus would also go to St Agnes', but the girls had nothing to do with that and weren't sorry as they sorted out elderly racquets and cricket bats, tennis balls with hardly a bounce left in them, and other sundries.

"Goodness! I'd no idea we'd collected such a mass of junk!" Peggy Burnett exclaimed as she looked at the pile. " 'Gwensi Howells'," she read from the handle of a racquet that seemed to be disintegrating altogether. "That takes us back a few years! Well, no one can use that thing, not even for rounders. Put it on a rubbish heap and gather what's fairly usable into another. The rubbish must be burned, but the rest can go to that place where they were appealing for sports stuff. Don't put the balls on the bonfire, by the way, or everyone on the island will hate us."

What with one thing and another, the school was busily occupied the whole morning in sorting out; for Lesley Pitt had marched another body over to the art rooms and they were fully employed in going through models, old drawings and paintings and all the rest of the et ceteras that had accumulated there. Anyone not working in one or other of the special departments set to work to turn out lockers and desks and form room cupboards, and when Griffiths, the school's head gardener, saw on Monday what they had done to his bonfire, his hair nearly stood on end!

Jean and the younger girls took the whole morning over the library, for it was not an easy task when so much of the lighter juvenile fiction was out of print. However, in the end, a fair selection had been set aside to go to Switzerland, the bulk being left in England; and that for two reasons. First, the Head had warned the prefects that they must economize on these things as far as they could. Secondly, the Middle School at St Agnes' would be a good deal larger than the Swiss one and they had all the Juniors, as well, so there would be a much bigger demand for the books.

In the afternoon, the Seniors had their turn at the library while the rest of the school worked off any steam left in games in the gym. It was while they were sorting out that Bride was moved to make what they all considered a really brilliant suggestion.

"It's going to cost the earth to move all our stuff, anyway," she said thoughtfully. "Suppose each one of us took charge of a few of the Fiction Library books and took them with us? How would that be?"

"It's quite an idea," Tom said, standing with her feet astride and her hands in her blazer pockets – an attitude that no one had yet succeeded in curing her of adopting when she was thinking really deeply. "The non-fic. isn't our pidgin is it? I mean, the Head and the staff will decide on those. How many of us are going altogether? Anyone know?"

"Counting those of us who go to Welsen, sixty-three, Auntie Jo said," Bride replied. "That needn't make any difference, though. We could take the books with us and then send them on to the Görnetz Platz when we had a chance. That would be easy enough. Let's finish this and find out how many books there are to go and then we'll know how many that would make for each of us to take."

They turned to, and half an hour later Bess announced that there were two hundred and forty-six.

"That would pan out at – let's see – four or so each, isn't it?" Bride asked with knitted brows. "Lesley, you're our sole mathematical genius. Am I right?"

"Near enough," Lesley replied. "Actually it means that thirty-nine must take four and the rest would have three each."

Bride nodded. "Good enough! We could all manage that, I'm sure. That would save the school having to pay carriage on that lot, anyhow. Bess, you're librarian. What about going to see the Head after tea and putting it to her. Jean could go with you to hold your hand if you'd rather not go alone," she added kindly.

Jean made a face at her. "How sweet of you!" Then she turned to the others. "Sauce for the gander is sauce for the goose. What's the matter with carrying the idea further. Mary-Lou and Vi and that kid, Clare Kennedy, and all that crowd are fairly responsible these days. Why not suggest it for the Junior Fic. and let them be responsible for that lot? We're leaving about two-thirds behind; but there are about a hundred and fifty to go. As Bride has pointed out, if *we* can see to all the fiction among us, quite a lot would be saved on carriage and also cases."

"Oh, jolly good!" Nancy exclaimed. "What do you say, Bride?"

Bride nodded. "I hadn't gone as far as that, but Jean's right. We couldn't trust *all* those Middles, but there are quite a number who could certainly see to it. I'll make a list and we'll see how many there are of them – and I *won't* be responsible for young Maeve," she added, "so don't suggest her, for pity's sake!"

The girls laughed. The youngest of the Bettany girls was noted in the school for being one of the most feather-brained young things it had ever known. They could quite believe that Bride objected to being responsible for her.

Meanwhile, that young lady had found a sheet of paper and was making a provisional list. They knew roughly who was going, so it was an easy matter. In the end, they decided that thirty-two girls might be trusted and that would be round about five books each. It was decided to ask the Head if she would agree to the proposal, and, if she did, to call those of the younger girls chosen and ask if they would take on the job.

"When do the rest of the books go over to St Agnes'?" Lesley asked.

"Oh, not till the end of term," Bride said quietly. "There's still four weeks to go – four weeks and three days, to be accurate. I vote we offer to cart them over ourselves on the Monday before we break up. We never have much to do that day, once our packing's finished."

"Well, I vote Bess and Jean bung in a request to see the Head at five," Nancy said. "Tell her what we suggest and find out if she'll agree. We may have four weeks and three days left of term, but that'll soon slip over. School Cert begins in a fortnight and we have the remainder of our matches to play off, never to mention practices for the Regatta. I'm thankful we aren't having our usual summer Pageant. I was sorry when the Head first told us it had to be called off as we were breaking up so soon, but I've been rejoicing nearly ever since. We'd never have managed to get in the rehearsals *or* see to the dresses."

"How right you are!" Tom was now squatting on the edge of a table. "As for packing, don't forget that *this* term means taking everything – house linen and all the junk we usually leave for another term and *everything*.

By the way, has anyone heard yet what we do about the things in the prefects' room?"

"Yes; I have," Bride told her. "We are to take all the stuff that came from Tirol. Auntie Madge says that most of that came from foreigners and ought to go back to the Continent. The stuff we've added since belongs to all of us, of course. We're to share it out fairly. She also says that we'd better choose only the most easily packed things to go to Switzerland. We'd better get cracking on that next week. I imagine it'll take some doing."

Julie Lucy, who during the weeks of term had recovered her colour and, though still rather thin, looked almost herself again, nodded her head until the short black curls that covered it danced madly. "It's going to be awfully difficult. How on earth are we to decide? Who'll be prees at St Agnes', by the way?"

"You'll have to ask the Head that," Bride said grinning. "Valerie Arnett for one, I should say. Probably Margaret Benn and Gwyn Jones." She cast a smile at the three who instantly blushed and looked sheepish. "Why aren't you three coming with us, anyhow?"

"I'm leaving school at Christmas," Margaret said. "Father said it wasn't worth going to Switzerland for just one term. If you come to that, I don't suppose I'll be a prefect either. Val will, though; and so will Gwyn."

"So will you," Valerie retorted. "Don't think you're likely to get out of it, for I'm jolly sure you won't. I say, hadn't we better do something about washing? Aren't books the filthiest things? My hands are *black*!"

Bride glanced at her watch. "Oh, we've twenty minutes before we need to shift," she said easily. "But Bess had better get that request in at the office. What are we doing this evening? Anyone got any idea?"

"Oh, games and dancing as usual, I expect," Nancy

said with a yawn. "It isn't anyone's specially. Paper games, perhaps. I shan't be sorry. My legs are still aching with all the perambulations of yesterday. I say–"

What she was going to say, no one ever knew for at that point the table, which was a light, folding affair which had been resenting the weight of Tom's eleven stone, suddenly gave way under her and landed on the floor with a crash that jarred her from head to foot, while the table, when they had hauled her off the remains, looked fit for nothing but to add to Peggy Burnett's bonfire.

"Are you hurt?" Bride demanded as she helped Lesley and Primrose to get Tom in to a chair. "Shall one of us go for Matey?"

"Not on your life!" Tom retorted, pulling herself together. "No; I'm not hurt – a bit bruised, perhaps, but nothing to make a song and dance about. Go for Matey? My good girl, are you off your head? I should think you *won't* go for her or anyone else. Serves me right for being such a goop as to trust to a flimsy bit of plywood like that! Let's have a dekko at it! Think anything can be done with it? Or had I just better get another to take its place?"

"What have you been doing now?" demanded a golden voice from the door; and the girls turned from an examination of the ruins to see Jo Maynard standing there.

"Auntie Jo!" Bride exclaimed. "I didn't know you were coming over today!"

Jo, who had only partly opened the door and was filling the aperture with her long self, now flung it wide and stepped aside to show a lady who had been standing behind her and who gave the girls a beaming smile. She was slighter than the lengthy Mrs Maynard, dark-eyed and black-haired, with a wide sensitive mouth and cheeks flushed with a soft pink. Most of the girls stared as if they could not believe their eyes and there was a dead silence.

Then Bride gave a queer sound, half squawk, half cheer, and flung herself on the newcomer with a cry of, "Auntie *Madge*! When did you come? Are you staying here here or at Carnbach? Have you got Kevin and Kester with you? How *long* are you staying?"

"Give me air!" her aunt gasped, wriggling free as soon as she could from Bride's bear-hug. "Really, Bride, for a Head Girl you sometimes behave like a K.G. infant! Hello, everyone! How much of me is left after Bride's assault?" She hurriedly repinned her wavy black hair into place and those who had known her from earlier days hurried to bid her welcome; for Bride's "Auntie Madge" was known to the outer world as Lady Russell, the founder of the Chalet School* in what Jo Maynard was wont to call "the dark ages" when she wanted to be rude.

"Why haven't you been here sooner?" Nancy asked reproachfully. "You came home from Canada the same time as Auntie Jo, didn't you? Don't you love us any more, Auntie Madge?"

Madge Russell laughed as she came in and sat down on the chair Primrose pulled forward for her. "What do *you* think? But for the first fortnight or so I was up to the eyes, trying to get the Round House straight. Oh, I know Marie kept it in beautiful order. That was the trouble. It was *too* beautiful! It looked like an exhibition house – not a home. By the time I'd managed to alter that, I had to go flying out to the Görnetz Platz on business and I only got home on Wednesday, so you can't say I've wasted much time in coming to see you. Now stand round and let me take a look at you. Good Heavens!" She suddenly looked blank. "What a bevy – a bevy of *giantesses* you've all grown to! Elfie's the only

* *The School at the Chalet.*

one who's stayed a reasonable height. Oh, and Madge Dawson. As for you, Tom, I wouldn't like to have the clothing of you! Whatever height are you?"

"Six foot and half an inch," Tom said with a grin. "I take after Pater. But I've stopped growing now – at least I think so. And Julie's not so very tall, Lady Russell. I shouldn't think she's as tall as you, even."

Julie went darkly red and Madge Russell chuckled. "Well, hurry up and introduce me to anyone I don't know. Then you'd better fly and clean up. Does *no* one ever dust the books? Hurry up, now! And we'll have a gab-fest before tea."

"A what?" Bride was on to the last remark like a knife.

Her aunt looked sheepish. "Sorry! That's a bit of Canadian I've picked up. It's awfully catching. I must watch my step with you folk, I can see that, or I'll be teaching you all sorts of new slang and then Miss Annersley will *not* love me. Besides, unless you've all reformed amazingly, I shouldn't have said you needed any encouragement along that line. Now carry on with the introductions."

Bride obliged and then the Seniors fled to make themselves fit to be seen, after which the prefects came back, explaining that she could talk to the others later; but she belonged to them and they wanted to see her after all this time.

Lady Russell laughed. She had been in England the previous autumn, but that had been on a very trying occasion when Bride's mother had had to undergo a major operation and it had seemed touch and go whether she would come through or not. Quite apart from the fact that Madge Russell and Mollie Bettany were great chums besides being sisters-in-law, the former and Mr Bettany were twins, and Lady Russell had been unable to leave her twin to go through what might have been tragedy alone. She had scarcely visited the school on that occasion and the girls had seen nothing of her, so it was two years since they had met as Bride reminded her.

"You must have known we'd grow a bit in two years. And most of us *are* a reasonable height. It's only Tom and Lesley and Prim and me that might be said to be really hefty. You stop insulting us and give us all the hanes." She wound up with the Welsh word for news.

"I don't know that I've so very much," her aunt said. "I've been to the Quadrant, Bride, and your mother is her old self again. You *will* see a big change in her when you go home. My twins? Oh, they're over at Carnbach in Rosa's charge at the moment. I'm staying there till Tuesday so you'll have a chance of meeting them at last. I think you'll quite like them, though they're demons for mischief, now they're on their feet."

"I see a big change in *you*," Bride said thoughtfully; but when her aunt rather indignantly demanded to know what she meant, she only laughed and shook her head. To herself she was thinking that the Auntie Madge who had come back from Canada was very different from the one who had gone there. *That* had been a sweet, gentle woman, very lovable, but definitely to be recognized as one of the older folk. *This* was as crisp and snappy as Aunt Jo ever was; and it was well known in the family that Jo Maynard might be fully grown-up in some ways, but in others she was still not very far from the schoolgirl Jo Bettany who had kept everyone on a stretch wondering what she would do or say next.

"Canada's done Auntie Madge an awful lot of good," Bride thought as Lady Russell exchanged news with the rest. "I believe if she'd just stayed in England, she'd have been definitely middle-aged by this time. Now she seems as young as Auntie Jo or Mummy. And goodness knows there's nothing middle-aged about either of *them*!"

The tea-bell rang at that point and Lady Russell jumped up. "I'm having tea with the Head. It won't do if I'm late. I'll see you all again, presently. We're staying till eight o'clock and then your Uncle Jack is rowing over to fetch us, Bride. I'll tell you about the Platz then. I've explored it from end to end and I think you're all going to love it. I only wish *we* were going to be there, too."

"Well, you had the choice," Jo said, suddenly entering the conversation. She had remained silent to give her sister a chance, as she explained later. "At the moment, though, I'd like to point out that you aren't the only one to have tea with the Head, and if *you* want to stay here nattering on, *I* don't. I want my tea and I'm going to seek it, whatever you may do!" She rose purposefully and strode to the door through which she vanished, followed by her sister, who ran after her, crying, "Wait for me, Jo! Wait for me!"

The prefects locked the cupboard doors and then promenaded into the dining room, every one of them five minutes late for the meal, much to the glee of all the Middle and Juniors who had had to suffer many things from them on the score of unpunctuality.

"After this," said Mary-Lou to Vi and Lesley as they sat munching bread and butter lavishly spread with blackberry jam, "I shouldn't think any of the prees will be able to say much to *us* if we're late for a meal – or not this term, anyhow! One up to us!"

And then Primrose from the prefects' table called over to ask if she knew that she was dropping jammy bread down the front of her frock!

CHAPTER FOURTEEN

Preparations for the Examinations

"That is all, I think. Oh, by the by, I should like to speak to the prefects in their own room in ten minutes' time. Will you go straight there? I won't keep you long." Miss Annersley thus wound up her after-Prayers speech which had dealt mainly with reminders to the girls that the term-end examinations would begin the next morning and they must be ready for them with pencils sharpened, pens in order and rubbers present. Then she said, "Stand! – Turn! – Forward - *march*!"

As one girl the school obeyed the orders. Miss Lawrence struck up Blake's "Grand March", which hoary perennial was a favourite at the school, and they marched out, form by form, to go and amuse themselves in the garden until the first bell took the Juniors off to bed.

Since the visit of Lady Russell, things had gone on normally. She had kept her promises and had thrilled everyone who was going to the Görnetz Platz by her descriptions of the place and the new school, while those who were not going frankly owned themselves green with envy. She had also brought Kevin and Kester over to show them off, and Bride, after inspecting her new cousins, remarked cheerfully that the school was going ravers over them and it was as well they wouldn't be there very often or they would get the most exalted ideas of their own importance! For which piece of impertinence her aunt rewarded her with a frown and a hint that the two tiny boys would be much too well brought up for anything like that.

When they had all gone home on the Tuesday, the school had settled down to intensive revision of its work, with spasms of clearing up, for time was going very quickly and there was a great deal to do.

"What's going to happen now?" Nancy Chester demanded when she and the rest were back in their own room, which they hastily tidied by the simple method of pushing everything into the cupboard and turning the key on it.

"Goodness knows!" Bride picked a few wilted-looking sweetpeas out of the jarful on the window-sill, tossed them into the waste-paper basket and then sat down on the nearest chair. "Ouf! It's hot! I'm simply melting! Well," she went on, feeling that talking about the heat would never help matters, "there's one thing for which we may be deeply thankful."

"What's that?" Julie Lucy asked as she manufactured a fan from a sheet of paper she had picked up.

"Do you folk realize that we've contrived to get through the term without *one* major incident. I don't call Pris Dawbarn's little effort on Vendell anything major and that's about the worst that's happened. And *we* had nothing to do with it, thank goodness! Besides, those Dawbarns are born to be hanged, anyhow!"

"The kids are too much excited about the coming changes to have much time to think about anything else," Bess said. "When the Head's finished with us, Bride, what about weeding the borders? We want the Christys to find the garden in decent order when they come back and those borders are getting overrun with chickweed and groundsel."

"Where it comes from, I simply don't know," Julie

remarked, wielding her now-finished fan vigorously. "Madge and Audrey and I were at it for two evenings and we really cleaned up. But there the wretched things are again, flourishing like the wicked! I call gardening a never-ending job!"

"How right you are!" Bride said. "But it's too ghastly hot for anything so strenuous as weeding, Bess. I can't say I'm looking forward to exams very much. If tomorrow's anything like today's been, I, for one, will be a spot of jelly on the chair with a fountain-pen in the middle of it!"

Primrose, who was fanning herself with an old exercise-book, nodded. "Even with all the windows and doors set to their widest limit the rooms have felt like ovens today whenever I've had to go into any of them. I call it cruelty to dumb animals to expect us to do exams in such sweltering heat as this! As for the poor souls with General Cert tomorrow, I should think they'll spend half their time passing out and having to be revived!"

The conversation came to an end there, for the sound of light footsteps came through the wide-open door and the girls rose to their feet as Miss Annersley, looking cool and unperturbed in her green cotton frock, came into the room.

"I won't keep you long, girls," she said as she crossed the room to the window where Nancy had pulled up a chair for her. She bent to sniff at the sweetpeas before she sat down. Then she went on, "It's about the exams tomorrow. According to the weather reports this evening, this heat is to go on for the next few days. I imagine your brains will be affected if we ask you to work indoors in such circumstances, so I have decided that we'll carry out all the folding desks and tables and chairs and put them all ready tonight and

185

you can do exams in the garden. Will you see to it, please, Bride?"

"Yes, Miss Annersley," Bride replied properly, though her eyes had lit up at the idea. Exams out-of-doors under the trees might even be bearable in the heat.

"Very well, then. Juniors at the bottom of the lawn under the copper beeches: Junior Middles in the orchard at this end, please: Senior Middles on the other front lawn round by the holly hedge – it will shield them from most of the sun until late afternoon, at any rate: and yourselves under the oaks. Ask some of the others to help with carrying the chairs and so on. Give the Juniors those trestle-tables out of the old Kindergarten, by the way, and see that they have safety-inkwells. If you will go to Miss Dene, she'll tell you the exact numbers in each section. Some of the mistresses are coming out presently to pin on name-slips. That's all, I think. See that the rest go in promptly when their bell rings, please. Now I must go. Thank you, girls."

She rose, left the room after smiling at them, and when the sound of her steps had died away Bride turned to grimace at Bess.

"And that puts paid to your nice little idea about weeding, my girl!" she said.

Bess, who was a thoroughly conscientious girl, looked troubled. "It only means we'll have to do it some other time. Those borders are looking like ragbags, and we do want to hand the place back in decent order."

"Don't fuss!" Tom said, getting up from her chair and stretching herself. "We'll get leave to get up at half-past five one morning and see to it."

"You've got a hope!" Nancy grinned. "Well, there's no end to do, so we'd better get cracking."

This was true. The girls left the room in a body, and, while Tom, Nancy and Audrey made a tour of the form rooms to discover where the folding desks and tables were, Bride went to the office to see Miss Dene, and the rest departed to the garden to rout up volunteers for the carrying.

Miss Dene had piles of packeted examination books on her table, and was tearing off the wrappings and counting them out, so many for each form. At the desk, Miss O'Ryan and Miss Burnett were tearing and folding sheets of blotting-paper. All three looked warm and their movements were languid. They all stopped work when the Head Girl came in and Biddy O'Ryan mopped her face with her handkerchief.

"Numbers?" Rosalie Dene said when Bride had explained what she wanted. "Here you are. Mind you don't muddle them while you're doing them. Mdlle, Miss Derwent and Miss Slater are coming along presently to see to the name-slips. Set the desks well apart and make sure that they're all securely set up."

"Yes, Miss Dene," Bride said meekly. But when she had left the office, she thought to herself that the heat must be affecting the staff as well as the girls. As if they didn't know everything there was to know about setting up those desks!

The Juniors had all gone to bed by the time she reached the garden and the Junior Middles were streaming up to the house, their bell having just rung.

"It's awful having to go to bed!" Emerence Hope said to the Head Girl as they met on the drive. "I know I shan't sleep – it's much too hot."

"What are you going to do, Bride?" demanded her young cousin Margot, who was with Emerence as usual, for the friendship still continued, though so far, they had

187

contrived to keep out of mischief.

Emerence had absorbed enough of the school atmosphere to be shocked at this cool question. She tugged Margot's sleeve. "You can't talk like that to the Head Girl!" she said reprovingly. "Come on, Margot. Matey'll tick us off if we're late."

Margot pulled herself free. "Bride's my cousin as well as Head Girl," she reminded her chum pettishly. "Go on, Bride; what are you gong to do?"

" 'Ask nae questions and ye'll be tellt nae lees!' " Bride quoted. "It's no business of yours, Margot, cousin or not."

She turned and ran off before Margot could reply. She was fond of the naughty triplet and had no wish to have to rebuke her. But Emerence had been quite right. However they might treat each other in private, it didn't do to be on too intimate terms in public. Neither Len nor Con would have dreamed of speaking to her like that when other girls were present. It took Margot to do it.

She found the others busily at work, setting up the desks and tables and placing chairs before them. The Senior Middles were bringing the long trestle tables from the old army hut which had been used as a kindergarten when the little ones had been on the island with them. Since the babies had been on the mainland, two of the other forms had been working there and one end had been used for storing things, among them the trestle tables. They were folding affairs, with clamps which held the legs properly extended when they were in use. Clem Barrass, Betsy Lucy, Polly Winterton, the Ozanne twins and Sally Winslow were engaged in setting them up. Bride watched Clem and Betsy for a moment or two and saw that they were being very careful to see that the clamps were secure, so she left it at that and went on to where Tom, Nancy and Elfie were helping to arrange the desks in long lines with plenty of space round each. Not that the girls were given to cheating, but some people wrote a large clear hand, and if you happened to be gazing round in search of inspiration you might catch sight of something before you knew it and then you might be in a quandary.

Blossom Willoughby and Katharine Gordon came out carrying trays of inkwells newly washed and ready for ink. Carola Johnstone followed with the big stone jar of school ink and Hilary Wilson and Meg Whyte trailed after them, each bearing a bouquet of the long-spouted fillers which were supposed to save messes.

"You can leave those inkwells here," Bride said. "Take the next lot to the orchard, will you? Set that ink down over there, Carola. The cork's in tight, isn't it? We don't want to water the grass with ink, and anyhow, no one will love us if we waste a whole jarful of it!"

Carola gave her a return grin as she set the jar down and gave the stopper a thump with her fist. "That's safe enough," she said. "Shall I begin filling the fillers, though, Bride?"

"No; you'd better take those other people and go and fetch the safeties for the kids. They're having the trestles, so it means inkwells for them. Let's see: you'll want fifty-seven." Bride consulted her lists. "See that they have one each. Juniors aren't allowed to use either fountain-pens or Biros, you know."

"Help! Have we as many as that in the school?" Carola asked.

"I expect so. You five go and hunt them up, anyhow. Aren't you General Cert girls going to bed early tonight? Then you'd better hurry up."

189

At this reminder, Meg and Carola fled, followed by the rest, and Bride turned to make her way to the orchard and see that all was going on as it should there.

When the bell rang for the Senior Middles and those Seniors who began the public examinations on the morrow, the mistresses had arrived and were pinning the name-slips at each place. That done, they said a word or two of approval at the way the girls had worked before they went off on their own lawful occasions. However, ten minutes later, Miss Derwent and Miss Slater appeared again, bearing trays of glasses and jugs of the lemonade Mdlle was famous for making. They invited the girls to help themselves and *not* to forget to bring everything in when they had finished before they said "Good night" and departed finally.

It was practically all done when the bell for the Seniors went, and the prefects, who by virtue of their office had an extra half-hour, were left alone. It was cooler in the garden now, and the sky was gorgeous with sunset colours. Bride looked round. "Well, apart from the inkwells, I think that's everything. Should we drop them into the holes, do you think?" she suggested. "You know the Head said at Prayers that Frühstück would be at half-past seven so that we could begin exams at half-past eight and do most of the work in the cool of the day."

"If you can call it 'the cool'!" Elfie sighed, pushing back her thick hair with a sticky hand. "I wish the Head would give us leave for a bathe!"

"Well, she won't, so you'd better stop wishing silly things," Audrey said.

Julie, who was standing by one of the trestle tables, filling the inkwells in readiness, stopped with the copper filler in one hand and the other resting on the surface of the table and said with a laugh, "Did any of you

190

hear young Emerence on the subject of the heat this afternoon?"

"No; and I don't know that I especially want to, either," Lesley said snubbingly.

"*You* mayn't, but *I* do!" Nancy had been scrapping on and off with Lesley all the evening, though normally they were quite good friends. She gave her cousin an encouraging smile. "What was it, Julie? Let's know the worst!"

"Well, apparently Emerence had been grousing about the heat to Margot Maynard and Margot replied that it might be hot, but she had known it hotter in Canada on occasion. She was by way of being most superior about it – I heard her myself, and if I'd been Emerence I'd have shaken her! – and Emerence has been fratchety, to say the least of it–"

"So have a good many other folk," Bride took it on herself to remark at this point. "It's the heat – makes people irritable."

Lesley and Nancy went red and one or two other people looked conscious. The fact was that a good many of them had been edgy and easily upset with the heat, and though the prefects were far too dignified to indulge in the spats that had been going on among the younger girls, there had been a certain amount of snapping. As Bride said later, when it came to sunshiny *Nancy* turning crabby, it was time to do something about it!

Julie shot a glance at her cousin, but made no comment and went on with her story. "Well, Margot, as I've said was most annoying and young Emerence replied, 'Are you sure you aren't talking about *Hell*? I should think that's the only other place that's likely to be any hotter than it's been here today.' "

The girls exploded at this startling remark and Nancy

and Lesley forgot their trouble. And then something happened that turned their thoughts away from the heat completely.

As Primrose remarked when they were discussing it in the interval between two exams next day, someone must have been abominably careless over the trestle table fastenings. Anyhow, in the interest of her story, Julie leaned her whole weight on it; the legs gracefully folded up and down it went, Julie on top of the inkwell tray going with it. Quite half the inkwells were brim full and, in the shock, she swung the filler upside down. As it was half full, it bedewed not only her, but all those standing near. Julie herself got to her feet dripping with ink from shoulder to hem. Her slide had come out during her performance and her curls were tumbling into her eyes. Instinctively, she put up an inky hand to brush them aside and the resultant part-coloured creature who stood before them finished the other girls completely. They all doubled up with mirth and the garden rang with their shrieks.

The noise brought Matron errupting from the house in short order. She was pardonably annoyed, for most of the Junior Middles slept in the dormitories at the front of the house. The windows were all wide open and the noise the prefects were making was enough to rouse even the Seven Sleepers.

"*Girls!* What do you think you are doing?" she demanded angrily as she neared them. "Have you forgotten that the younger girls have been in bed for the last hour and a half and should all be asleep by this time? What do you mean by making such a noise and waking them up at this hour? You might be a set of Kindergarten–" This was where she had a full view of Julie and stopped short, her mouth open with amazement.

The girls pealed with laughter again, though they tried to smother it. Matron furious was Matron to be avoided! But control themselves once they had glimpsed her expression, they could not. Bride subsided on the ground and moaned feebly. Lesley and Nancy, forgetting their differences, held each other up. Even Julie, opening her own lips to say something – no one ever knew what – stopped short and giggled madly.

Matron shut her mouth with a snap. "*Well!* And what, may I ask, do you think *you* have been doing to bathe in the ink?" she demanded of Julie, who ceased her giggles so abruptly that she started a violent attack of hiccoughs instead. "Look at your dress! And your face!"

"Hic – I'm – hic – very sorry – hic – Matron, but the – hic – table – hic – col – hic – collapsed," Julie got out before she went off into a series of hiccoughs which made the school's beloved tyrant cease her fulminations for the time being.

"Into the house with you!" she said sharply. "Try to hold your breath, Julie. I'm coming at once!" And when Julie, still hiccoughing madly, had set off for the house, she turned to the others. "Set that table up again and see it's done *properly* and finish your work. Go straight up to bed as soon as you go in, take those dresses off and bring them to my room. They must all go into water at once before the ink has time to dry into the fabric or they'll be ruined. Hurry, girls! It's after nine now."

"It's school ink, Matron," Bride ventured. "It isn't permanent."

Matron gave her a glare that reduced her to the tiresome child she had been two years and more ago and made her forget that she was that very important person, the Head Girl. Not that that was anything new. Old Girls who returned to teach had been known to say that when

193

Matron gave them a certain look, they returned to their Middle School days and shook in their shoes.

When she felt that Bride was sufficiently reduced to humility, Matron spoke. "Kindly do as you're told without any more argument," she snapped, before she turned to speed after Julie to the house.

Somewhat subdued, the prefects set the table up again. Elfie made certain that the legs were safe this time and Nancy and Lesley amiably finished the inkwells together as if they had never had a cross word between them.

"We'll put them under this tree, shall we, Bride?" Lesley asked of the Head Girl who was busy printing fresh name-slips to take the place of those included in Julie's accident, while Bess and Primrose distributed the safety inkwells on the tables. "They'll be safe enough there till the morning."

"OK," Bride said absently as she removed the inky slips and pinned the fresh ones in place. "There! That's done! Finished, you people? Then we'd better scram. Tiptoe, once we're inside, you folk, and for Heaven's sake keep your voices down and don't fall over anything. We don't want Matey on our tracks again!"

They definitely did not. They carried the ink-fillers to the shelf outside the office, where they left them for Miss Dene to deal with next day. Then they went upstairs on tiptoe. Those who had escaped the ink-bath went off to do dormitory rounds while the others fled to their cubicles, where they removed their frocks and took them to Matron's room in some trepidation as to what else she might say.

Luckily for them, she was not there. Julie had got well away with her hiccoughs and Matron was a little anxious. The girl had been so ill with peritonitis the term before and had so barely come through a dangerous operation, that it was not until she was sleeping quietly at last that Matron left her. By that time it was nearly eleven and Julie looked exhausted. However, the hiccoughs had stopped and Matron hoped there had been no harm done, though before she herself went to bed after midnight, having taken the frocks to the laundry, where she put them to soak, she slipped along to Julie's dormitory. The patient was peacefully asleep and the colour was returning to her lips and cheeks.

"But I'll come in for a look at her before the rising-bell goes," Matron thought as she shed her clothes and got into her nightdress. "A severe shaking up like that isn't the ideal treatment for anyone who had to go through such an operation as hers less than five months ago."

Then, having said her prayers and plaited her hair, she switched off her bedside lamp and lay down to fall asleep at once and slumber as soundly as any of her charges.

CHAPTER FIFTEEN

Pigs in the Old Orchard!

Bride Bettany was not the only member of the Chalet
School to realize that, all things considered, they had
got through the term with remarkably little incident.
Mary-Lou Trelawney had discovered it, too, and being
Mary-Lou it never occurred to her to keep it to herself.
She had voiced it aloud during the afternoon rest. Usually, the girls were expected to read or lie quiet; but the
rule was always relaxed the last afternoon before exams
and the girls might talk quietly.

On this occasion, some of them had dropped off to
sleep, but among Mary-Lou's clan, she herself, Vi Lucy,
Lesley Malcolm and Doris Hill were all wide awake. They
talked quietly among themselves in case anyone should
suddenly decide that they were doing too much gossiping.
However, all four had clear voices and their words carried
to a group a little to the right of them. This was made
up of the Dawbarns, Emerence Hope, Margot Maynard
and Peggy Harper. Four of them only heard a word here
and there; but Priscilla had ears that were fit to hear
the grass growing, and she caught Mary-Lou's remark,
"I say, you lot, d'you realize that we haven't had one
big row this term? And it's our last here, too."

"So much the better," Vi Lucy yawned. "It's *time*
those Dawbarn kids began to reform. They'll be fourteen
sometime next term, won't they? Well, then!"

This from Vi Lucy, whose fourteenth birthday was

only four months old while Mary-Lou's had come just three weeks before, was an insult and Priscilla might have told them so; but at that moment Bride Bettany and Elfie Woodward appeared, strolling across the lawn between the clusters of chairs holding their juniors, so for once Priscilla decided to be discreet.

She said nothing until the rest period was ended and they were folding their deck-chairs preparatory to carrying them off to the pile at the side of the house. Then she repeated to the rest what she had heard and they were suitably annoyed.

"Vi Lucy does think she's someone!" Prudence fumed. "She's not all that much older than us. And Mary Lou's even *less*! I do think they've a cheek!"

"All the same," said Peggy Harper thoughtfully, "it's true about nothing much happening, you know. It seems a pity, don't you think? I mean this is our last term here and all that. Things'll be different at St Agnes'."

Peggy was an imp of the first water. She, like the Dawbarns, was condemned to St Agnes' until she was fifteen and she was very disgruntled about it. But she had been one of the people to come to the Chalet School from the Tanswick one when it closed down the previous Christmas term and her family considered that one big move was enough for her at present.

"What could we do?" Priscilla ruminated. "It does seem a pity to let Bride's last term as Head Girl end without giving her a *little* fun, doesn't it?"

Her twin's eyes lit up with the impish gleam that made people in authority look sharply after her when they saw it. "You're right; it does. Anyone got anything to suggest?" She looked round them hopefully.

A suggestion *was* forthcoming at once – though not from any of her fellow sinners. Rosalind Yolland, the prefect on duty, glanced their way and saw that they were making very little effort at putting their chairs away. She strolled across to them to mention sweetly, "The bell for lessons is just about to ring. Don't you think it would be a good idea if you all stopped talking and put those chairs in their proper place?"

They had nothing to say, of course. Rosalind might be the least of all the prefects, as they were shrewd enough to know, but no one argued with *any* prefect at the Chalet School – not if she knew what was good for her! It was too apt to have unpleasant repercussions, since the prefects were, by tradition, a close-knit body who backed each other up on all occasions. They stopped talking as desired and meekly carried away their chairs to add them to the pile over which Madge Dawson was keeping watch. But it had needed only this to decide Priscilla on finding something to do that would leave its mark on the present term.

The trouble was that neither she nor the rest could think of anything sensational enough to satisfy them. Furthermore, they were handicapped by the fact that both Emerence and Margot, who could generally be relied on to produce original ideas, knew that they were more or less on probation so far as going to the new Swiss school was concerned, and flatly refused to be mixed up in anything that might mean their being sent to St Agnes' for another year.

"Oh, all right!" Prudence finally said disgustedly when all her coaxing brought no result. "If you two can't be sports, we'll just hoick Primrose Trevoase in – and Carol Soames. I don't suppose *they'll* be so fussy!"

This seemed probable, since Primrose was as great a scamp as the Dawbarns or Peggy, and Carol always did what the rest wanted. It was an added advantage that neither was going to Switzerland, either. Primrose, like Peggy, had come from Tanswick, and her first term's report at St Briavel's had brought from her father the fiat that there would be no Switzerland for her until she had at least three terms' good reports to show. Caroline's people had simply declined without giving any reason.

This promising pair, approached by Priscilla later in the afternoon, eagerly agreed to come to the meeting she proposed to hold when tea was over.

"And see if you can't think of some *smashing* lark for us to do before the term ends," Priscilla said, thus tempting Providence, since "smashing" used in the sense she used it, was strictly forbidden to them.

However, for once, Providence let her off and she was saved a penny in the fines' box which was more than she deserved. Providence, as it turned out, was simply holding its hand. When it really got going, Priscilla was in such a state that she wouldn't have cared if she had had to put an entire week's pocket money in the fines' box. And, as if that were not enough, the exam results following on it all were so awful that their subsequent reports moved their parents to tell them what they thought of them with a forthrightness that reduced Carol to floods of tears and the Dawbarns to three days of sulks. The other two were too much accustomed to this sort of thing to worry, and it was water off a duck's back so far as they were concerned.

No one had thought of anything by the time their evening preparation hour was ended and they were set free to amuse themselves until the bell rang for their evening meal. In fact, it looked rather as if Priscilla's great idea must go by the board, but for a happening that no one had ever dreamed could inspire the most sinful Middle to even greater depths of sinfulness.

They were standing in the courtyard at the back of the house when there came a terrific noise of squeals and grunts and Carol Soames cried, "Pigs! Where are they? We haven't *got* pigs here! Where'd they come from?"

Cherry Christy, standing near, turned. "In the Old Orchard," she said eagerly. "I saw Daddy for a minute after morning school when he came to see the Head and he told me that he'd agreed to let Mr Evans put one lot of his pigs in the Old Orchard because the tree that shaded their pigscot got blown down in the gale last winter and it's too hot for them just now."

"Do pigs mind heat?" Prudence asked curiously.

Cherry giggled. "Believe it or not, they do. If they're too much in the sun they may have apoplectic fits. Mr Evans is moving the pigscot – it was a blessing the tree fell the opposite way from it – but he hasn't got round to it yet. Come on and let's see him put them in!"

She turned and limped quickly away to the door and the rest followed her in time to see the last of the pigs being turned out of the small trailer in which they had been brought from the farm at the other side of the island.

"Hello, Mr Evans," Cherry called across the gate over which they were all hanging. "Why didn't you just drive them here instead of using the trailer? Is it Sukey and her babies?"

Mr Evans turned an indulgent smile on her. "Well, now, Miss Cherry, pigs ain't that easy druv and I've no time to spare, what with the harvest and all. Besides, it's too hot on the road, even now. Easier to bring them this way."

"I see." Cherry was eyeing the big mother pig warily. "Bad-tempered old thing, isn't she?" she said.

"Well, aye; that's so," he admitted. "Don't any of you young ladies be trying to get in to 'em. Sukey's a cranky sow, 'specially when she has little 'uns, and a pig can give you a real nasty bite whatever."

"We can't get in – not from here, anyhow," Primrose said. "I saw Griffiths wiring the gate up this morning when we were having art."

"Aye; well, that's good indeed," he said in his soft, sing-song Welsh voice. "That the last of 'em, Madoc? Then we'd best get back. Evening, young ladies."

"Sukey won't try to get through the hedge here, will she?" Cherry asked.

"No, no," he said soothingly. "Keep to the far end where there's more trees and the grass is longer."

Then he and his helper climbed back into the battered old car and drove off. The indignant pigs, finding themselves under trees in long grass, with windfalls here and there to be picked up, and therefore, in a pig's paradise, decided to stop their furious noise and enjoy life. Mary-Lou appeared at the same time to summon Cherry to some ploy of their own. She stayed long enough to exclaim at the new inhabitants of the Old Orchard and peal with laughter over the rings through their noses. Then she tucked a hand through the younger girl's arm and bore her off, leaving the Dawbarns and Co. to their own devices.

"*Why* do they have rings through their noses?" Primrose, born and bred in a city, wanted to know before they turned away.

Carol, whose father farmed in a big way, explained. "To keep them from barking the trees. If they didn't have rings or something of that kind, they'd nibble all the bark they could reach – especially from the young trees. Then the trees would die after a while. You always ring pigs for that reason."

"I think it's horrid!" Peggy said decidedly. "It must hurt, poor things!"

"But you couldn't let them destroy the trees," Carol expostulated.

"No; but I wouldn't let them be where there *are* trees," Peggy said.

"Oh, come on!" Prudence said impatiently. "We don't want to stand here all the night! Hasn't anyone got any ideas yet?"

The pigs were forgotten as Primrose announced, "Yes; I have!"

"Oh, Primrose, what?" they chorused eagerly.

Primrose eyed them cautiously for a moment, for she knew that what she was going to propose was against all rules and as thoroughly naughty as it could be. If they were caught, there would be heavy penalties. But it was too good to lose.

"Which of you have any tuck left?" she asked as they turned away from the orchard and made their way towards the rock garden.

"I've got half a cake – and some jam," Peggy said promptly.

"I've a box of dates and another of figs and some gingerbread. Oh, and Mother sent me a seedcake yesterday," Carol added.

"What've we got, Pris?" Prudence turned to her sister.

Priscilla thought. "There's some of the date loaf left, I know. Oh, and that tin of sardines Mum's sent for the picnic and we forgot it. She sent one of the old keys to open it as well. But I rather think that's the lot."

"What've you got yourself, Primrose?" Peggy asked. "And what's it all in aid of, anyway?"

"Blob, so far as tuck goes," Primrose said sadly. "We had the last for the picnic last Saturday."

"Oh, well, we can share ours. Go on, Primrose! What're you getting at?"

"It was the pigs that made me think of it really," Primrose began.

"Oh, get *on* with it!" Priscilla said crossly. "The bell will go for Abendessen in two secs – and if anyone catches us talking English when this is a French day, there'll be a row," she added righteously.

"Well, I like that! You've done as much talking in English as anyone!" Prudence rounded on her. "Never mind her, Prim! Tell us what you've thought of."

Primrose stood stock-still and eyed them all again. Then she said, "I propose we have a picnic in the Old Orchard after everyone's gone to bed."

There was a startled silence. Then Peggy said, "But what about the pigs? If they're awake, won't they squeal and give us away? And didn't Mr Evans say the mother pig would bite?"

"Yes; but he said, too, that they'd stay at the other end where there are more trees. Anyhow, it's full moon now and we'd see them if they came near. Besides, don't pigs sleep awfully soundly?"

They all looked at Carol, who said cautiously, "So far as I know they do. I've never seen them, though. And how are we going to get the tuck? Matey keeps it all locked up."

"That's where we're lucky," Primrose said. "This afternoon when I was getting my sweets, Matey was grumbling that the lock of the sweet cupboard had gone funny and she'd have to leave the door open as Griffiths went home this morning for his daughter's wedding and he won't be back till late tomorrow. Matey said it *would* happen when he wasn't there to put it right!"

"But what's all this got to do with our tuck?" Prudence demanded.

"Well, if you can get your arm down between the

bottom shelf of the sweet cupboard and the doors, you can move the button on the inside of the tuck cupboard door which is where *our* tuck is kept. Matey has a hook she does it with and she never locks the door. But we could easily *squeege* an arm through and then we can get out tuck and – and there you are!" Primrose replied.

The bell rang for their evening meal and they had to go, but when it was over they made their final arrangements, for all of them were thrilled at the idea of a moonlight picnic in the Old Orchard. They went up to bed fully resolved to keep awake until the sounds in the house had ceased. Then they would get up and go out and have a glorious time. Of the fact that Matron was sure to miss the tuck and institute instant inquiries about it, they didn't trouble to think. Neither did they question Mr Evans' careless statement that the pigs were likely to keep to the far end of the place.

What they did find, however, was that it is one thing to say you will stay awake when you are healthily tired with a day's work and play, and quite another to do it. By nine o'clock, every last one of them was fast asleep and it was not until one o'clock that Primrose woke up. She remembered their scheme instantly and was out of bed in a moment and going round, cautiously rousing her boon companions.

Luckily for their plans, all five slept in the same dormitory. Julie Lucy was dormitory prefect, but Matron had taken her to San to recover from her hiccoughs, though they could not know that. They took it for granted that she was asleep in the big corner cubicle, and moved on tiptoe and in silence, since not even Prudence, most imprudent of girls, dreamed of peeping in on a prefect. They tossed off their pyjamas and donned frocks and knickers and wriggled their feet into their sandals. Then they slipped noiselessly out of the dormitory and downstairs to the little room where Matron kept all forms of tuck. It was full moon that night and the Big House was well supplied with large windows, so they were able to see their way quite easily.

As Primrose had said, the sweet cupboard door was open and it was easy enough for Priscilla, the thinnest of them, to slip her arm between the shelf and the door, reach down and turn the button which kept the lower cupboard door fastened.

"What about a few sweets?" Carol asked, eyeing her own box longingly.

Priscilla shook her head with a shocked look. "Certainly not! Matey is trusting us not to touch them if we know the door's unlocked."

Considering what they proposed to do, this had its humorous side; but they were all much too childish to see it for themselves. Later on, when it was pointed out to them, they were horrified at what they had done.

They loaded themselves with what was left of their tuck and then, having closed the doors again, they climbed out of the window down to the back lawn on which it looked, and keeping well in the shadow of the house, scurried softly over the grass to the Old Orchard.

Everything was quiet and the primrose light of the full moon made it easy for them to climb over the gate and choose a spot a little way along the hedge where they sat down and unloaded themselves.

"We'll have to eat the sardines with our fingers," Prudence said with a giggle. "No one thought of bringing any forks."

As it turned out, they never got those sardines opened at all. Mrs Dawbarn had enclosed an elderly key, which snapped off short the moment Peggy put any force on and that settled *that*!

"Never mind! We can put the tin back when we go in and we've plenty without," Prudence said easily.

On the whole it was just as well they were unable to add the fish to their very mixed bag. They had brought everything of their own they could find, Primrose even discovering an unopened tin of chicken and ham paste which they spread on the gingerbread. By the time they had eaten that and all the rest of the stuff, including dollops of cherry jam on seedcake, all of them felt more than satisfied. They wiped their sticky fingers on the sun-dried grass and wished they had thought of bringing something to drink, even if it was only water. Then Peggy suggested that they should go to the brook and they could have all the water they wanted. They could use the jar which had held Primrose's paste as a cup.

"Smashing idea!" Prudence exclaimed; and set off without any more thought.

The way passed under a big old tree, heavy with its summer foliage, and between the semi-darkness under the boughs and her own heedlessness in not looking where she was going, she brought catastrophe on them all. She tripped over an independent young pig who had chosen to sleep away from his brethren. Up rose the pig with a lamentable squeal and down went Prudence with a wild yell and then, as Primrose said later, the fat *was* in the fire!

The noise the pair of them made roused all the other pigs who came grunting furiously to see what had happened to their brother. Much more alarming, Sukey also bustled along. Her son was squealing continuously and loudly and the old mother, convinced that something awful was happening to him, made for the first person she saw, which happened to be Carol. That young lady turned and fled up the orchard, shrieking with terror at the top of her voice while the rest scattered, Priscilla only waiting to yank her twin to her feet, grasp her hand and rush madly to the far hedge, where they tried to squeeze through vainly.

All thought of caution had left the girls, and between their screams and the pigs' squeals they made noise enough to have roused the whole island. They *did* rouse a large section of the school, and by the time the howling twins had contrived to work their way round the Old Orchard, clamber over the gate and topple to the ground on the other side, while the demoralized pigs rushed about, colliding with each other and the trees and making the night hideous with their protesting shrill yells, a small procession, headed by Matron with a coat pulled over her nightdress and bare feet, hurtled across the grass to where the five were picking themselves up; for it is a fact that every last one of them quite literally *fell* over the gate, and Carol, who had been first and had received the full weight of Primrose, was severely bruised.

As for Primrose herself, she had struggled to her feet and was standing with eyes screwed tightly shut, screaming at the full pitch of healthy lungs. Matron saw her and made a beeline for her. She shook her sharply and Primrose bit her tongue smartly with the shock and stopped screaming to burst into noisy sobs of pain.

"Stop that noise at once!" Matron said severely. "You are far too big to be such a baby. Do you hear me? Stop it, I say!"

In her relief at hearing the familiar voice, even though Matron sounded about as furious as she could possibly be, Primrose nearly flung her arms around her. She did retain enough sense not to do it, but she clutched at the little lady as her sobs were reduced in volume and wailed, "Oh, Matron, I'm so frightened!"

"As you richly deserve to be!" Matron snapped, having seen that her colleagues had taken charge of the other culprits. "Come indoors at once and tell me the meaning of this disgraceful conduct!"

The sobbing, shivering group were ushered into the house and taken to the study, where they were interviewed by a Miss Annersley, who contrived to look as stately in her silk kimono with her hair hastily twisted into a knob as ever she did in her M.A. gown with its glowing scarlet hood. She asked few questions, for the girls were in a state bordering on hysteria. She forbade them to say another word then, though Peggy and Prudence were ready to burst into talk.

"I wish to hear nothing from you now," she said icily – so icily that the five shook in their shoes at the thought of what would happen to them when the Head was as angry as this. "You will go to bed at once and stay there until you are told to get up in the morning. I will see you after Frühstück. Until then, you are in silence. Now go with Matron."

Matron, at her very grimmest, marched them off and saw them into bed. So cowed were they that they scurried out of their clothes and between the sheets as fast as they could. Then their tyrant left them to return with a tray of five cups each containing hot milk, and even Peggy Harper, who hated hot milk, downed it without a word.

"Now lie down and go to sleep," Matron said when she had collected the last cup. "Let us hear no more of you for the rest of the night."

Then she went off to set the tray on a table and make the rounds of the dormitories to make sure that everyone else had settled down again. The only one she found awake was Bride Bettany, who had taken charge on her own landing and seen to it that the disturbed girls got no chance to rush out to find out what was happening. In fact, as the staff agreed the next day, the prefects had kept their heads and behaved with remarkable common sense.

When Matron appeared in the door of the tiny room which Bride occupied as Head Girl, that young lady sat up, shaking the thick straight hair out of her eyes, and demanded, "Who was it, Matey?"

"The Dawbarns, Peggy Harper, Primrose Trevoase and Carol Soames," Matron told her. "Why aren't you asleep?"

"Oh, I'll get off soon." Bride smothered a yawn. "The Dawbarns and Co? I *might* have known! It *would* be them!" This time the yawn refused to be suppressed. Bride gaped till Matron, gazing at her, fascinated, wondered how much more strain her jaws could stand. When the girl, pink with confusion, apologized, she gave her short shrift.

"Well, now you know that much, I hope you'll manage to go to sleep again! You have exams tomorrow, in case you've forgotten. Good night!" And she went out, switching off the light.

Left to herself, Bride continued to giggle between yawns for a minute or two. "Why did I talk? I might have *known* something would happen, considering we've still a good fortnight of term to go! It jolly well serves me right!"

She yawned again, turned over with a final giggle, and fell asleep almost as she turned.

CHAPTER SIXTEEN

The Regatta

Nemesis arrived next morning.

The five were left to sleep until eight o'clock, when five very icy prefects appeared with trays bearing what was known in the school as "prison fare". This consisted of a large cup of milk and a plate of brown bread very thinly spread with butter. The sinners were roused and told to sit up, eat their breakfast and then dress at once as Miss Annersley wished to see them as soon as they were ready.

To keep an angry Head waiting a moment longer than was necessary was unthinkable. They got through the meal in record time and hurried into their clothes. Matron had brought them fresh frocks as the night's adventures had finished the ones they had had clean the day before. Indeed, the Dawbarns had torn theirs in their endeavours to get through the far hedge.

"And there'll be another row about that!" Carol meditated mournfully as she pulled hers on.

Matron insisted that summer dresses must last at least three days, and those had lasted only one. If there had been time, Carol would have had a weep at the thought of having to face an irate Matron on the subject. Time, however, there was not. She hurriedly saw to it that she was immaculate and then joined the doleful group standing by the door, where the Head Girl was waiting to escort them to the study.

On the whole, it might have been worse. Miss Annersley was lenient – though *they* did not think so. She reminded them that they had broken rules and proved themselves untrustworthy by using their knowledge about the unlocked sweet cupboard. They had also been utterly inconsiderate in disturbing the school, especially those girls who began their General Certificate that day. They had also upset the pigs, which had been upset enough by their journey across the island. As the indictment was piled up against them, Carol did dissolve into tears and Peggy followed suit. Primrose and Priscilla only managed to avoid it by biting their lips. It was left to Prudence most characteristically to put in the only plea that was uttered.

"Please, Miss Annersley, we never touched the sweets. Priscilla told us that Matron was trusting us who knew about the lock not to."

Miss Annersley treated this ungrammatical remark with a glare that made Prudence wish the floor would open and swallow her up. Then she said in such chilling tones that the pleader literally shivered, "Indeed? I am thankful to know that *any* of you could show even that small amount of honesty."

This finished Priscilla, who gulped hard and then began to cry stormily, whereupon both Primrose and Prudence followed suit. Miss Annersley surveyed the five Niobes before her with eyes that, if they had but known, only just did not twinkle. Some hours after the event, she was able to see the funny side of it – and parts of it had been very funny. Not that the culprits ever knew.

"Yes; you may well cry," she said impressively. "I would not have believed that we had five girls so disobedient, selfish and untrustworthy in the school. I am utterly ashamed of you all. I am ashamed to think that you *are* members of the Chalet School!"

This brought a low kind of howl from Carol and loud sobs from the rest and all fully made up their minds that they were to be expelled on the spot. However, when judgment came, it was not quite so bad as that. Bad enough, though, from their point of view. The Head said that for the rest of the term they would sleep in other dormitories as it was clear that they could not be trusted together. They would not be allowed to join in any of the form picnics and, finally, they would not be allowed to compete in the Regatta.

This was by far the worst part of their punishment. Peggy Harper had had hopes of the under-fourteen swimming, now that Mary-Lou was over-age for it. The Dawbarns had entered for the greasy-pole event and Carol was in for the under-fourteen diving. And all of them had entered for the tub race. If the Head had tried the whole term with both hands to find a punishment that would really hurt them and make a deep impression, she could not have succeeded better.

She dismissed them after that, and they left the study still sobbing. Mercifully for them, the exams had begun by that time and the house was deserted except for the maids, Miss Dene who was in her office sorting the contents of the postbag, Matron, and Nurse who was busy going through the sheets and other bedding in San. Even those mistresses who were not invigilating had removed themselves and their work to the rose garden.

They were not very sure where to go or what to do, for the Head had simply told them to go away as she had seen enough of them. They were not to know that the moment the door closed on them, she had rung Matron on the house phone by previous arrangement, and when they reached their form room, where they had instinctively gone, that lady was waiting for them.

"Now then," she said briskly, "crying won't help matters. You've had your fun and you must pay for it. I suppose you know that exams began twenty minutes ago? What do you have first?"

"Dud—dicta—ation!" Primrose contrived to swallow her sobs long enough to give her the information.

"Then it's no use sending you out for that now. Go upstairs and wash your faces and then go and make your beds and tidy your cubicles. I'll come along in twenty minutes' time to see what you've done. And stop crying *at once*!"

They crawled upstairs, choking down their sobs, and by the time she arrived to inspect their work, though they were still red-eyed and shaken, the worst was over. She desired Prudence to refold her pyjamas and put them under the pillow and called Primrose's attention to the fact that she had not tucked in her bedclothes neatly. When these errors were rectified, she looked at her watch.

"Well, you still have twenty-five minutes left before your next exam begins. I'll see to the dictation myself after tea, so you won't miss your marks. In the meantime, I want one or two things from the village. Go and get your hats and you can walk down with me. It'll freshen you up for your arithmetic."

It certainly did. By the time they were back and sitting in their places, looking at the arithmetic paper with horrified eyes, they were all more or less calm again. It is true that Carol made a mess of two-thirds of her paper, but that was Carol in any case. But for the rest of that week, the whole five were as good as they knew how to be and for the rest of the term they remained meek and subdued and gave very little trouble.

As for the school at large, once that first day was over, they found they had too much to do to worry greatly over what was past. It is true that Josette Russell gleefully informed Mary-Lou that with her and Peggy out of the under-fourteen race, there was a chance for other folk.

"I suppose you mean you," that young woman retorted. "Well, I'll give you a tip, Josette. When the race comes off, keep your mind glued to it and if anyone even screams, 'Sharks!' don't pay any attention. You'll have a chance then. And don't try to push too hard, either, or you'll overdo it. I know you!"

Josette grinned. "It won't happen, I guess. We don't get sharks around here as a rule. And anyway," she added, "they'd be way out to sea and not in the Cove. But thanks a million for the other tip. I'll remember."

"Well, see you do," Mary-Lou said as she departed for the tennis court.

The Saturday of the Regatta dawned hot and hazy with every sign of sweltering heat later on. Miss Moore, the geography mistress, informed Biddy O'Ryan as they went down to the Cove before Frühstück to see that all was in readiness for ten o'clock when the Regatta was scheduled to start, that they would all be melting by noon.

"Well, at any rate we'll all be *in* or *by* the water," Biddy replied. "We'll have a chance of being coolish. Just you forget it and be counting those chairs, will ye? We shan't have many parents today, but *some* will be coming and there'll be other people as well, I expect. I'll go and see that everything in the tent's ready. Sure, we haven't any too much time, anyhow."

She left Miss Moore counting chairs and forms and made her way to the quay first to inspect the greasy pole which Griffiths had fixed up the night before.

"What's the leg of mutton?" she asked curiously, pointing to the peculiar-looking bundle that hung from the end.

214

Miss Slater looked up and laughed. "Well, not *mutton*, you may be sure!"

"It never was," Biddy retorted. "Sure, what would our girls be doing with a chunk of meat at all, at all? What have you stuffed it with, Pam?"

"It's a sack filled with shavings and other oddments to give it weight," the maths mistress said. "What are you doing, Biddy?"

"Going to the tents to make sure everything's there. The girls are bringing down their second bathing suits after Frühstück, but I want to make sure they have everything else they need."

She went off and was busy until the bell for Frühstück, rung violently by Mary-Lou who had been sent on the job from the top of the cliff, recalled them to school.

The Regatta was to begin with the boat-races, the authorities having decreed that it would be best to have those before the greatest heat of the day. By half-past nine, St Agnes' had arrived in full force. There was a swimming race and a floating event for them, and in any case this would be their last chance to be together as a complete school. Jo Maynard was with them, accompanied by her husband and three elder boys. The twins, as she told the girls when they asked where they were, had been left at home with Anna, since Regattas were no place for ten-month babies. She also brought Lady Russell and Sir James with her as he and Jack Maynard were to be two of the judges. The third was Commander Christy, and Mr Bettany was to be the starter.

By ten o'clock, the chairs for the visitors were full, many more friends and relatives having turned up than had been expected. Those mistresses who would be in the guard boats had already paddled off to take up their stations, armed against the heat with wide-brimmed hats, coloured glasses and flasks of lemonade. Mr Willoughby, father of Blossom, had sailed his yacht, the *Sea Witch*, round the coast and she was to be used as the Judges' boat, so the judges, with their wives and such of the families as were there, were rowed off to it when he had picked up moorings. The Head went with them, leaving Mdlle to take her place as hostess and took Miss Dene with her, whose job was to mark down the winners. When they were all ready, with two of the men from the *Sea Witch* to hold the final tape ready, a string of flags fluttered up her mainmast and the Regatta began.

It opened with the Senior pair-oars. They came into line and Mr Bettany began his chant. The gun went off with a bang that made everyone but the competitors jump and the race was on. There were a good many of them in for it, but they soon thinned out, and it became clear that it lay between Nancy Chester, Ruth Wilson and a dark horse from Upper V, one Nora Penley, who had come from Tanswick the term before. Nora had been marked down as good, but no one had realized quite how good she was until they saw her going all out against the other two. In the end, she beat Ruth and it was such a close finish with Nancy that the judges had to consult on it before it was finally announced – by Commander Christy, roaring it through his megaphone – that Nancy had won.

The Junior pair-oars was won by Betsy Lucy, who was accustomed to any amount of rowing and swimming during the holidays and who easily beat all her rivals, even paddling the last few strokes home quietly. It was followed by an open canoe race – open, that is, to everyone of fourteen or over – and this went to Lesley Pitt with Tom Gay and Katharine Gordon dead-heating for second place.

After this came a race peculiar to the school and

generally called paddling race. A large loose ring was clipped on to the stern of the pair-oars and paddles slipped through. The idea was to paddle from the stern in much the same way as a gondolier manoeuvres his gondola through the waterways of Venice. It was Tom who won this by shooting ahead at the very beginning and never letting up on her efforts until she reached the tape, when she turned round to see a long string of paddlers tailing after her.

Next came the inter-house races. The Junior inter-house was rowed off first and St Agnes' proudly raced against the other Juniors and, as Bride observed, did themselves proud, coming in third, with St Clare's first and Ste Thérèse second. St Scholastika should have been third, but Stella Porter, rowing at bow, plunged in her oar too deep and caught a magnificent crab, landing flat on her back, and throwing the rest of the crew into such complete confusion that the wonder was that they did not capsize their boat. Stella's little friends and companions had quite a lot to say to her later on when the visitors had gone!

"Those infants from St Agnes' should have a prize for keeping their little heads and rowing as well as they do," Jo remarked to her sister. "We've some very decent oarsmen coming along there, or I miss my guess."

"It's too late, unfortunately," Madge Russell said.

"Too late be sugared!" Jo suddenly stood up. "Nigel, I want your dinghy. I'll be back anon."

"OK; take it if you like, but mind how you get into it," Mr Willoughby replied amiably. "You'll miss the rest of the boat-races, Jo, if you're going off to Carnbach in quest of sweets for the kids."

"Never mind! I've seen it all before and a little encouragement at that age can go a long way," Jo responded.

217

"Give me a pound, Madge. I haven't much more than ten bob with me and it's *your* school after all."

"Modesty always *was* one of your virtues!" her sister retorted as she felt in her bag. "Here you are – and don't kill yourself trying to get back in a hurry. It's growing fearfully hot."

"You're telling *me*! I'll have the tide with me, anyhow, and I'll row to the landing-stage at the village and walk across from there," Jo answered. "Nigel can pick up his dinghy later on."

She dropped into the dinghy, cast off the painter, and rowed away with long practised strokes which took her the maximum distance with the minimum of effort.

"Where's she going?" demanded lovely Mrs Willoughby, who was sitting further along the deck, her frail little son, Aubrey, in her lap, and who had missed the dialogue.

"To buy sweets as prizes for St Agnes'," Madge Russell replied.

"Oh, but that's not fair! Jo oughtn't to have to pay for the lot."

"Don't you worry! She's just rooked me of a pound for the purpose. Now don't fuss, Rosamund," Lady Russell said firmly. "The Seniors are just getting under way." She lifted her glasses to inspect them. "What a strong set they seem! Who's that stroking St Scholastika's, Hilda?" She raised her voice and Miss Annersley turned round.

"What's that? Stroking St Scholastika's? Lesley Pitt. She's very good, I hear. I shouldn't wonder if St Scholastika's didn't win this." She raised her own glasses and looked across to the quay where the Seniors were entering their boats and settling to their oars.

Unaware of the excitement they were causing on the Judges' boat, the big girls, in their shorts and loose shirts, paddled over to the holding-boats whose occupants were seniors not in the race. The coxes handed one end of the starting chains to them and then the boats were gently paddled into position, everyone being mindful of the fact that, if a boat moves too promptly, the starting chain will tauten and drag the stern round. The coxes, holding the other end of the chains, also had the ticklish job of keeping them apart from the rudder-lines, as well as being prepared to drop their ends of the chain when the gun went off.

It seemed ages to the spectators before, across the glassy water, they heard Mr Bettany's voice chanting: "Five – four – three – two –" *Bang!* The pistol shot rang out, the coxes let go the chains and concentrated on their steering and the boats were off – to an excellent start, too. For a few seconds, they rowed side by side, leaving everyone else in a state of pleasing indecision as to which was likely to set the pace. Then St Scholastika's, stroked by Lesley, began to draw very slightly ahead, with St Clare and St Thérèse still level, and keeping up quite well.

The course was quite a good distance for schoolgirls. It began near the quay. The girls rowed across the mouth of the Cove, round what was known as the Table Rock at the far side, back to the starting-point and then straight across to the point close to the Judges' boat, where the two seamen were waiting to draw the tape taut as the boats neared them. The then P.T. mistress, Hilary Burn,* now Hilary Graves, had marked it out two years ago, since they had to be careful about the east-flowing branch of the Wreckers' Race, and they had adhered to it since. It gave the girls a long enough stretch and kept them well inside of the Race.

* *The Chalet School and the Island.*

"Thirty to the minute," observed the knowledgeable Mr Willoughby, who had rowed for his College when he was at Oxford and spent all his spare time on the water. "They're keeping well within themselves. Lesley's right not to bustle them yet. There they go – round the Table Rock! Oh, very neat work!"

"Bride's quickening!" her father exclaimed as St Clare's quickened stroke and began to creep up on their leader. "Silly little *ass*! She'll row them out before they're ready. Jolly bad judgment!"

Tom, stroking St Scholastika's, thought the same. It was a great temptation to follow Bride's example and quicken, but she knew that Jean Donald at five could manage a final spurt, but if asked to quicken too soon was apt to weary and lose stroke. So she kept her crew down to the steady thirty.

The boats were all round the Table Rock now, and sweeping across the bay in fine style, St Clare's now level with St Scholastika's while Ste Thérèse was a full length behind. Halfway over, Lesley quickened to thirty-two and once more Tom had to resist temptation and keep her spurt for the final stretch. She glanced at her cox, Hilary Bennett, who was steering with every ounce in her.

"Quicken?" she asked as she met Tom's eye.

"Not – yet!" Tom gasped. "After starting-point!"

Hilary nodded and directed her attention to keeping out of the wake of St Clare, where Vi Lucy was trying to do the same thing by St Scholastika. They neared the starters' boats where the starters were all standing up and cheering. Loud cheers came from the shore, too, and the startled sea birds added to the noise with their mewing and crying. Then they were past and on the long last lap. Tom caught Hilary's eye.

220

"Quicken-thirty-two!" she panted. Then, a minute later, "Thirty-four!"

Bawling at the top of her voice, Hilary passed on the command and the stroke quickened. Lesley would have quickened again, but dared not, for her crew were already rowing all out, since she had quickened when they had swung round the boats by the quay and she knew that one or two of them could do no more.

Bride had also called for more, but she had miscalculated her crew's strength. They were already tiring and thirty-four proved to be their downfall. Annis, at bow, missed her stroke and the boat lost course. Bride, by means of Catriona Watson's yells, tried to get them together again: but it was useless. St Clare's rowed gamely on to the end, but they were three lengths behind the others.

Meanwhile, St Scholastika's and Ste Thérèse's, were fighting it out, neck and neck. Jean was nearly done, but she forced herself to go on, though the sweat was pouring off her, and the oar felt a ton weight every time she moved it. But they were nearly there, she *must* not let the House down. Finally, amid a thunder of applause, the two boats cut through the tape at exactly the same minute. St Scholastika's and Ste Thérèse had made a dead heat of it!

CHAPTER SEVENTEEN

Finale!

The inter-house race finished the rowing part of the Regatta, and as it was now half-past twelve Miss Annersley decreed that lunch would be served. Unfortunately, Jo had gone off with the dinghy belonging to the Judges' boat and had not returned yet. Even if she had, she had announced her intention of leaving it at the village landing. The tide was just on the turn, so the water near the quay was not deep enough for the *Sea Witch*, and as Mrs Willoughby said it looked rather as if everyone aboard her must go lunchless.

"Nonsense!" Lady Russell said firmly. "What are the guard boats for?"

"To guard the course and keep an eye on the girls," the Head said with equal firmness.

"They aren't needed for that at the moment." She turned to Commander Christy. "Michael, give them a hail, will you? They can take us off very nicely."

He obliged with a hail that brought up two of the guard boats in a hurry to ask what was wrong. However, when they learned why they were needed, they rowed in and presently were making for shore, each carrying four passengers. The other guard boats rallied round on hearing of the dilemma, and between them all the visitors and Judges from the yacht reached the shore in plenty of time to enjoy the delicious cold lunch which Frau Mieders, head of the domestic science department, had concocted with the aid of the Seniors.

Halfway through, Jo arrived, swinging a fish-basket which bulged and which she handed over to Peggy Burnett, who was responsible for the prizes.

"There you are," she said, sitting down and accepting a plate of iced salad and cold chicken. "That's for St Agnes' – bless them! They *deserve* prizes for putting up such a good effort."

"What have you got them?" Peggy asked suspiciously as she took the basket.

"Jigsaw puzzles from Courthope's," Jo applied herself to her lunch.

"Had you enough money?" her sister demanded.

"Just. I had your pound and my own ten bob and there are nine of them. I had to spend ninepence on the fish-basket to carry them, so I have about five bob left. The puzzles were half-a-crown each."

"It's just like Jo," Madge Russell murmured dreamily to Miss Annersley. "Will she ever grow up, d'you think, Hilda?"

"Who wants her to?" the Head demanded. "I like her as she is."

Lady Russell giggled and let the subject drop. In any case, she was being offered a most delectable-looking compound by Julie Lucy, who had had to miss her rowing and swimming as well as all other games this term. She helped herself and Julie passed on to her Aunt Rosamund and Jo and her doings were left in abeyance for the time being.

The swimming events began at half-past one with the race for the Under-Tens which was won by Nancy Chester's small sister Janice. Janice was a regular little fish in the water and she shot straight ahead of everyone and reached the tape well in front of such leggy people as Ailie Russell, Josette's youngest sister, and Signa Björnessen who was also a good little swimmer for her age, which was more than a year-and-a-half older than eight-year-old Janice.

The school cheered that small person when her little dripping form scuttled up the beach to the tents where she was rubbed down and seen into her second bathing suit by Matron from St Agnes'.

"Not bad for a kid of eight," Nancy said casually. "She should make quite a swimmer some day if she only keeps it up." But her eyes were very proud.

"I call it super," Bride retorted. "I only wish young Maeve was as good. She can swim, of course, but she's much keener on cricket than swimming or rowing. And she prefers riding to all the rest put together. What's next? Oh, the Under-Twelves. Enid Roberts should get that. None of that batch is anything special and Enid has quite a pretty style when she tries."

Enid won her race, and, much to her own delight, Josette Russell simply walked away with the Under-Fourteens. The next race, the Under-Sixteens, was a gift to Mary-Lou, who gave promise of becoming the finest swimmer the school had ever known. She had both style and pace to a remarkable degree for a girl of fourteen, and, which mattered most as much, she showed amazingly good judgment in timing her spurts. The Over-Sixteens and the Open went to Bride herself, though Mary-Lou came second in the Open, and gave her a hard fight most of the way. But Bride at nearly eighteen had just that amount more of staying power and she outpaced Mary-Lou in the end, though that young woman left all the rest of the competitors in Open also-rans.

The two life-saving classes came next and were won

by Beth Lane and Audrey Simpson respectively. The neat way in which Beth pinioned her "body" before taking her on her shoulder being particularly admired by the judges. Audrey, to quote Tom Gay, had always been a dead cert for this. She was easily the best at it in the school and Sir Jem, as they all called him, complimented her on the professional way she did things.

The inter-house races were great thrills, naturally. Tom represented St Clare's for the Seniors, with Bride for Ste Thérèse and Gwynneth Jones for St Scholastika's. All three were strong swimmers and very evenly matched. It was a fight from beginning to end, and when Tom finally touched the tape a second before either of the others, she fully deserved the lusty cheers that greeted her win. The Junior Race was a very flat affair after this, for Mary-Lou left her rivals behind as usual, and it was clear from the start that they had no chance against her, though they put up a game fight.

"What's happening to the diving?" Jo asked her eldest daughter when that young lady came racing up to her for a moment.

"We're having it at the same time as the greasy pole," Len explained.

"We couldn't get everything in any other way. You'll come and watch Con and me, won't you, Mamma? We lost our swimming heats, but we both hope to win the diving. Margot said she wouldn't go in for anything but the greasy pole."

"I'll come and watch of course. Off the Table Rock as usual, I suppose? OK; I'll be there. Now you'd better fly. Someone's yelling herself blind for you," Jo replied. "What a rowdy lot you all are! I'm sure *we* never made so much noise when we were kids."

"Didn't you just!" Madge Russell put in, overhearing

this. "Don't you believe her, Len. She could out-yell anyone when she liked."

Len chuckled. "I know. That's what's so nice about her. OK; I'm going." And she shot off, leaving her aunt and mother laughing until Madge Russell said, "Remember when all your crowd got into a row for shouting at the tops of your voices the whole time, Joey?"*

"*And* had to write out those mushy lines from *King Lear* dozens of times," Jo nodded. "But that was the fault of that ghastly Matron we had then."

They both went off into peals of mirth at this reminiscence, from which they were called by Biddy O'Ryan who wanted to know the joke. Both refused to tell – then; but Jo promised her the whole story later on. Then they settled down to watching the relay races. In the Seniors, Team A, captained by Elfie Woodward, beat B and C hollow; and in the Juniors, C won with seconds to spare.

Apart from the diving, this was the last of what might be described as the serious races. Commander Christy announced a porpoise race which was open to all over fourteen and a string of girls entered the water and waded out until they were waist-deep. They lined up, and when the pistol-shot rang out they set off with a vim that made the older members of the audience wonder aloud how they managed to do it.

The porpoise race had been evolved by Hilary Graves in one of her more frivolous moments. It consisted of swimming six strokes and then turning a standing somersault in the water and was a huge favourite with the girls, who alternately swam and twirled until Mrs Willoughby vowed it made her giddy to watch them.

* *The Princess of the Chalet School.*

"As for that girl Clem Barrass, she's a boneless wonder!" she said. "I never in my life saw anyone fling herself round the way she does."

"Your own young Blossom isn't far behind her!" Jo retorted. "There she goes! Over like a – a – a catherine wheel!"

"If Blossom isn't careful, she's going to get someone in the face," Lady Russell declared. "There! I *knew* it!" As Blossom gave an extra wild whirl and kicked Katharine Gordon smartly on one cheek, causing that young lady, who was swimming, to go under with a howl which was half-smothered as she swallowed a large dose of salt water.

Blossom, who was nothing if not insouciant, went straight ahead, shouting over her shoulder, "Sorry! I'll apologize later!" Then she finished her sixth stroke and made a porpoise of herself again.

"Carry me home and bury me decently!" Jo half-sobbed as she rocked with laughter. "Oh, *why* did no one ever think of this when *I* was at school?"

"It took Hilary Burn to think up such a thing," said the Head with conviction. "Miss Nalder was P.T. in your time, Joey, and she lacked the – er – *brighter* ideas that Hilary produced on occasion. There! Clem's home and there goes Blossom just after her. Now which are you people going to do – stay here and watch the greasy pole fun; or go to the other end of the shore and see the diving?"

"Me for the diving! I seem to have two daughters in for it so I must go and cheer them on or I'll never hear the last of it," Jo said as she gave her eyes a final scrub, got to her feet and set off along the shore, together with a number of other parents, all bent on the same good deed.

Her sister stayed where she was, with Rosamund

Willoughby, little Mrs Christy and the Commander. The two doctors were judging the diving, so had to go. The guard boats at the quay end of the beach moved in closer, though there was little need of them, since no one was allowed to enter for the greasy pole who could not swim properly. Madge Russell gave a little chuckle as she prepared herself for some fun by fishing in her bag for her second handkerchief.

"It's bound to be an utter scream," she explained to Rosamund, "and this one's damp already." She glanced round casually. "Hello, the sun seems to be going in. I hope it's not going to rain."

Carey Christy glanced round, too. "Oh, I don't think so. It's just a cloud come up. It'll pass. Just as well, too, I think. It takes the glare off the water. Oh, why isn't Jo here? It's her Margot who leads off."

"Well, she can't be in two places at once," the lady's sister pointed out sensibly. "She had to go to watch the other two diving. I wonder how far Margot will get?"

The competitors began by dipping their feet into a dish of water to wash off any loose sand. They then set off on their walk along the pole which Griffiths, who was watching from the cliffs, had greased thoroughly with cartwheel grease. Margot contrived to go three paces along. Then her foot slipped, and with a squall she fell with a huge splash into the water, which was now deepening fast as the tide came in. She vanished from view, but was at the surface again in a moment and swimming for shore, where she was caught by her cousin Bride and sent off to rub down and change into her frock, since this was the only event for which she had entered.

Norah Fitzgerald followed and fell off at once. So did most of the younger fry, including Emerence Hope, who varied proceedings by contriving to turn a somersault in mid-air before she touched the water, where she vanished with a screech that Biddy O'Ryan declared would have outdone any banshee of her own native land. Finally, as girl after girl followed, only to end ignominiously in the sea before she had taken more than half-a-dozen paces at most, it came to the Sixths and at last only Elfie, Tom, Nancy, Audrey and Bride were left.

Jo had come back by this time, the proud mother of a winning diver, for Len had beaten everyone in her class and wound up with a beautiful swallow dive – or so her mother declared. Later on, the young lady's father said you could call it a swallow dive if you liked. To him it looked like the contortion of someone who had taken strychnine by accident! Still, there was no doubt that Len was the best diver of them all, and Jo was, as her friends and relatives declared, as proud as a cat with nine tails!

Audrey came first and she set off with arms extended, eyes fixed on the bundle swaying at the end of the pole and feet moving slowly and carefully. She had made up her mind that the safest way would be to set each foot forward in the first position so that she could get some grip on the pole with her insteps. It took some doing, but she forged slowly ahead while the rest held their breath and watched her excitedly. Would she do it?

Audrey got a little past the half-way mark, which was further than anyone else had managed. Then she made the fatal mistake of glancing aside for a second. Her foot came down on the heel instead of the instep; it slid off the pole, leaving her in a squatting attitude for a second, and then away she went, ending in a mighty splash that sent the water flying far enough to baptize Miss Armitage, who was standing close to the end of the quay. Miss Armitage's cry of protest mingled with Audrey's wild yell and the school broke into peals of laughter mixed with frantic cheering.

Miss Moore rushed forward to her colleague with a towel and then Elfie took her place at the beginning. But this was not Elfie's day for balance walking. She took three steps and fell in, even as Margot had done, and Tom came striding up to see what she could do.

Tom tried a different method. She had decided that if you went slowly and carefully, you stood more chance of slipping; so she made a dive for it and went running with enormous strides. It nearly came off – nearly; but not quite! Just as she was almost within reach of the bundle, her foot slipped and down she went with a howl that outdid anything that had gone before. Nancy was no luckier, for she came off halfway, contriving to swing her legs up so that she made a dive of it and cleft the water with a neatness to be expected of the girl who had won the Over-Sixteen diving event.

It was Bride's turn, and if she failed, then no one would have won.

"What happens to the prize?" Jo asked at large.

"It goes to whoever got farthest – Tom, so far," Peggy Burnett said. The next moment she had doubled up with laughter. "Oh – *oh*! I knew they'd be funny, but I didn't think they'd be as funny as this!"

Bride had also decided to try a new method. She neither ran, nor tried fancy dancing steps, nor behaved in the usual way. Instead, she *shuffled*! She had started off on her left foot and it remained in front the whole way along. How she did it, even she could not tell when it was all over, but she actually did reach the farther end and bent for what was the most difficult part of the job – taking the bundle off the hook driven into the end of the pole. For almost a moment it looked as if she were going to do it. Then the inevitable happened. Her foot slipped; she caught hold of the pole and for quite fifteen seconds she contrived to hang on to the pole with both hands – long enough, at any rate, for Elfie, who had brought her Kodak to snap the win, to take one which Bride's peers treasured ever after – and then her fingers slipped on the treacherous grease and down she plunged, feet first. But she *had* reached the end, being the only one to do so, and she *had* hung on, so the Judges announced her as winner.

"Only the tub race now," the Head said with a glance at her watch. "I hope–"

She had turned seawards as she spoke and now she gave a gasp at what she saw.

"Right!" Commander Christy told her. "*No* tub race! And you'd better see about getting everything cleared at the double. I'll warn 'em!" And he seized his megaphone and roared through it, "That's the end of the Regatta. Fog is coming up. Will all visitors please hurry up the cliff to the school? Girls who have not changed get your clothes and run as hard as you can. Those who have, please help carry the prizes up to school. Guard boats, come i–i–in!"

He was obeyed at once. Everyone could see how the horizon had dimmed and no one wanted to be caught if it could be avoided. The guests, headed by Miss Annersley, Lady Russell and Mrs Bettany, scurried up the cliff path, across the rough turf and down the lane and reached school in clear weather. The rest, headed by St Agnes', with Bride, Elfie and Primrose tailing off, were fortunate to get to the top of the cliff before the mist came down and they had to make their way back through a wet-clinging blanket of white. However, they got back safely.

As Mdlle said much later on, it might have been so very much worse. What if they had begun the tub race and the girls had been out on the water?

Miss Annersley, picturing what might have happened if this had been the case, had fully agreed with her.

However, the immediate prospect was the prize-giving. It had been decided that Madge herself must give the prizes away as it was so long since she had been at any of the school's public functions. First, though, they had tea with raspberries – and cream from Mr Evans' cows – and as it had been intended to have that down at the Cove, people had to rush round with small tables and chairs in Hall. However, everyone was served at last. The girls themselves had theirs in the dining room. Then, while the visitors were still seated at the tables, Peggy Burnett and Biddy O'Ryan marshalled the winners of prizes into line and sent the rest to Hall with orders to sit on the floor and keep out of the way as far as they could. The prize-table, well laden, appeared on the dais and Mr Willoughby, who was chairman, appeared with Lady Russell, the Head, the two doctors and Commander Christy, and while the guests finished their tea the prizes were presented.

The Christys had provided several of them by special permission, and excited girls became the possessors of brooches and lockets and other trinkets, selected from what remained of Dai Lloyd's hoard. Jo's consolation prizes of jigsaw puzzles for the St Agnes' crew were greeted with ringing cheers as the little girls headed by Ailie Russell marched up on to the dais, looking very pleased with themselves. The House cups for rowing and swimming were handed over with due ceremony and at last there remained only the greasy pole.

Bride came forward to take it looking very flushed, with shining eyes and a smile on her lips. For once she, the plainest of the three Bettany girls, looked supremely pretty, as Lady Russell told her brother and sister-in-law later, and prophesied that in a year's time they would have *three* pretty daughters of which to boast instead of only two.

Lady Russell turned to take the prize from Commander Christy, who was seeing to that part of the business. She stared as he gravely put into her hands an elderly toy monkey. Then she saw that twisted round it was a string of seed pearls, very small and of no great value, but very dainty and girlish, and she nearly disgraced herself by exploding on the dais. She pulled herself together and presented the shabby object to her niece with all solemnity.

Suddenly, from among the girls on the floor, there rose a wail of, "That's my Monkey Jacko! I never said Bride could have him! Oh, Daddy, you *are* mean!"

Small Gaynor Christy was hushed at once by shocked elder girls, but the hall rang with the shouts of laughter. Bride herself went crimson and hurriedly jumped down off the dais and hid herself as well as she could among the rest. She was so overcome, she never even remembered her curtsy and thanks. As for the inveterate practical joker, Commander Christy, he chuckled richly over the way his joke had come off.

Gaynor was consoled very quickly, once the prize-giving was ended, for Bride brought the beloved Jacko which the Commander had sent Cherry home to seek, and returned him to his sorrowing owner once she had removed the pearls. Then the guests had to make a move, for the ferry would be waiting to take them back to the mainland. The Willoughbys had to wait until the mist cleared, which it did shortly after seven. They were going home in the yacht and taking the Bettanys with them. But by half-past seven they had gone and so had St Agnes', and the rest of the school, having hastily tidied up, marched to the dining room for the Regatta supper.

It was, as Emerence said to Margot and Len who were sitting on either side of her, a luscious meal! Karen and Megan, the people responsible for the housekeeping, had outdone themselves and the girls feasted royally. Chicken salad, trifle, jellies, creams, dishes of raspberries and cream, and, as a grand wind-up, ices, sent across from Carnbach by Joey, who had longed to stay for the affair but was obliged to hurry home to her twins, made the sort of supper the girls would remember as their last big one on St Briavel's all their lives.

Then, supper ended, they called for speeches. First the Head; then Lady Russell who, with her husband, was staying on the island for the night, since *her* twins could be left to her faithful Marie. Then there came the call for the Head Girl, and Bride, sitting among the prefects, rose to her feet feeling suddenly grave, for this was the last time she would officiate at any big ceremony as Head Girl. On Tuesday, school on the island would finish, and though a good many of them would meet next term, there were others whose schooldays would end then. Madge Dawson would be going to the Royal College of Music and three of the others to training hospitals. Her own special chum, Elfie, was one of them, for she was to have a year's work at massage and remedials before she went to Chelsea to train as a P.T. mistress. Others again would be going on to St Agnes', and though a number of them might finish at the branch at Welsen she herself would have done with school then.

"I haven't much to say," she began slowly. "I should just like to thank you all for helping to make my two terms as Head Girl so jolly decent. And I would like to ask Miss Annersley to tell Commander and Mrs Christy what I know we all feel – that these two years on the island have been simply marvellous." Here she had to wait, for the girls all clapped until Miss Annersley rang her bell for silence again. Bride continued: "We've had three Regattas, now, but I think you'll all agree that the last has been the best, even if the mist *did* do us out of the tub race! It really has been a splendid wind-up to our time here." She raised her glass of lemonade. "Girls, I want us all to drink a toast! Here's to the Chalet School, wherever it may be! May it go on and prosper!"

Like one body, they all sprang to their feet, mistresses as well as girls, and their voices rang out: "The Chalet School – may it go on and prosper."

Then, when the toast had been drunk and they were sitting again, the school outdid itself in wild cheers for its Head Girl and the Chalet School.

No Chalet School collection
will be complete without

Elinor M. Brent-Dyer's Chalet School

*by Elinor M. Brent-Dyer
and Helen McClelland*

Elinor M. Brent-Dyer's famous Chalet School series, begun in 1925, is still as popular as ever – and this fascinating compendium of Chalet School facts is a must for Chalet School fans of any age.

Included are:

★ **Articles about the history of the school and its main characters**

★ **Information about the mysterious Miss Brent-Dyer**

★ **Two short stories, unpublished since the 1940s**

★ **Quizzes**

★ **Competitions**

Find out about the ideas behind these delightful stories, only available in Armada.

£3.99 ☐

ARMADA

Heartbreak Café
JANET QUIN-HARKIN

Deborah Lesley started working at the Heartbreak Café when her parents split up. She's up-market, drives her own car to school, and she's never had a job before, but she needs the money.

Joe Garbarini runs the Heartbreak Café when he's not at school. He's cool and confident – and he doesn't think Debbie will last a month. But she's determined to put up with his wisecracks and prove him wrong.

The Heartbreak Café is a noisy hangout on the north Californian coast. Meet Debbie, Joe and the rest of the gang in this exciting new series by best-selling author Janet Quin-Harkin.

ARMADA

The Chalet School
Series

ELINOR M. BRENT-DYER

Elinor M. Brent-Dyer has written many books about life at the famous alpine school. Follow the thrilling adventures of Joey, Mary-Lou and all the other well-loved characters in these delightful stories, available only in Armada.

Enid Blyton
School Stories
in Armada

Malory Towers series

First Term at Malory Towers	£2.25	☐
Second Form at Malory Towers	£2.25	☐
Third Year at Malory Towers	£2.25	☐
Upper Fourth a Malory Towers	£2.25	☐
In the Fifth at Malory Towers	£2.25	☐
Last Term at Malory Towers	£2.25	☐

St. Clare's series

The Twins at St. Clare's	£2.25	☐
The O'Sullivan Twins	£2.25	☐
Summer Term at St. Clare's	£2.25	☐
Second Form at St. Clare's	£2.25	☐
Claudine at St. Clare's	£2.25	☐
Fifth Formers at St. Clare's	£2.25	☐

ARMADA

Other titles by
Enid Blyton
in Armada

ARMADA

All these books are available at your local bookshop or newsagent, or can be ordered from the publisher. To order direct from the publishers just tick the title you want and fill in the form below:

Name _____

Address _____

_____

Send to: Collins Childrens Cash Sales
         PO Box 11
         Falmouth
         Cornwall
         TR10 9EN

Please enclose a cheque or postal order or debit my Visa/ Access –

  Credit card no:

  Expiry date:

  Signature:

– to the value of the cover price plus:

UK: 60p for the first book, 25p for the second book, plus 15p per copy for each additional book ordered to a maximum charge of £1.90.

BFPO: 60p for the first book, 25p for the second book plus 15p per copy for the next 7 books, thereafter 9p per book.

Overseas and Eire: £1.25 for the first book, 75p for the second book. Thereafter 28p per book.

Armada reserve the right to show new retail prices on covers which may differ from those previously advertised in the text or elsewhere.

ARMADA